I0589196

HEAD-TRIPPED

Ad Agency Series, Book 2

NICOLE ARCHER

Twist Idea Lab, LLC

)

Head-Tripped Copyright © 2017 by Nicole Archer 1-472407831

All rights reserved. No part of this publication may be reproduced, distributed or transmitted in any form or by any means, including photocopying, recording, or other electronic or mechanical methods, without the prior written permission of the publisher, except in the case of brief quotations embodied in critical reviews and certain other noncommercial uses permitted by copyright law. For permission requests, write to the publisher:

Twist Idea Lab, LLC
707 Parkview Circle
Richardson, TX 75080

This is a work of fiction. Names, characters, places, and incidents are a product of the author's imagination. Locales and public names are sometimes used for atmospheric purposes. Any resemblance to actual people, living or dead, or to businesses, companies, events, institutions, or locales is completely coincidental.

Third edition

Cover design 2017: Letitia Hasser I RBA Designs

ISBN: 978-0-692-87467-7

To all the book bloggers who work tirelessly to promote the authors they love.

HEAD-TRIPPED SOUNDTRACK

This book comes with its own soundtrack. If you're reading on a device with Internet access, simply click the link at the beginning of each scene. If you don't already have a Spotify account, you'll need to sign up for the free streaming service. You can play it online or from your mobile device.

If you're reading a print version or have a device without Internet access, you can find the Head-Tripped playlist on the website: nicolearcher.com, as well as on Spotify.com under the user name: nicolearcherauthor.

QUICK NOTE

At the end of the book, there is a glossary to help decipher the foreign languages spoken in the story.

Also, all the quotes are from *Alice in Wonderland* and *Through the Looking Glass,* by Lewis Carroll. Effie is loosely based on Alice.

Hope you enjoy the adventure.

Love, Nicole

URBAN'S EUROPEAN TOUR

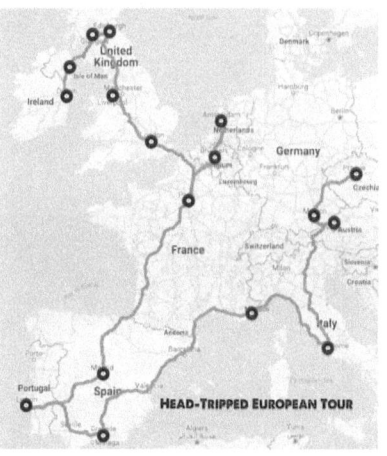

"Before Alice got to Wonderland she had to fall pretty hard down a deep hole."

— ANONYMOUS

OVERATURE
Overture

"'Only it is so VERY lonely here!' Alice said in a melancholy voice; and at the thought of her loneliness, two large tears came rolling down her cheeks."

Soundtrack: *"Empathy," Crystal Castles*

This was no ordinary audition—it was an audition for a new life. *This is it*, Effie Murphy told herself, *my way out of the hole*.

How could she possibly fail? She'd been practicing this song since the age of three. She didn't even have to think while she played. Even with only two hours of sleep, nothing to eat all day, and her hands riddled with pain, she could still play it by heart.

At the end of her performance, however, there was no standing ovation. And no one threw roses at her feet. No one clapped or shouted "bravo." In fact, the only sound in the auditorium was a theater seat flapping closed after someone walked out.

"Would you care to explain, Miss Murphy, what that offal was?" Professor Frommer's sharp Israeli accent sliced through the silence.

Effie shielded her eyes from the spotlights. "It was awful?"

"No, not awful," he clarified. "*Offal*. As in the rotting carcass of a dead animal. This is what you present? After six months of preparation? This tripe?"

Her heartbeat shot up to two hundred and eighteen BPM.

"I played with your mother in Berlin many years ago, you know," he said. "Had she seen this performance she would have disowned you."

Too late. Her mother had already disowned her years ago. That witch didn't care about her.

"Your left-handedness is a tragic handicap," he said. "Perhaps you should rethink this instrument. I suggest over the summer you take time to consider your career as a violinist. You're one of ten child prodigies in this class, Miss Murphy. Here, you're not exceptional—you're average. In fact, after that performance, I'd say you're less than average—you're sub-par." He dismissed her with a wave and called for the next student.

Now what? Her only job opportunity had just flown out the door with one of the other faculty members. What would she do for money? How would she pay for school? How was she going to eat?

A trigger in her brain fired. If she ran fast enough, she could get high in thirty minutes. She tossed her bow in her case and bolted off the stage.

Outside, a chilly spring wind whipped her face on the way to the corner drug store. Two months ago she'd quit smoking because the cost of cigarettes had become as expensive as a coke habit. But she needed one now—desperately. *Just one, then I'll throw the rest away. Just one hit, and that's it.*

At the counter, she grabbed a handful of lollipops instead, and shoved money in the clerk's hand.

She staggered toward Central Park with the candy gripped between her teeth and parked herself on a bench underneath a canopy of cherry trees. A pink petal blew off and stuck to her sucker. *Stupid spring. Stupid, ugly trees. Stupid, ugly day. Stupid, ugly city.* What an awful place to start over. An *offal* place.

A couple strolled through her tainted view. The woman laughed at the man's private joke, and he tousled her hair and kissed her cheek. They giggled and smooched some more then disappeared around the bend, dragging Effie's broken spirit behind them.

New love—the worst thing to witness when you're alone.

How did they find each other in that mass of people? Did they just run into each other by happenstance? And what did it feel like when they met? Was it like being shocked by static electricity? Or more like huddling in front of a warm fire? Or maybe it was like a deep breath?

She couldn't even picture holding hands with someone, let alone falling in love with them. Men didn't fall in love with damaged goods.

Her phone vibrated. Skip Shimura's name flashed on the screen. Her savior.

"Yo," he said. "Where you at? I'm outside your school. I know I'm early, but the award show is in an hour, and traffic is a bitch."

She groaned. "Oh, no. I forgot. I'm sorry. You'll have to go without me. I'm not dressed—"

"F-bomb," he was gritting his teeth, she could hear it in his voice. "I know I shouldn't point this out, but you owe me."

She did. She owed him her life.

"I don't care if you're dressed up like a braless hippie. Get out here."

It almost required supernatural determination to lift herself off the bench and head in his direction. "I'm around the corner in

Central Park. I'll be there in five." Forty BPM—the slowest beat possible—that's how fast she walked.

Skip's driver opened the door and a cloud of pot smoke blew out. Skip jumped out, wearing a black suit with a black tie and a black shirt. He was also wearing glasses—yellow-tinted horn-rimmed glasses. "Dude, get in."

She plopped down across from him. "I didn't know you wore glasses."

"I don't."

"Then why are you wearing them?"

"They make me look smart."

"No, they don't."

"Who gives a shit? Let's go over the plan." He fished out a folded-up piece of paper from his suit pocket and handed it to her. "Memorize your sister's acceptance speech."

"How do you know she'll win?"

"Not she. *You.* You are Callie tonight. If anyone figures out you're her twin, I'll be in deep doo-doo, so mum's-the-fucking word." He flopped back on the seat. "One night. One damned night. That's all I asked for. But, nooo, she and Rhodes are too busy screwing somewhere out in the boonies. They wouldn't even be together if it weren't for me. And this is the thanks I get?" Skip's normal demeanor was somewhere between comatose and dead. He was definitely on edge. Surprising, given the weed he just smoked.

"Dude, you're freaking out." She rubbed his shoulder. "Calm down."

He flicked her off. "Winning this award is a big deal. Awards attract new clients. The agency is in the hole. I need out of the hole." He poured himself a shot of something. "I'd offer you one, but . . ." He gave her a one-sided smirk. "Anywho, Hot PR chick has an insider at One Club. That woman is co-neck-ted. The word on the street is your sister's campaign won best in show. Now memorize that speech, wonder child, and make papa proud."

"Did you just refer to yourself as papa?"

"Read the damn thing."

"*Yada, yada, yada* . . . 'I'd like to say a special thanks to Skip Shimura, owner of the agency. Without his creativity, entrepreneurial drive, and excellent leadership, I wouldn't be here —" She snorted then crumpled it up and threw on the floor. "Callie would never say that."

"Please, F-bomb." He clasped his hands in prayer. "Just read the script."

"Don't worry. I got this."

He took off his fake glasses and eyeballed her. Skip was an attractive man. With his Scandinavian mother's high cheekbones and his Japanese father's smooth olive skin and thick black hair— he could have played an exotic male lead in any movie.

If he weren't such a stoner, and she weren't such a mess, she'd almost consider doing him. She was just that lonely.

"Stop looking at me like that," he said.

"Like what?"

"Like you're gonna pull some devious shit at the award show. I'm serious, F-bomb, this is a big fucking deal." He drank another shot.

"You haven't called me F-bomb in a while."

"Yeah, well, you haven't been 'bombed Effie' in a while. Hey, I forgot to ask, did everyone get boners after you played? Did you get the spot in the symphony?"

"I don't know yet." Lately, she lied so much she couldn't keep her story straight. But if she told the truth, that she was out of money, couldn't pay for school, and hated New York, he and her sister would send in the relapse army. Or worse, they'd pity her. And she was tired of that.

"I'm fine," she'd lied to her sister. "Yep, got my scholarship back. Everything's covered."

In reality, Juilliard didn't give her one red cent. If it hadn't been for her meager financial aid, a burgeoning student loan, and Walker's free digs, she'd still be living in a halfway house back in California.

Help wasn't something she could ask for anymore. Not after all the horrible things she'd done. Everyone had been covering her ass for far too long, and as far as favors went, she was in debt up to her eyeballs.

Skip unwrapped a box and pulled out a short black wig. "Put this on."

She examined it. "Callie dyed her hair back to blonde, you know?"

"No one else knows. And even if they did, it didn't grow down to her butt overnight."

"This is beyond ridiculous." She bunched her hair on the top of her head.

He looked at his watch. "We're looking good on time." He pushed a button and called to his driver. "Hey, Alan, pull over in front of Dolce & Gabbana. I'm gonna run in and buy Train-wreck here something besides this hippie garb she's got on."

"No, Skip—"

"Shut it and put that damn wig on."

Alan double-parked and opened the door. Not even fifteen minutes later, Effie slid back in the limo, wearing stilettos and a blue dress that barely covered her crotch. Red rhinestones spelled out the word 'princess' on the front. As if that weren't bad enough, Skip made her wear a bra and thong underwear that felt like razor-wire up her butt. A perfectly uncomfortable outfit for a perfectly uncomfortable situation.

"Looking fly, F-Bomb," he said.

"I look like a jackass."

"Whatever. Better than a broke hippie. Now, down a couple Red Bulls before we get there and catch a nice caffeine buzz while I blaze up."

VERISMO

Verismo

Soundtrack *"The Month of May,"* Arcade Fire

Elias Lovaro dropkicked a soccer ball against his fifteen-thousand-dollar custom-made guitar.

"Goooooooaaal," he shouted, then drilled a shot against the studio wall. It bounced off and hit a half-full blender of wheatgrass, carrot juice, apples, and some other crap, and knocked it over into the mixing board.

The music died abruptly. His DJ roommate, Eli St. James (a.k.a. "The Saint"), sprinted to the mixing board and grabbed the blender. "What the fuck!"

Elias pushed a pile of old takeout boxes off the sofa and sat down.

St. James gripped his hair with both fists while he surveyed the damage. "What the fuck! No eating and drinking in the studio. That was your rule. You better cough up the dough to fix this shit. I've got a gig in here tomorrow." St. James grabbed a Styrofoam container off the board and chucked it into the trash. "Our crib looks like a crack den. What happened to the housekeeper?"

"I fired her," Elias said.

"What was it this time?"

"I caught her taking a naked selfie on my bed."

St. James waved his arms out wide. "So?"

"She was wearing the gag gift Annie bought Cato for Christmas."

"That pink studded g-string with the words Lil' Bitch on the front?"

Elias nodded. "After Cato's gay bar incident, if those pictures got out . . ." He kicked the ball against the microphone stand and toppled it over. "My tour is already toast. I can't handle any more bad publicity."

St. James set the stand upright. "Why's the tour toast?"

"No new music."

"Then write some damn songs." St. James threw the soccer ball at him.

He slapped it away. "Fuck off, *puto*. Think I haven't been trying?"

St. James smirked. "Fuck off, bitch? Is that how you talk to your roommate? Tell me to fuck off. What's wrong with you? You're all dark and broody. You on your period or something?"

If only this problem *would* have disappeared in a few days. But this block had been going on for months. He grasped his hands behind his neck and closed his eyes. "I don't know, man. I'm just not feeling it. Nothing's coming to me."

"No wonder, since you've been living in the studio for a month." St. James picked up a soiled napkin with a pair of chopsticks, presenting it as evidence. "You need to get out. See people. Take the night off. Plus, you're getting on my fucking nerves. I only agreed to be your roommate because you're never here."

Elias fought off the urge to punch his roommate by cursing at the ceiling. "*La puta madre!* Think I want to be trapped in here?"

St. James sighed and sat next to him. "The agency is having a party tonight—an award show. Come be my wingman."

"You still work there?" Elias asked. "Thought you were making bank producing?"

He shrugged. "I love designing shit. Free health insurance. The people are cool. Not fake like the music industry."

That was reason enough for Elias. Other than St. James, his band, and his mom, everyone else wanted something from him.

"Come on. It'll be fun." His roommate punched his shoulder. "Plus, I need someone to keep me from sleeping with Sabrina again."

"The chica you work with? You're not with her anymore? Why not? She was hot as fuck."

"Yeah, a hot mind fuck. I didn't like her little games. She's always trying to make me jealous. I don't need that shit in my life." He picked up the soccer ball and threw it against the wall.

"I'm not in the mood to deal with the paparazzi tonight," Elias said. *Or parties. Or people. Or small talk.* His ideal night out was staying in. Otherwise, photographers circled him like vultures, just waiting for him to make an asshole out of himself. The minute he stepped outside, another headline made the news.

EL LOVE LOVES FAST FOOD

That story pissed him off more than it should have. After spending much of his life broke as hell, fast food had become a symbol of his poverty. McDonald's, peanut butter, and especially ramen noodles were high on his list of things never to eat again.

EL LOVE WINS WORST DRESSED

He made that list after someone took a picture of him taking out the trash in a pair of sweat pants.

HOT GAY CELEBRITIES

Cato Lawson, his closeted bassist, made the list after he was caught outside a gay bar in Los Angeles. His face was partially hidden in the photo, so the label claimed it was a case of mistaken identity.

EL LOVE LOSES LOVE

That headline became a top Google search hit after a one-night stand faked a pregnancy. It cost him almost a million dollars in legal fees just to shut her up. No one cared whether she'd lied, he was still made out to be the bad guy.

Step into the spotlight and your private life no longer exists. Which is why he had no desire to go out in public.

"It's an ad show, not the GRAMMY's," his friend said. "I'll tell everyone you're my jobless roommate. No one will know you're a famous rock star."

"Don't call me rock star. I hate that."

"Babes aplenty will be there." St. James bounced his brows. "Lots of sexy song inspiration."

Since screwing someone required a signed legal release now, women were a pain-in-the-ass Elias didn't need. "Think I'm just gonna stick around here and try to hash out some songs."

His roommate strode toward the door. "You're going. Now go pick out something sexy for the party tonight, rock star."

Elias tossed the soccer ball at St. James' head. "*Gil*, don't call me rock star!"

St. James ducked and shot him the finger.

For the rest of the day, until St. James forced him out that evening, Elias lay on the studio floor, staring up at the ceiling, wondering what his new career flipping burgers would be like.

TOTAL MUSIC MAGAZINE

URBAN'S UPCOMING EUROPEAN TOUR: A BAD TRIP
By Len Neal, Editor

SIX YEARS AGO, I saw El Love and his band Urban play in a small Manhattan venue. He was everything you could ever want in a front man. It was a beautiful thing to watch—the way he strutted up on stage like he had the biggest pair of cojónes in the biz. And after the show, he left the stage flanked by two adoring female fans. El Love was the epitome of a rock star.

And his songs were just as cool. His mind-melting music, perfectly layered with the pumping beats and hard-driving angst. Generational theme songs they were, the kind of music that never dies.

Back in the day, I'd drive up to the Adirondacks with my ex-wife and play Urban's entire catalogue. That's the kind of music one plays while getting a blowjob in a beautiful setting.

Unfortunately, fame and fortune has since spanked Urban's booty, with scandal after scandal plaguing the band this year. At times, I felt like I was reporting on a pop teen idol gone bad, instead of the coolest f*cking band that ever walked this earth.

Their partnership with Heart Records may have made them the highest grossing act of all time, but it also watered down Urban's vibe to appeal to the masses, including my ninety-year-old grandmother. And I've got news for you, that sound is as worn out as her house slippers.

It's been a year-and-a-half since they released an album, and their songs have been playing on repeat at my neighborhood Whole Foods that entire time. I can barely stand to buy my almond milk anymore.

With nothing new on the horizon, Urban's fans will be paying 150 Euros a pop to watch the demise of a great band. And I, for one, will shed many a man-tear when it happens.

TREMOLO

Tremolo

"'Curiouser and curiouser!' cried Alice."

Soundtrack *"Shoo-B-Doop and Cop Him," Betty Davis*

"Are we at a funeral?" Effie asked Skip at the awards ceremony. "Why is everyone wearing black?"

Skip threw a burning glare her way. "Do not ask me fucked-up questions right now. In fact, don't talk at all. Just blend in. Act normal."

She took in the crowd's so-called normality. How did one blend in with this primitive tribe of Manhattan hipsters without a socially acceptable drink in her hand?

Her scalp itched, and her feet hurt, and life sucked, and boy, wouldn't a buzz be nice? Except, alcohol was never her thing. The giddy clarity, zippy bolt of energy, and blissful numbness of cocaine was what she craved.

Skip slapped a few backs and laughed a few fake laughs, then dragged her to the auditorium. Bloated yellow flower arrangements adorned every table and gold stars dangled from the ceiling. Was this the Oscars or an ad show?

Did anyone even watch commercials anymore? She didn't even own a TV. Or furniture. Or a computer. Or anything except an expensive violin. But that was beside the point.

A few of Skip's employees were already seated at the table. Skip directed her to her chair. "Sit. Don't move. I need to schmooze. Don't say a word."

While he fake-laughed his way around the auditorium, a blonde woman with oversized lips struck up a conversation in a foreign hipster language.

Only twenty-eight and Effie could barely understand what these youngsters were saying. For example, Blondie kept asking her where "Walkie" was.

Effie winced and shrugged.

Blondie hiked up a lip. "Like, is he, like hardcore missing the NYC?"

On occasion, Effie's supernatural hearing made up for what she lacked in social skills—according to her sister, anyway. She could detect even the minutest change in pitch, which made her a master at gauging emotion. But in this case, she had no clue what this woman was talking about. None whatsoever.

Rather than pretend to comprehend her foreign tongue, she searched the crowd for that bastard, Skip. She glanced over her shoulder and spotted two hot guys near the entrance. One guy was bearded and tatted, and far too hip for her. The other guy though . . .

Her heart stopped beating for a second as the perfect male specimen strutted down the aisle in slow motion, all smooth and confident, like sex on legs.

She may or may not have let out an orgasmic moan.

The universe had molded a man to her exact standards. His dark wavy hair fell just above his broad shoulders. And his skin— the color of a warm sugar cookie—hinted at an exotic ancestry. South American perhaps? Latino for sure. *Ay, chihuahua.*

Even his attire made her want to weep like a child—vintage brown leather jacket, dark denim jeans, and retro-mirrored shades.

And he was headed her way! And he was sitting right next to her!

A halo of heat blazed out from his body and zapped her skin. She suppressed a whimper and smelled him instead. *Mm.* Fresh and clean. Like holy water and soap.

Would he notice if she hopped up on his lap?

She pressed her bare thigh against his jean-clad leg.

He glanced down then up at her. The corner of his mouth ticked up.

That time she moaned.

The corner ticked up a little higher.

Say something! Ask for my number. Lick me. What was the perfect conversational opener? Something subtly flirtatious? Something like, want to touch my vagina later? Or, I'm a thousand percent available? Or, I'll hike up my skirt if you take off your pants?

Or, how about this: "Hi."

"Hi," he said. One word. One velvety deep word with a hint of an exotic accent.

"Hi," she said again.

His smile said, "Get in my lap," but his mouth said nothing.

Geez, Louise. That's it. Forget violin. She was going into advertising.

Her sister's fiancé was hot as hell, but this guy? Jesus, Callie must have spent all of her free time masturbating at her desk.

"What's your name?" she asked.

He bumped his shoulder against hers. "Elias."

"I'm Effie. Oh, wait, no. Shit. I'm Callie." She smacked her forehead.

The bearded guy next to him leaned back. "What up, Murph? Didn't think I'd see you here tonight."

Skip showed up right then and did some sort of man-shake with the Beard. "Eli St. James. Thought you'd be at a gig tonight."

Skip's stoned greeting spanned a few moments longer then he sat next to Effie.

She leaned over and whispered to him, "Leave me alone again and I'll tell everyone about that time you dated Vanilla Ice's mom."

He sliced a finger through the air. "I went out for sushi, that's all."

"That's not what I heard."

Before he could respond, a brown-haired, buxom woman interrupted.

"Callie? What are you doing here? I just talked to Walker . . . Wait a minute." The woman tilted her head and eyed Effie with ample suspicion. "You're not Callie."

Skip air-pinched the woman's lips together. "Sit down and shut it, Avery."

The Avery woman glared at Skip and shook her head. "You didn't."

Skip grabbed a glass of wine off a waiter's tray and downed it. "Listen up, team." He gestured them in for a huddle. "This is Callie's twin sister, Effie. You can call her F-bomb."

"No, they can't."

He ignored her. "She's accepting the award for her lust-crazed sister who ran off with my creative director." He sat back and straightened his tie. "Anywho, tell anyone and you're fired."

"Are you insane?" Avery said.

"This award means new clients, Miss Adams. And that means I can hire more people so I don't have to keep riding your postpartum ass. So, zip-the-fuck it." He violently closed a pretend zipper on his mouth about twenty times.

Avery gave him a withering look. "You are the worst boss." She waved at Effie. "Hi, I'm Avery. I was sick as a dog and had to give up my place on the RoadStream tour. That's how your sister and Walker met."

Effie jumped up and hugged her. "You changed my sister's life."

Avery laughed and gave her a warm hug back. "You're not like your sister, are you?"

"Totally different," Effie said and sat back down.

Blondie snapped her gum. "How did Avery's barfing change Callie's life?"

Skip turned to her. "Sabrina, when they were handing out brains, were you shopping for shoes?"

Of course! Blondie was Account Manager Barbie—the woman who'd been a constant pain in her sister's ass. "Oh, I get it now." Effie smacked her forehead again. "That's what you meant earlier. You kept saying *Walkie*. But you meant Walk-*er*."

The bearded guy scoffed. "That's all she does. Talk about *Walkie* this and *Walkie* that."

A dramatic silence passed between Barbie and the Beard.

Effie leaned over to Skip. "Does everyone at your agency screw each other? If so, sign me up to sleep with Elvis." She flicked a look at the man-meat on her left.

"That guy doesn't work for me. Hey, St. James," Skip yelled. "Who's your date?"

"My jobless roommate," St. James said, grinning sideways. "He's just here for the free appetizers."

Skip rubbed his chin. "He looks familiar. Have we met before?"

Elvis shook his head once and squirmed a little in his seat.

"Huh," Skip eyed him for a few seconds longer.

The waiter came by and poured more wine.

"No thanks." She blocked her cup.

Elvis denied the wine as well.

"You don't drink?" she asked him.

"No."

"Ever?"

His brows lowered under the rims of his shades. "You're not going to put that on Facebook, are you?"

"What do you mean?"

"Never mind."

She scooted her chair closer to him. "So what kind of work are you looking for, Elvis?"

His mouth opened then quickly shut. Not a good sign. He probably worked in some shady field, like the stock market. *Figures.* No one could be that delectable and have a non-shady job.

Shrill music blasted out, and soon after, commercials flashed on the big screen. She yawned and sank down in her chair.

"Sleepy?" Elvis asked

Oh, boy, he was talking to her again. "Bored. You?"

He tweaked his right cheek in facial agreement.

Subtle. She liked that. No obnoxious blather from him. Quiet mouth. Loud body. Could this guy be any more perfect?

She regarded her reflection in his mirrored sunglasses. Was that her? Was she smiling? *How weird.* "I wish I could see your eyes."

His glasses slid down and revealed a pair of light coppery-brownish-green eyes.

"Wow, I love you," she said. *Oh shit,* did she just say she loved him? She puffed out a laugh. "You didn't hear that, did you?"

He shot her a big grin. "That you love me?"

"No, no." She waved a finger. "I love ewes, not you. As in female sheep."

So much for her first attempt at flirting. It was fun while it lasted. She didn't even bother to glance at him again. He was probably checking the exit doors for the nearest escape.

"F-bomb." Skip pulled out her chair. "That's us." He hooked her elbow and put on a weird smile.

She tripped her way down the aisle to the podium.

"Thank me, the agency, and the committee," he said through his weird smile, "and that's it. Got it?"

"I can't walk in these things." She kicked off her heels.

Skip's weird smile wilted. "Tell me you did not just take off your shoes in the middle of an award show."

They clambered up on stage. "New plan," he stage-whispered. "Take the award and leave. That's it. Nothing else. I'll do the talking."

"I know. I know."

The sharp corners of Skip's Nordic cheekbones tightened. "Do not screw this up, F-bomb."

"I've got this."

Someone handed her a . . . *golden pencil.* "Seriously?" she said into the microphone. "A pencil? What happened to cold, hard cash for a prize?" She rubbed her fingers together and laughed heartily. Screeching feedback blasted out of the microphone. "Oh shit. Sorry."

More feedback.

Skip pinched her thigh.

"Ow! Right! Okay, I've always wanted a big gold pencil."

Skip jabbed her in the side.

Effie stifled a yelp. "Thanks to my wonderful boss, Skip"—she stomped on his foot—"for sending me on the trip of a lifetime." *Literally.* Her sister hated that word, but literally, she wouldn't be alive without Skip. She leaned closer to the microphone. "Skip introduced me to my hot fiancé—"

Skip ripped the microphone away. "Thanks Eff, er, *Callie.* Our agency is incredibly lucky to have the most talented staff in the country. Thanks to everyone who voted for us. We're honored to be here." He blew a kiss at the audience then quickly escorted her off the stage, out through the back door.

Out in the hallway, he clasped his hands behind his neck and bent over.

She rubbed his back. "It's okay, buddy, you're fine. Take a deep breath."

He straightened. "Yeah, you're right. Speaking of deep breaths—" He patted down his pocket and pulled out a mini vaporizer. "I'm gonna hit the john." He pushed open the bathroom door and stabbed a finger at her. "Stay here. Do not move. I mean it."

Ugh, the wig was driving her crazy. It was probably all cock-eyed. She barged into the ladies' room and found Avery on the floor with a machine stuck to her boobs.

"Eesh," Effie said. "Does that hurt? Looks like a torture device."

Avery sniffled. "It is."

"Hey, are you okay?"

"No." She sobbed a little. "I'm exhausted. My baby is with a sitter who's probably a pedophile. I can barely pump enough milk to feed him, and this is the only moment I've had to myself in three months."

Effie turned to leave. "I'll give you some privacy."

"No, stay. I don't get to talk to adults very often. How's Walker? I miss him."

"He's good. He's great. I think. I don't talk to him very much."

Avery smiled. "I'm so happy for him." Then she began to wail. "I'll never know what that's like. To fall in love."

Effie yanked out dry paper towels from the machine and dabbed her face. "Your baby loves you. What's his name?"

"Austin."

"That's nice. Does he look like you?"

"I don't know. Besides the sitter, I'm the only one who's seen him." Her shoulders shook. The machine gurgled and started pumping again. "You're so much nicer than your sister." Avery smacked her head back against the wall. "I'm sorry. That was rude. I'm sleep deprived."

"No worries. I'll let you get back to . . ." she nodded down at her boobs.

"Tearing off my nipples?"

She grimaced "Yeah, that."

After Effie checked her wig, she hurried out of the bathroom and ran smack into . . .

"Daniel."

Her sister's ex pushed out an evil smile. "Hello, Callie. I see you've changed your hair."

"Fuck you very much, Daniel." She turned to the woman next to him. "I see you've got the backstabber with you. How's this abusive asshole treating you, Hillary? Having fun fucking my ex?"

"Oh, I've been having fun fucking him for the last three years," Hillary said with a cute laugh.

Effie cocked back her fist and rammed it into Hillary's face. And since that wasn't nearly satisfying enough, she grabbed Daniel by the tie and kneed him in the crotch.

He doubled over and groaned.

She smiled at her sister's ex best friend. "Looks like you won't be fucking him tonight."

Daniel yanked off her black wig. "You bitch."

Hillary jumped on Effie's back and tackled her to the ground.

Then they both turned on her like a pack of dogs.

A large shape came out of nowhere and hammered Daniel in the face.

Elvis.

Elvis in a stone-cold rage.

He did some sort of ninja move and knocked both her attackers on their asses. *"Hijo de puta."* He kicked Daniel's leg. "What kind of man beats up a woman?"

Daniel dabbed the blood off his lip with his shirttail. "She hit me first."

"Guard!" Hillary screamed. "These two just attacked us."

An overweight rent-a-cop jiggled and jangled toward them with his baton out.

Effie grabbed Elvis's hand. "Run!"

They bolted out the back entrance and set off the fire alarm.

She ran across the street, bare feet slapping on the asphalt, and just barely missed getting hit by a car.

Horns blared. Middle fingers flew. Swear words sounded.

A block away, she stopped to catch her breath in an alley.

Elvis, not the slightest bit winded, flattened his back against the building. "Did anyone see us?" He peeked around the corner. "Besides that cop?"

She jumped up and punched the air. "That was incredible. *You* were incredible. The way you laid him out." She shadowboxed him, giggling like a maniac.

He gripped his forehead and paced the alley. "What the hell? Why did that guy hit you?"

"He thought I was my sister. That guy's such a dick. I can't wait to tell her you avenged her honor. My hero." She clasped her hands and fluttered her eyelashes.

Her hero stared at her like she'd just escaped from the mental hospital. "*Estás más loca que la mierda.*"

"Was that Spanish?"

"Maybe."

"Where are you from?"

"Here, but my parents were from Argentina."

"I'm moving to Argentina."

The tension eased from his expression. "They have beautiful sheep."

"Even better." Why not go for the gusto and humiliate herself a little more? "So where to next, Elvis?"

"Elias, not Elvis. F-bomb was it?" He held out a hand.

She hugged him instead. He was so strong and hard. And he wasn't hugging her back. She tore herself away and smoothed out her dress. "I'm Effie," *but you can call me yours.* "Do you have a girlfriend, Elias?"

"No."

"Wife?"

"I'm single."

She tried not to do a split-leap. "Well then, where are you taking me?"

He gestured to the street. "Wherever you go, I'll follow, *mujer salvaje.*"

"Does that mean I love you in Spanish?"

"Sort of."

CAPRICCIO

Capriccio

"'Have I gone mad?'

'I'm afraid so, but let me tell you something, the best people usually are.'"

Soundtrack *"Bad Ideas," Alle Farben*
Soundtrack *"Let's Groove," Earth Wind & Fire*

How in the hell did he end up in a dark alley with this crazy woman? And why was she wearing that wig? Her hair was beautiful—all tangled and wild. He could see her galloping off down the street, naked on a white unicorn, her blonde tresses flowing behind her.

This woman intrigued him. There was something unusual about her, something soulful and spiritual. *Ella tenía una buena onda.* She excited him and soothed him at the same time.

Also, she was completely *loca.*

And even crazier, she had no clue who he was. For all she knew, he really was St. James's unemployed roommate.

"Think we're safe." She peered behind the dumpster. "Let's go." She pranced out of the alley, barefoot and floating like a butterfly in flight, wearing that tiny blue dress with the word 'princess' bejeweled on the front. "I need to get my stuff out of Skip's car first."

He hesitated. This was a bad idea. Effie was a walking headline on the front page of *TMM*. His manager, Gail, would have his ass in a sling if he ended up on the news with her. *Bad idea,* his voice of reason said, *horrible idea.*

But, for some reason, he followed her anyway—didn't even try to fight her, just gave in.

Up ahead, her tiny tight ass bounced underneath the thin fabric of her dress. *No panties.*

Suddenly, the bad idea seemed like a good idea. A very good idea. *A great fucking idea.*

He caught up to her, and she jogged across the street in the middle of traffic. He ran behind waving apologies at the drivers.

A line of limos stretched in front of the event's entrance. She peeked through the tinted windows until she found the car.

"Hi, Alan. I'm just grabbing my stuff. This is Elvis."

"Elias," he corrected.

"Sorry, I'm bad with names. But I'm great with voices!"

From her backpack, she pulled out a pair of sandals with bells on the straps and put them on. Then she dug under her dress and peeled off a black-netted thong. So she *was* wearing underwear, albeit not anymore.

As hot as this *mina* was, he wasn't about to do her in a limo after knowing her for an hour—not after that last one-night stand. "Whoa. Whoa! Slow down. Put your clothes back on." He slid over to the side, covering his eyes.

"Sorry, didn't mean to flash you. I just can't handle this torture device any longer." She shot the thong across the limo and pulled out a pair of underwear from her bag.

"Are those little boy boxer briefs?" He examined them. "Little boy Batman boxer briefs?"

"Not very sexy, I know, but they're sooo comfortable." She pulled some crazy maneuver where she took off her bra without taking off her dress, then shot it across the limo, too. Without her bra, her hard nipples poked out, just begging for a suck.

"Sooo much better." She blew out a sigh. "Skip made me wear that stuff. Said he didn't want me to go to the show like a braless hippie. My boobs aren't big enough for a two-hundred-dollar bra. I should return it for cash, but I doubt they'll take it back." She braided her hair and tied it with a red ribbon from her bag.

He closed his mouth—it was gaping open.

"Ready?" she asked.

"Wait a minute. Why were you wearing a wig?"

"Long story." She opened the door. "Let's go."

"Where?"

"For a walk."

"A walk?"

"I haven't had a chance to see much of the city since I moved here. I figured you could take me on a tour. You live here, right?"

"For the most part."

She blinked. "What does that mean?"

"I travel a lot."

"We can just wander. I'm not picky." She hit a button, and the divider slid down. "Hey, Alan? Can you pop the trunk?"

He nodded, and the glass slid back up.

"One thing before we go." She gave him the "gimme" gesture. "I'm going to need you to lose those glasses."

Before he opened his mouth to refuse, she shimmied next to him and tore them off his face. "Wow. Your eyes are really green now. They were brown a while ago." For a moment, she gazed at him, her blue orbs sparkling.

A throbbing desire to kiss her took hold. Very few people made eye contact with him anymore. Something about fame and fortune made people think he wasn't real. But not her. No, she was completely comfortable staring right at him.

She licked her lips. "Like a pickle."

"Huh?"

"Your eyes—they're the color of a dill pickle."

"That's . . . different."

Her mouth pulled into a little girl's pout. "I'm sorry. Did I hurt your feelings? I'm not very good with people. I never say the right thing."

"Do you like pickles?"

"I love them."

"*Flaquita*, you didn't hurt my feelings."

"My name is Effie, not *Flaquita*."

"That's a term of endearment in Spanish."

"Oh, phew." She smiled and opened the door. "We better go before Skip gets back." From the trunk, she heaved out a black case.

"What's that?"

"My violin."

"You play?"

Her shoulders slumped. "Not really."

"Sure you want to haul that around?"

"I don't go anywhere without it. Skip forced me to leave it here."

"Forced you?"

"I owed him a favor."

"What kind of favor?" He tried to take the violin.

She grabbed it back and breezed up the street, the bells on her shoes tinkling. A few times she paused, admired something in a window, then kept moving.

He prepared himself for the exhaustion that typically followed after talking to a woman at length. Chicks were so noisy.

But this one said nothing for several blocks until she halted mid-stride and smacked her forehead. "I forgot to ask what you do. I read somewhere men like it when you ask a lot of questions."

"Where'd you read that?"

"Some magazine." She looked so serious.

He tried not to laugh. "I'm a musician."

Her eyes widened. "Me, too."

"I figured." He nodded to her case.

"Are you in a band? What do you play? Where do you play?"

"Yes, I'm in a band." Although lately, they were more like sideshow freaks. "And I play guitar and sing."

"You look like a rock star."

He tensed. "I hate that word."

"Why?"

"I don't know."

"Will you show me how to play guitar?"

"Sure," he said, but didn't mean it. The chances of them hanging out again were *cero*.

She bounced on her toes. "I'm trying to learn every instrument. I taught myself how to play trumpet last week."

"In a week?"

"It's a lot easier than the violin. I watched a few *YouTube* lessons."

In other words, she didn't have a clue how to play. "What else do you play?" He immediately regretted the question. Small talk— he hated it. But she was making him do crazy things, like stroll aimlessly around New York, making small talk.

"Let's see"—she ticked off her fingers—"Piano, xylophone, cello, viola, double bass, pretty much all the strings. Trumpet, bassoon. I know quite a few percussion instruments. Oh, and the saxophone. I'm not an expert or anything. But, I've got the whole summer to learn."

This *mina* was a trip. "No bagpipes or sitar?"

"I'm sticking with orchestra stuff for now."

"So that's what you do? Learn instruments?"

"I'm in school. Juilliard. I'm trying to get out of the violin program and into the composer one, but I have to learn music theory first. I figured I might as well learn to play everything I'm composing for."

A bunch of people in traffic started honking and yelling. She covered her ears and winced. "Can we go somewhere else? The noise bothers me."

He steered her down a quieter street.

"So where do you work?" she asked.

Didn't he just tell her he was a musician? "I don't work."

"You don't have a job?"

"No. No job." He fought a smile.

She gave him a probing glance then shrugged and trotted off down the street.

A few blocks up in front of the wax museum, she examined the fake celebrities. "They're so life-like." She pointed to a replica of Angelina Jolie. "Who's that?"

"Really?"

"I don't have a TV. Is she a movie star?"

"You could say that."

"Hey, look in the back." Her forehead pressed against the window. "That one kinda looks like you."

Mierda, he forgot about that stupid thing. He grabbed her hand and tugged her down the sidewalk.

She stumbled next to him, eyes still trained on his wax figure.

"Let me show you a cool place," he said. Five blocks later, he stopped in front of the Diamond Horseshoe. His mouth dried out thinking of himself onstage there as a teenager. Back then, he couldn't control his stage fright. It was amazing how far he'd come.

Crazy Woman skipped past a sign in the entrance that said *Mazel Tov Mr. & Mrs. Daniel Leibowitz* and marched into the private reception as if she'd received an engraved invitation.

"Stop! What are you doing?" he shouted.

She ignored him and floated into the ballroom. "This is so coooool. I've never been to a wedding."

A cover band played fifties' songs on the stage. And yarmulke-topped old men danced with bridesmaids in bright pink dresses.

He glanced around. "Where can we hide?"

"I'm gonna go cut a rug. Watch this." She dropped her case at his feet and bounced down to the stage.

For the next few minutes, she busted a groove to Kool & the Gang with a bunch of drunken old women.

He hid behind a planter and watched her dance.

She tossed her hair and twerked against an old man.

He slapped his shades back on his face.

Once in a while, her underwear peeked out from the bottom of her dress. He felt a smile build.

A tiny man, no bigger than her, boogied up next to her, disco-pointing his fingers.

Crazy Woman mimicked his moves, then the guy swung her around and dipped her.

She giggled and squealed.

The Isley Brothers' "Shout" started playing. Crazy Woman did a breakdance-caterpillar move on the floor in front then twisted and shouted with the bride and groom.

He laughed to himself. She was having so much fun.

The band switched to a slow number. She snap-danced back to him. "I like this song. Know what it's called?"

"I believe this is *Earth, Wind & Fire*."

"Me likie. Wanna dance?"

"I don't dance."

She shrugged and bounced off to find another victim.

The next song, much to his horror, was his own. And they played it terribly.

"This song sucks," she said. "Ready to go?"

Her insult hit him right in the groin. "What's wrong with it?"

"Ugh, the guitar isn't tuned. And the lyrics make me want to cry in a corner."

"The lyrics are sad?"

"'Skin like the clouds of May, Sweet Grace? Above me you lay, Sweet Grace? Next to you I play, Sweet Grace? Over me you stay, Sweet Grace. Grinding away my days, Sweet Grace.' Who plays a song about death at a wedding?"

A prick of sorrow hit him. Everyone thought the song was about having sex with a woman named Grace, but he'd written it about his mother.

She touched his hand. "Are you like me? Do you feel everything as deeply as me?"

His heart banged. *Yes,* he didn't say. "What planet are you from?"

"Los Angeles."

He laughed.

"Hey, Love!" A kid shouted.

Elias glanced over his shoulder.

"Holy shit! It is him," the kid said.

"Time to go." He grabbed her hand and ran to the exit.

Behind him someone shouted, "Yo, man! Urban's at the wedding!"

Elias yanked her into an alley and crouched behind a stinking dumpster.

A few feet away, his pre-teen hunters stopped then turned back. "Where'd he go?" a kid said.

"Bet he took off in a cab," said one of his friends.

"Dumbass."

"Ow! Why'd you hit me?" his friend shouted.

"Think El Love would take a cab?"

"He was at your sister's wedding, wasn't he?"

"Damn. Wish I woulda had my phone. Nobody'll believe me."

The boys shut up for a second.

"Grant stole a bottle of booze," one of them said. "Let's go get shit-faced and hit on the rabbi's hot daughter."

Effie snorted.

After the kids left, Elias peeked around the dumpster. "Think they're gone." He helped her up.

She plugged her nose. "What was that about?"

"Long story."

"What were they screaming? Urban? Is that a new slang word? I can't keep track."

"You hungry? Come on. I'll buy you dinner."

They stopped in front of a cash machine. He swiped his card and punched in the numbers. A big red "declined" flashed on the screen. Since his net worth was well over a half-billion, he tried again, but got the same message. "Something's up." He pulled out his phone and texted his mother, Annie.

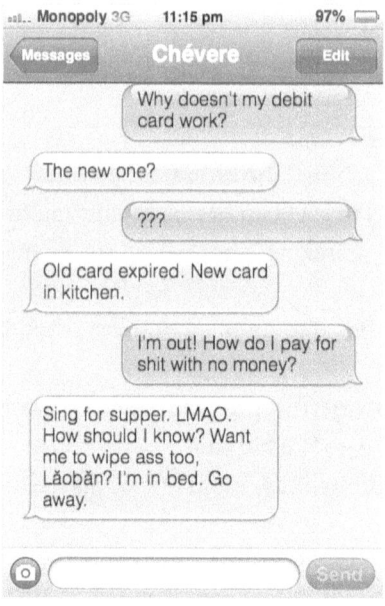

Tomorrow, he was firing his mother.

"My card is expired, and I don't have a dime on me." He brushed his hand through his hair. "I'm sorry. Can I make it up to you another time?" Like that would ever happen. She probably thought he was the biggest loser.

"Which way is Grand Central?" She glanced around.

"That way. Why?"

"I'll get money there."

Mid-sentence, she sprinted across traffic.

He joined her on the other side, and they strolled in silence for the next few blocks. "Usually, I'm the quiet one," he said.

"Oh, sorry. I was composing music in my head. Did you want to ask me something?"

Yes. No. "Tell me about yourself. Who are you, Effie? Inquiring minds want to know."

She paused on the corner, her eyes dimmer. "Is it okay if we don't talk about personal stuff? I don't feel like being Effie right now."

That was a first. Usually, women were dying to tell him their whole life story. "Who do you want to be?"

"Somebody else."

He studied her for a moment, searching for information.

"What?"

He shook his head. "Nothing."

Soundtrack *"Violin Concerto in D Major, Op 77: 111" Johannes Brahms*

UNDER THE SEA-BLUE dome of Grand Central Station, across from the gold clock by the elevators, Effie unpacked her violin.

"What are you doing?" Elias asked.

"Making some moola."

"*¡Qué!* You're gonna beg?" He waved a finger. "No, no, no. I can't allow you to do that."

She ignored him and lifted the violin to her chin.

Boiling hot blood rushed to his face. He backed away and hid near the exit. A woman was begging for his dinner. How humiliating. He should just go. Run out of there. Escape.

But then her music drifted over the white noise, sweet and delicate, yet powerful and mysterious. Like her.

She wasn't lying about playing the violin. What she wasn't honest about was how good she was.

An old lady listened for a moment then threw a dollar in the case. A guy in a suit stopped and checked her out then kept walking. Pennies for the performance of a lifetime. He would have given her five hundred bucks, maybe even a thousand. Instead, he stood there and gawked.

After the song, she bent down and counted the money in the case. "Fifteen bucks. Enough for a couple slices of pizza."

He pinched his bottom lip until it hurt. "I can't let you do that," he said. "It's against my religion to let a woman pay for dinner."

"We can eat at my place," she said timidly. "But it's in Brooklyn. And I only have ramen noodles."

"I love ramen noodles," he said.

SONATA

Sonata

"'Pretend to be two people! Why, there's hardly enough of me left to make one respectable person!'"

Soundtrack *"Room in Here," Anderson. Paak, The Game*

On the subway, Elias unfolded a newspaper and hid behind it.

Effie peered over the top. "Are you a spy?"

"I'm not crazy about the subway."

"Really? I love it. It's fascinating. All these people in one place. Close your eyes," she said.

"What? No. That's dangerous."

"Just do it. Come on."

He gave her a sideways glance then closed his eyes.

"Now, listen to the music."

"The music?"

"Yeah, the symphony of humanity." The train screeched along the tracks and scratchy bass thumped through someone's ear buds.

Amidst the sneezes and coughs and conversational buzz, an elderly couple chatted.

"I like that hat," the woman said.

"That's her hair," the man said.

"Oh, my! It looks warm."

Elias chuckled.

"Did you hear that?" Effie asked.

"Yeah."

"Keep listening."

Two guys argued at the other end of the train. The first one whined, "Look, I'm just saying, if you still loved me, you'd stop talking to your ex so much."

"If you don't shut your mouth, I will fuck it," the other guy said.

"I'll have to remember that line," Elias whispered.

She laughed.

At the next station, a guy stood beside them and screamed into his phone. "Motherfucker, I don't need you organizing my love life. You've been stabbed by two different women. The second one cut you with a SWORD. Dagger, sword, whatever. They come at you with blades, man."

Elias snorted.

"See? What did I tell you? It's fun, huh?"

"Pretty entertaining," he said.

"That guy looks just like El Love." A young woman pointed at Elias.

Her friend didn't look up from his book. "Yeah, like El Love rides the C train."

Paper crinkled next to her. Elias ducked behind the newspaper again.

She peered behind it. "You okay?"

"How many more stops?"

"Two more."

He looked really nervous. Maybe he suffered from anxiety. "Okay," she said. "I'll let you get back to the Gay Times."

He tossed the paper on the seat, draped an arm around her, and spread his thighs wide.

"You're not gay, right?" she asked.

"I'm definitely not gay." He moved in closer, his lips within kissing distance.

A freezing burn engulfed her—hot attraction laced with fear. Her first kiss in years was about to take place on a urine-soaked subway in front of a crowd of people. Another inch and she'd taste him. Was she ready for this? It didn't feel right. She drew back.

"What's wrong?" he asked.

Between her shoulder blades, the sting of her past throbbed. She rubbed the spot while a rambling schizophrenic captured Elias's attention. A minute later, they arrived at her station.

On the way to her place, she didn't speak. Instead, she worried.

Her therapist told her sex was as addictive as drugs. If Effie were seeking something lasting, she needed to take it slow, become friends first and build a solid foundation that way.

Plus, she'd vowed never to sleep with someone again unless they were serious, unless she was in love.

By the time they arrived at her door, she was so frantic she dropped the key twice.

Elias picked it up the second time and moved toward the lock.

"I'm a virgin!" she blurted out.

His hand froze.

"Well, not technically," she added. "I've had sex, but bad sex doesn't count."

"How much bad sex have you had?"

She swept a dramatic hand across her forehead. "Any bad sex is too much."

"True." He shoved a hand in his pocket. "Should I leave?"

No, don't leave. Please stay. "That depends, are you expecting sex?"

"I'm just here for the ramen noodles."

"Oh."

He chuckled. "F-bomb, *porfa*. I'm kidding." He caressed her cheek. "I'm cool with just chillin.'"

"Is it all right if we don't go any further than first base?" She winced.

"What's first base?"

"Anal."

"I'm down with that."

"It was a joke."

"I know. Let me in."

"Just so we're clear, anal is way out in left-field, not even close to the bases."

"Effie?"

"Yeah?"

"You gonna let me in?"

"I guess."

"Want me to open the door?"

"Please."

Inside, he took off his coat then rubbed his hands together. "Where's that ramen?"

"Never seen anyone so excited about ramen."

"I'm not." He stepped closer. "I just can't wait to see you bending over a hot stove in that little dress."

Their gazes collided, and her lamp flickered. The brick walls blurred to an abstract painting. A drip from the faucet hit the steel sink with a clang. In the distance, a siren whirred and her lungs trapped a panicky breath.

She was hooked.

The curves of his mouth. The pattern of his scruff. The cut of his cheekbones. His coppery-green irises. She memorized every detail, because as sure as the sun would set tomorrow, that man would break her heart.

He captured a tendril of hair stuck to her lips and pushed it behind her ear. "You're nervous."

She shook her head then nodded. "A little."

"Me, too."

"Really?" She perked up. "Why?"

"Because MSG does terrible things to me." He cracked a sly grin.

She wagged her finger. "You're dangerous."

He clutched his chest. "Me? What about you, wild woman? I never crashed a wedding before you showed up. And I've never been chased by the cops." He wagged a finger. "You're a bad influence."

That sinking feeling swept in again. Time to change the subject. "Ready for some ramen? Still hungry?"

His gaze traveled the length of her body. "Starving."

CADENZA

Cadenza

Soundtrack *"I Put A Spell On You," Annie Lennox*

This was the weirdest dream. Surely, he wasn't really in Brooklyn, sitting on the floor between a scuffed-up cello and an old electric piano, eating ramen noodles.

"We can eat on my bed," she'd suggested.

"Too risky."

"Yeah, we might spill."

Or he might end up dry-humping her like a pre-pubescent boy.

After he ate a bowl of the shitty noodles, he patted his belly and said, *"Riquísimo."*

A shy smile crept up. "Flattery will get you everywhere."

Except her bed. He was dying to get his hands on her sweet little ass.

But even if she miraculously changed her mind, there was no doubt she'd expect something from him afterwards, and other than an orgasm or two and a goodnight kiss, he had *nada* to give.

Women usually begged him for sex, not the other way around. Why then, was he hanging out in Brooklyn, making light conversation—something he hated—eating ramen—something he swore off years ago—with a complete stranger, albeit a spicy hot one—who wasn't going to let him get past first base?

What the fuck was first base, anyway? Kissing? Finger-banging? Clitoral massage?

Whatever. It didn't matter. He wasn't getting any.

So why was he there, then?

Because this woman, this tiny *tesoro,* with her long golden hair, freckled nose, and milky skin, had cast a spell on him. Most likely with those eyes of hers. No one had eyes that blue.

Sí, that was the only answer—she'd bewitched him.

That's why he was acting like a fool—punching people, allowing women to beg for his supper. *Dios.*

Amped up—that's what he was. Ready to explode. Like he'd gone feral. His muscles twitched involuntarily as if he were subconsciously getting ready to pounce on her.

But also, he felt strangely at ease—*tranquilo*—like he belonged there with her.

As she rinsed off the dishes, she hummed. She probably didn't even realize it. Music just naturally flowed out of her.

Shaking off the urge to bend her over the sink, he bounced on his feet. "You really play all these instruments?" he asked.

She wiped her hands on a towel and joined him. "I'm learning."

He passed her a beat-up trumpet. "Let's hear what you got."

She puffed her cheeks and played the military "Reveille" as if she'd done it every morning for the past ten years.

It turned into a game: he'd hand her an instrument and she'd blow him away.

After the third time, she stopped and frowned. "Why are you looking at me like that?"

"Like what?"

"Like I'm a circus freak?"

"No, *princesa.* You impress me. And inspire me. I feel like writing music." He picked up her crappy guitar. "You mind? I've got a song stuck in my head."

"Be my guest." She sat cross-legged on the bed.

He strummed a few chords.

"You're left-handed?" she asked.

"Yeah, it's a pain."

"Me, too."

"You play violin with your right, though."

"I have to. There aren't any left-handed violin players."

"None?"

"It's rare."

In awe, he stared at her. "You play that well with your bad hand?"

"I got a raw deal in the womb." She twirled her hair around her finger. "My sister and I are mirror twins. We look alike, except everything is opposite. She's right-handed, I'm left."

"*Me estás jodiendo!* There are two of you?" He made the sign of the cross. *Two of them! Ay ay ay!* If he didn't channel his sexual energy into something soon, he'd have to beat off in her bathroom.

He blew out a loud breath, strummed a few chords, and then let his brain go on autopilot.

She jumped up and grabbed the cello, adding harmony to his melody.

"I like that," he said. "It's different."

"Pick up the tempo, like this." She tapped her foot faster.

He added a beat on the side of the guitar.

She slammed her eyes closed.

"What?"

"It doesn't sound right. It needs something. Ever heard of chaos theory?"

"Like random events?"

"Sort of. Everything in nature is chaotic—rivers, clouds, trees. This song needs a pinch of nature. It's too predictable. Here, I'll show you." She picked up the violin and played his song. "Now, here's chaos theory applied."

He shot up from his seat, electrified by the sound. "I get it. You're building tension. It's sexy."

"Yes!" She hooted and clapped and danced in a circle.

He chuckled. *Such a silly woman.* "They teach you chaos theory at Juilliard?"

She bit her lip. "I . . . um . . . spent a lot of time at the library."

Why did she seem embarrassed by this? As a kid, he actually lived in his elementary school library. But he wasn't about to share that with her.

Instead, he shared music. They wrote five songs together—one every hour.

For two months, he'd been stuck, and all of a sudden she comes along, and he was a songwriting machine.

"Okay if I play these songs with my band?" he asked.

"Only if you invite me to the next show."

And just like that, his excitement shriveled up like a prune. The next show was in Europe. In a week. In front of a crowd of fifty-thousand. *Game over.* Exhaustion washed over him.

He set down his guitar and stretched his arms. "I'm beat. Mind if I crash here?" He put his hand over his heart. "I won't touch you, not even if you beg."

"It's not that I don't trust you," she said. "I don't trust me."

"No *problemo.* Touch me all you want. Mind if I take off my shirt?"

She pretended to cry and warded him off with cross fingers. "Yes."

He shook his head and laughed.

"Stop being so hot!" she whined.

"You first."

"Get in bed before I change my mind." She turned her back and yanked off her dress. Before she slipped on a t-shirt, he caught a precious glimpse of side-boob and nipple.

He adjusted his pants and lay down.

She twirled around and locked her gaze on his hard-on. "Oh come on!" she shouted at the ceiling. "I'm not strong enough for this."

"Sorry." He raised his hands "Can't control him. He does whatever he wants."

She scrunched her eyes closed and turned off the lamp. The streetlight outside cast a yellow crescent on her profile. Side-by-side, gazes bonded, neither moved, nor spoke.

How many women had he fucked in his lifetime? Too many to count. Even though he never touched drugs or alcohol, it took work for a woman to get him off. But all she had to do was look at him and he was ready.

"Can I kiss you?"

She hesitated for too long.

"Not on the first date."

"This is a date?"

"It isn't?"

"I don't make my dates beg for food. And I rarely assault people on the first date."

"What about the Bar Mitzvah gang?"

"Now them, I planned."

She stroked his chin. "I like you, Elvis."

"I like you too, F-bomb."

Her breathing evened out, and just as the morning birds started chirping, she fell asleep. And just like a total creeper, he watched her until her pretty face blurred and then disappeared in his dream.

PORTAMENTO

Portamento

"For, you see, so many out-of-the-way things had happened lately, that Alice had begun to think that very few things indeed were really impossible."

Soundtrack *"Light of the Morning," Band of Skulls*

Effie woke up in a pool of her own spit—on Elias's tummy—right next to his raging erection. *Well, someone was awake.*

She sat up and wiped her mouth. "Sorry about that."

"I love it when hot women drool all over me." He nodded to his morning wood. "Obviously."

The desire to mount him overwhelmed her. She covered her eyes. "Put that away, would you?"

"Podría metértela en la boca."

"You just said something naughty, didn't you?"

He winked. "Maybe."

"Never mind." She ripped her attention off his lap. "What time is it?"

"Noon."

Reality hit like a bolt of lightning. She tore off her clothes and ran to the bathroom.

"Where are you going?"

"I have to teach a lesson in thirty minutes." She hopped in the shower with her toothbrush.

A minute later, he opened the door and stepped in. She spit out her toothbrush and dropped the shampoo.

They knocked heads bending over to retrieve the bottle.

He massaged his temple. "Jesus, I'm batting a thousand in the smooth move department."

She slapped her hands over her eyes. "Oh my God, I can't."

"Can't what?"

He was grinning. She heard it in his voice. "You can't be in here!"

"I'm just gonna rinse off real quick."

She peeked through her fingers. "Are you out yet?"

Yep, he was grinning.

"Hard, isn't it?" he said.

"Yes! Now get your hard penis out of here."

"Not me, you!"

She flattened her back against the wall and fake-cried under her forearm.

"First, you took off your panties and bra in the limo." He folded down a finger for every offense. "Then, you whipped off your dress in front of me. You slept on *mi pija* all night! And then you took off your clothes again. I didn't sleep at ALL. Not *un minuto*." His feigned rage was as adorable as his penis.

His sexy stink-eye stayed stuck to her as he rinsed off then stepped out of the shower. "Paybacks are a bitch, aren't they?"

"You wicked man."

"Me?" he said innocently. "You're the evil one. Can I use your toothpaste?"

Yes, twice a day for the rest of my life. She gurgled nonsense under the shower.

"Eh?"

She peeked through the door and busted him snooping through her stuff. "I see you've found my gonorrhea cream."

He read the instructions on the tube. "Think it'll take care of this pesky erection?"

She yanked a towel off the rack and tucked it around her. "If you put that on your penis, you'll never get another erection again."

He shoved the medicine back in the drawer.

"I'm kidding."

"I know."

"Everything in there is for arthritis."

He unfurled her fingers then kissed them. "For your hands?"

Her stomach fluttered. "Hands, wrist, neck, shoulders, elbows."

"I have a good doc who works with musicians. She can hook you up with steroids and some pain pills."

"No pain medicine!" She closed her eyes and counted to three. "I'm . . . they make me sick." That was only a half-lie, considering codeine had started her slow descent into addiction.

"You should try acupuncture."

"Are you kidding? I can't afford acupuncture."

"My mom's an acupuncturist. I'll call her later."

Aw, he was worried about her. *And!* He wanted to introduce her to his mother. In the mirror, her cheeks glowed as pink as the cherry trees, bursting with new life.

A new life.

It all made sense now. That's why she'd moved there—to meet this man.

Everything had led up to this moment. This moment, with this man, and his pretty muscles, and long wet hair, and bronze treasure trail.

Her metaphorical chastity belt tightened.

How long did she have to hold off? How many dates did it take to fall in love? Four? Five? When would she know for sure? Was there an online test somewhere? Because, *man oh man,* she was so in love with the idea of falling in love with him.

They could make music before, after, and during sex. How cool would that be?

What if he was the "one?" What if he stayed with her forever?

"Don't you have somewhere to be?" he asked.

Her smile deflated. He wanted to leave. "I do, but . . ."

"But?"

"But I don't want to go."

"How long is your lesson?"

"An hour."

"I could come with you," he said.

Too bad her mother never let her try out for the cheerleading squad, because her routine right then—with the jumping jacks and sky punches and loud whoops—would have won the gold medal in team spirit. *Go team Effie and Elias!*

"Could you do that again?" He leaned against the sink and rubbed his scruff. "But with pigtails in your hair and without the towel?"

She tossed him a teasing glance. "Maybe after the lesson."

"Let's go. Let's go." He clapped. "*Vamos.*"

"I'm joking."

"I know." He blew her a kiss. "Go get dressed. I'll stay here so my dick doesn't get any ideas."

She gasped. "My good-sex virgin ears!"

"Better get out of here before I bust your good-sex cherry."

"La la la!" She stuck her fingers in her ears. "I can't hear you."

But I can feel you, she thought, *and you feel so good.*

VIRTUOSO

Virtuoso

Soundtrack *"Souvenir de Florence; d moll, op 70," Tchaikovsky*

Overnight, Elias had received one hundred text messages, forty-two voicemails, and three hundred and two emails. His real life tightened like a noose around his neck. *Just one more day.* Just one more day of normalcy. Just one more day with her.

The only text he returned was Annie's, asking her to swing by his place and grab his new card. "Mind if we meet my mom for dim sum later?" he asked Effie.

She grabbed her throat. "You want me to meet your mom? Already?"

Mierda. It wasn't like that. He'd hired his mom, Annie, as his new personal assistant. Even though she was the worst employee ever, his adoptive father had passed recently, and Annie needed something to take her mind off him.

"If we're getting married, you need to meet *mi mama.*"

She dropped her violin case, picked it up, and dropped it again.

"Let me get that for you."

"No, no, I got it."

"Sure?"

"Frrrrrgh." She closed her eyes and started over. "It's an heirloom."

"You don't trust your soon-to-be husband?"

She rubbed the wrinkles off her brow. "If anything happens to this, we're getting a divorce."

"I'll guard it with my life."

They strolled for at least half a mile until piles of garbage and old mattresses replaced the spring landscaping of Park Slope. A drug runner darted off his stoop and did a drive-by deal. Her pace quickened.

"You don't come here by yourself, do you?" he asked.

"Who else would I come here with?"

"This isn't a good neighborhood. It's not safe."

"I've been in worse places."

He glanced around at the graffiti-covered buildings with broken windows. She'd seen worse than the projects? "Where'd you grow up?"

"Los Angeles."

"Then you should know better."

She stopped and gave him a bright smile. "Thank you."

"For what?"

"For caring. It's very chivalrous of you."

If that were the case, he'd have called a limo. But El Love wasn't who he wanted to be. He wanted to be an average guy, walking his beautiful girl to her violin lesson in the *ghetto de mierda*.

They rounded the corner and entered an elementary school. In the gymnasium, six kids with violins awaited her in foldout chairs. "Hello, my little stars." Effie set down her case. "This is my, uh, *friend*, Elias."

A small boy in a giant football jersey glared at him. "Damn, shawty, why you so late?"

"Aw, did you miss me, Antoine?" She took out her violin.

"I missed your sweet tits."

Elias stalked over and crouched down in front of the kid. "Disrespect her again, and you'll be wearing that violin."

"He's kidding," Effie said.

"No, I'm not," Elias said.

"No, I mean Antoine's kidding. He's as harmless as a lamb. Aren't you, Antoine?"

"I ain't no lamb."

She pointed Elias toward the stand. "Have a seat. He'll shut up once we start."

A girl in braids waved a sassy hand. "Nuh-uh, he never shuts his fat mouth."

"Yo momma has a fat mouth." Antoine gripped his crotch. "And it felt good."

The girl sprung from her chair and knocked him upside the head.

Elias spun around, ready to give old Antoine another lesson in manners, but a woman in the bleachers shot up and yelled, "I know all your mommas, and if you don't sit down and shut up, you're out of the program!"

Their backs snapped straight in their chairs. "Yes, ma'am," they said in unison.

"Flip open your books to page seventy-five," Effie said. "From the beginning."

He sat next to the woman in the bleachers.

After the first song, she leaned in and whispered, "Good, aren't they?"

"Yeah, not bad."

She flashed a proud smile. "I'm Ms. Matthews, the principal."

He shook her outstretched hand. "Elias."

"It's my day off, but I love seeing these kids play. I busted my behind to get the grant for this program. You wouldn't believe the difference it's made in their lives. Thanks to Miss Murphy. If she didn't volunteer her time, they'd be out on the streets."

Music had kept him off the streets, too. "She does this for free?"

"Effie didn't tell you? She's got a big heart." She paused and listened for a moment. "Antoine, the kid with the big mouth? His older brother was killed in a shooting last week. His momma works three jobs. I leave the gym door unlocked so he can practice after school."

"Feel where the bow changes strings?" Effie said. "Don't move your arm too much, or you'll overshoot the A-string on the way to the E-string." She went around the circle and adjusted their elbows. "Keisha, speed it up. That's it. Good."

Toward the end of the lesson the principal stepped down from the stands. "I promised I'd check in on a student. Nice to meet you, Mr. Elias."

"Hold on a sec. Let me get your email." He'd send her a fat check so maybe she'd pay Effie.

She gave him a card and tossed a pointed look in Effie's direction. "Hold on tight to that one. She's super special."

The stranglehold around his neck tightened. Unfortunately, he couldn't keep her. One more day, and he'd have to turn back into El Love.

GRAZIOSO

Grazioso

"Alice thought the whole thing very absurd, but they all looked so grave that she did not dare to laugh."

Soundtrack *"Slipped, Tripped, and Fell in Love," Ann Peebles*

At the entrance of the dim sum restaurant in Chinatown, a middle-aged Asian woman with white spiky hair and a sharp chin jumped out from behind a giant lucky cat statue and shrieked. *"Aieee!* You late!"

Elias flinched and clutched his heart. *"Mierda,* don't sneak up on me like that!"

The woman doubled over and cackled. "Wha? You think I was reporter, *lǎobǎn?"*

"Don't call me that. I'm not your boss." He grimaced. "What did you do to your hair?"

She fluffed her hairdo. "You like? I look like a rock star?"

"More like an anime character."

The woman muttered something in Chinese. He replied in Chinese.

"Bah! Who's this?"

"Effie meet Annie, my mother."

It took her a minute to wipe the shock off of her face. "Nice to meet you, Annie."

"We look just like each other, eh?" Annie elbowed her in the side and cracked up.

"Annie adopted me when I was thirteen," Elias said.

"He ruined my life," Annie said with a dramatic head roll.

Effie jerked back in horror.

Through a razor-thin squint, his mother inspected her. "Your friend has no sense of humor."

"My sarcasm meter must be off." Her own mother had said the very same thing about her. She didn't find that funny at all.

Annie gave her another once-over then sprinted to an empty table.

The restaurant looked like a Vegas casino. Blue and pink neon ceiling lights cast a cartoonish light on the patrons, and the servers doled out food from their carts like dealers.

"You been here before, girl?" Annie asked.

"No, I just moved to New York."

"I'll order for you, then." Annie called for the server and ordered in Chinese. The waitress set several steaming baskets on the table and Annie dished a little from each onto Effie's plate.

She pointed to the fried claws. "What are those?"

"Chicken feet." Annie said, digging into her rice. "Make you run faster."

Elias unwrapped his chopsticks. "Don't eat those. She tells everyone they're a delicacy."

"Everyone?" Her appetite vanished. Just how many women had he taken to dim sum with his mother?

"My band comes here a lot," he said.

And her appetite came roaring back. She picked up a foot and took a tiny bite.

Annie stared at her while she chewed.

"Hmm, tastes like chicken," she said with a broad smile. "And suddenly I feel like running."

"You'll be running to the bathroom if you eat any more," Elias said.

Despite his frequent warnings, she tried everything on the plate —the jellyfish, the pig's ear, the cow intestines, and the duck blood —and afterwards, proclaimed everything delicious.

Annie scrutinized her every move. It was clear this was his mother's Princess-and-the-Pea test—if she didn't complain or barf, she passed.

Elias excused himself to make a call and Annie leapt in for the kill. "How long you known my son?"

"Since 'Nam," Effie said.

The restaurant grew eerily quiet. "You funny girl," she said straight-faced.

Didn't China have something to do with the Vietnam war? *Good grief*, she'd probably offended the entire restaurant.

Effie shifted in her seat. "Well, um, thanks so much for lunch. How do you say 'thank you' in Mandarin?"

Annie shot her a pointy-chinned smile. "*Jianren.*"

She repeated the phrase several times. "*Jianren?*"

Annie gave her the thumbs up.

Another wall of silence stretched between them.

"Did my son tell you about the hoopies?" Annie asked.

"Hoopies?"

"Genital rash."

"Oh! You mean herpes!" Effie flapped a hand. "Yes, he told me all about them." His mother was lying of course. At least she was about sixty-seven percent certain. "It's amazing he's able to sit down."

Annie reared back and roared.

Right then, Elias came back. He narrowed his eyes. "What was it this time? Syphilis?"

Effie answered for his mother. "Herpes."

Annie refolded her napkin into a neat square and placed it on the table.

"At least that's treatable," Elias said. "Last time, she made up an incurable disease. She likes to torture my dates."

"Dates!" Annie cried. "What dates? You don't date."

Effie did an imaginary cheerleader routine in her head.

"All right, time to go." He pushed out his chair. "You have my bank card?"

"Yes, *lǎobǎn*." Annie slapped the card in his hand.

"Don't call me that."

She bowed her head. "Yes, *lǎobǎn*."

He helped Effie up and gave his mom a kiss on the cheek. "You staying?"

"For a bit," his mother said. "I want to finish my tea."

Effie waved. "See you later, Annie."

His mother propped her cheek on a fist and frowned. "I doubt it."

Geez. That woman would make the worst mother-in-law. But that didn't deter her from daydreaming about her future husband.

"Am I winning the award for the worst date ever?" her future husband asked on the way up front.

Since that was only the second date she'd been on, she didn't really have a good benchmark. "Not yet," she said. "But you still have time."

He handed the cashier his card. "Next, we'll swing by the portable toilets up the street and see if I can't clinch the deal."

"Can't wait."

"Did you enjoy your meal?" the cashier asked.

"Yes," Effie said cheerfully. "*Jianren.*"

The cashier's mouth fell open.

Elias apologized then rushed her out the door. "Why'd you call that lady a slut?"

"What? No! I said thank you, didn't I?"

"Did Annie tell you to say that?"

She wince-nodded.

He sighed. "I'm not related to her. In case you were wondering."

"Your mom hates me."

"Nah, she would have ignored you then."

"Sheesh."

A man popped up behind a parked car and aimed a camera in their direction. It was the third time she'd seen him. "That guy's following us." She pointed over Elias's shoulder.

He spun around. "What guy?"

"He just ducked behind that red car. Look! There he is again. The guy with the camera. See?"

Elias tore off his coat and threw it over them.

"What's going on?" she asked.

"Do me a favor. Meet me around the block in front of the teahouse. I'll wait for you there."

"Are you in trouble?"

"Yes. No. I'll explain everything in a minute."

"You're not trying to get rid of me, are you?"

"No! Shit, there he is again. See you in a minute." He smiled and waved for the photographer's benefit and took off in the opposite direction.

Wind whipped through the trees and rained pink blossoms down on her. "Nice meeting you, Elvis!" she shouted. "*Jianren!*"

10

FERMATA

Fermata

Soundtrack *"Wild Love," Cashmere Cat, The Weeknd, Francis & the Lights*

Elias paced in front of the teashop. Effie should have been there by now. It wouldn't have surprised him if she didn't show up. No sane person wanted to be hunted down like an animal.

With their hidden cameras and telephoto lenses—the paparazzi were an elaborate network of spies. They'd stop at nothing to get a juicy bit of gossip.

They trailed him constantly, which was pointless since he led a pretty boring life. All he did was play music, work out, and sleep. Once in a while, he shared a purely physical relationship with a woman who'd signed the non-disclosure, but other than that, he wasn't the slightest bit interesting. That didn't stop them from making up shit though.

In a matter of hours, those pictures of Effie would be splashed across a web page with a new bullshit headline.

Losing the wild genius he'd known for less than a day shouldn't have upset him. But it did. He felt like driving a nail into someone's skull. "Fuck!" he shouted.

"Not on the second date."

He crushed her into a hug. "Where have you been?"

"I stopped at the Chinese medicine store." She shook a paper bag. "They gave me something for arthritis. No idea what it is, but I maxed out my credit card buying it."

He took out the bottle and pretended to read the label. "Dragon balls. Good for enhancing sex life and curing carpel tunnel."

She grabbed the bottle, ripped off the cap, shook two pills into her hand, and downed them dry.

He laughed and traced her bottom lip with his thumb. "You're the bomb, F-bomb."

She kissed the tip of his finger.

Flames of heat roared inside him. He wanted to grip the back of her hair and consume her. But the photographer could be lurking.

"Where to next, *flaquita*?"

"Take me on a tour," she said. "Show me the secrets of the city."

"All right, a secret tour it is." He bowed like a ringmaster. "We'll start here. See the sharp curve of the street? It's known as the 'Bloody Angle.' Chinese gangs use to ambush each other right over there. Underneath, there are tunnels where the Tong Gang hid their artillery."

She clapped and jumped. "Cooooooool."

They hopped into a cab, took a five-minute ride north, and got out in front of a bakery.

"Not sure I can stomach more food." She patted her non-existent belly.

"We're not here to eat." He led her to the back of the shop and unlocked the door.

"What is this place?" She glanced around.

"Used to be a theater. Now it's a recording studio."

"How did you find it?"

A realtor had showed it to him a few years ago, and he bought it that day. But he didn't tell her that. "Did some recording here."

"And you still have the key?"

He pushed a button on the jukebox and music poured out.

She played with an old microphone then bounced down the stairs. Stage curtains billowed around a velvet seating arrangement. She tossed a couple pillows off and patted the seat.

He crept toward her like a tiger waiting to pounce on his prey. He sat next to her, and she crawled into his lap.

A breathy moan slipped out of her. "You're so hot." She pressed her fingertips under his neck and gave him a flirty little smile. "One hundred and forty BPM. You're excited."

That he was. He wanted inside this beautiful creature, starting with her mouth. The scent of her skin made him drunk with desire. He brushed light kisses along her collarbone, trying like hell not to bite her. *Slow.* That's how it needed to be. *Slow,* so she'd savor every second.

He'd build her up one kiss at a time, one caress at a time, one lick at a time, one mouthful at a time. Then he'd bust her good-sex cherry with a long, slow fuck right before he left.

In three days.

He missed her already.

"Can I run to first base?" he asked.

"Yes, please." She closed her eyes and parted her lips.

He hovered above her mouth, feeling like an asshole all of a sudden. She clearly had feelings for him. This wasn't a wham-bam-thank-you-ma'am type of situation. He should have told her he was leaving. That's what a nice guy would do.

He traced her mouth with his thumb. *"Tenés una boca tan hermosa."*

The tip of her tongue darted out and invited him in.

Forget being a nice guy. He captured her tongue between his teeth and reeled her in.

The second their mouths met, a blast of white heat hit him. It was almost spiritual. That wasn't a kiss, it was a meeting of souls.

"Did you feel that?" he said against her mouth.

"Yes," she whispered. "Do it again."

For an hour, all they did was kiss. At one point, he almost came in his pants. He didn't even touch her boobs!

He nibbled her neck. "You're like a drug. I can't get enough."

Her body tensed, and then she shot up and smoothed out her shirt. "What next?"

Something upset her. He didn't ask though, because they needed to keep things light and airy—just like her.

A fuck buddy of his, who lived in Europe half the year, had a place nearby with a garden. She'd given him the keys a while ago and asked him to check in on the place when he was in town.

"You up for a little fun in the sun?" he asked.

"It's a beautiful day." She reached for his hand.

He swallowed the sadness building in the back of his throat and threw an arm around her instead.

PASTORAL

Pastoral

"She found herself at last in the beautiful garden, among the bright flower-beds and the cool fountains."

Soundtrack *"Wish I Knew You," The Revivalists*

The world seemed brighter, and the air sweeter. New York had changed in the last twenty-four hours. Thanks to Elias.

For the past six months, she'd gone from work to lessons to school—the same route every day—never paying attention to her surroundings. That day, though, she was fully present.

Except when he'd mentioned drugs earlier. Anytime that word came up, guilt barged in and accused her of a crime she didn't commit. It was a ridiculous reaction, of course, but often her past showed up unannounced.

"Wait here," he said. "I forgot something." He disappeared back inside the bakery and came out with a gift-wrapped box.

"What's that?" she asked.

"A surprise."

She shook pretend pompoms and did a one-legged toe touch. "Yay! Gimme. Gimme!"

"I'll give it to you when we get there." He kissed her on the cheek. "But only if you do that again, naked."

"Let's run." She took off jogging.

He caught her hand and nodded across the street. "It's right there."

"That apartment building?"

"You'll see." He climbed the stoop and put in a code at the entrance. At the end of the hallway, he pushed in another code and opened a door. Except for a few boxes it was empty inside. "Is this your dump?" she asked.

"Friend's place. But this isn't what I want to show you." He opened a sliding glass door and stepped onto the patio. "Unfortunately, I don't have the gate key, so we'll have to scale the fence." He hooked his hands. "Come on, F-bomb."

On the other side, she slapped her palms on her cheeks and gasped. Trees, lit up with spring buds, surrounded the private park, and butterflies danced over wildflowers. "A secret garden," she whispered.

He rolled his shoulders back and tilted his face to the sun. The light tinted his hair the color of rich chocolate syrup. She yearned to run her fingers through it.

"See the playground?" He pointed to a clearing where a slide poked out.

She made a beeline for it. "Yippee! There's a seesaw!" She straddled the seat. "Get on."

They bounced each other up and down, uncontrollable giggles pouring out of them. While he was still in the air, she hopped off and sent him crashing to the ground. "Ha ha!"

"You little—" He chased her around the park, pinching her bottom when he came within reach.

She slid under the jungle gym dome and thumbed her nose. *"Nah nah nah nah.* Can't catch me."

Somehow, he squeezed his tall body through the bars and

tackled her to the ground. His gaze stole her breath and sent tingles traveling down her belly.

She needed another kiss. The first one was so intense, she'd almost wept.

Eyes anchored to his, she snatched his bottom lip and sucked it into her mouth. His tongue greeted hers hungrily.

Soon, she was zooming into outer space.

"Quiero comerte la boca," he murmured, nibbling her neck. After another long-lingering kiss, he rolled over and made a sound like a missile speeding towards earth. *"Mierda."* He scrubbed a hand down his face and shook his head.

"What does that mean?"

"Shit."

"Good shit or bad shit?"

"Both."

She tried not to dwell on the statement and focused on the passing seconds instead, willing time to slow down.

"I forgot your surprise." He crawled out and handed her the box.

She tore off the ribbon and peeled back the tissue paper. Inside was the most perfect chocolate tart in the world. A peculiar feeling swelled inside her. Something she couldn't pinpoint. No man had ever given her anything . . . except drugs.

"It's . . . oh my gosh." She fanned her face to keep from crying.

"Is this your first dessert?" he mused.

"My first one from you. *Gracias.*"

"*De nada.* Try it." He fed her a piece.

It melted on her tongue. "Mm. Tastes like a chocolate cloud."

"Good, yeah?" He licked his finger and took a bite.

After they ate every crumb, he stretched out on his back and gazed at the sky.

She settled next to him and watched the clouds drift by. "Doesn't that one look like a snowman?" she said.

He angled his head to the side. "Looks like boobs to me."

She turned to him and snorted.

"What can I say? I love boobs." He positively oozed machismo. And she drank it right up.

"How free the clouds are, lying around all day long." She sighed. "Bob Ross said that."

"Who's Bob Ross?"

She propped herself on an elbow. "Only the most brilliant philosopher ever. He had a painting show on public television back in the seventies. I watch *YouTube* reruns on my phone. His voice is so sooooooooothing, and he says the most profound things. Total genius."

"'If you look into the clouds long enough, you'll find what you're looking for,'" she said, imitating Bob's voice.

He pulled a leaf from her hair. "What *are* you looking for?"

Love, she thought. "Success, I guess."

"At what?"

"Anything."

A spell of silence passed. "Success isn't all it's cracked up to be."

"How do you know?" Wasn't he unemployed?

"I don't know many happy wealthy people."

"So you think success means money?"

He turned back to the sky. "What else did Bob say?"

"This one's my favorite: 'You need the dark to show the light.'"

"Very Zen."

"Indeed."

"I don't remember the last time I stared at the clouds." His tone was wistful, sad almost.

As a homeless addict, all she did was get stoned, lie on the beach, and stare up at the clouds. But she kept that to herself, because as of this moment, that person didn't exist anymore.

"I can't remember the last time I went to a playground," she said. "Maybe when I was three?"

"That long ago?"

"I didn't have much of a childhood." Her mother had stolen it from her. "I was always practicing violin or performing somewhere."

He paused for a beat. "I didn't have much of a childhood, either."

"Annie was strict?"

"She didn't adopt me until I was thirteen."

"So your real mother was mean?" If so, they had a lot more in common than she thought.

"You could say that." He sat up and brushed the grass off his shirt.

"Where is she now?"

"Dead."

"I'm sorry."

"I'm not."

The conversation had taken an unpleasant turn. And since this day was all about pleasure, she steered it in another direction. "If you could be a kid again, what would you do?"

"Go to Disneyland, for sure," he said without hesitation.

A memory of her mother flashed in her mind. She'd refused to let Effie go to Disneyland with her father. They argued about it for weeks until he finally gave up. "I've never been there, either."

"What about you?" he asked. "What would you do differently?"

For starters, she'd never play violin. "I've never been on a Ferris wheel."

"I don't think I've ever been on one." He picked up a leaf and twirled it. "I've always wanted a tree house. Growing up in Manhattan made it impossible."

"A tree house would be great," she said. "If I could, I'd play Candy Land all the time."

"What's that?"

"A board game." Her mother had hidden it from her and her sister, claiming it was too much of a distraction.

For a second, he regarded her. "I bet you were the cutest little girl."

Not for long. "What else would you do?" she asked.

"I never went trick-or-treating."

"Shut up! Me, neither. I'd be a fairy princess." She flapped her pretend wings.

"Why not do it now? Dress up for Halloween?"

"Guess I've been too"—*High? Broke? Homeless?*—"focused on other things." She pulled out her phone and typed in their conversation.

"What are you doing?"

"Making our bucket list."

His smile wilted.

"What's wrong?"

"*Nada.* Tell me what else you'd do."

"I've always wanted to ride a horse."

"I'd learn to ride a bike."

"Get out!" She shoved him to the ground. "I don't know how to ride a bike!"

Their gazes collided and a zap of energy hit her with a bang. "We've lived parallel lives, it seems."

"Excuse me!" someone shouted. "You don't have permission to be here." Two cops and elderly woman pushing a walker headed their way.

They crawled out from under the jungle gym. "My friend lives here," he said. "I'm watching the place for her."

The lady scooted her walker closer. "And which friend would that be?"

He tapped his forehead then snapped his fingers. "Jenny. Yeah, that's it."

The lines around the old woman's eyes crinkled together. "How did you get in here?"

"A key."

"Jenny moved six months ago."

"Run," he whispered.

They darted toward the fence. He picked her up, tossed her over the gate, then ninja-jumped it.

One cop called in a break-in and the other pounded after them.

They dashed out to the street right as a cab drove by. He flagged it down, and they jumped in.

A burly female driver with a dollar sign on her front tooth asked the rearview mirror, "Where to?"

"Just go," he said. "Drive!"

A trumpeting laugh erupted out of her. "Why don't I just take you back to my house then? Have a little party?"

He stuffed cash in the box. "Drive."

"That's right. Let the money talk." The cab peeled out.

"I think we're safe." He slumped down in his seat and winced. "You must think I'm some kind of criminal."

"Never crossed my mind." *On second thought.* "Are you?"

"No. But don't you want to know who Jenny is?"

"Um, no." As far as she was concerned, his old girlfriends didn't exist.

"Really?"

She bounced in her seat. "Where to next? I'm having a blast."

He gripped the back of her neck and gave her a hard kiss. "*Cásate conmigo!*"

"Yes!"

A gigantic grin appeared. "Know what that means?"

"No! But it sounds amazing." She climbed into his lap and kissed him back.

The driver pounded on the safety glass. "Hey, no sex in the cab!"

"What about heavy petting?" he asked.

The driver slammed on the brakes. "Get out."

He boomed out a laugh. "Okay, okay. Drop us off in front of the Music Shack on Broadway."

"Say please."

"*Por favor*, please, kind lady, would you take us to the Music Shack?"

The driver blasted them with a look that would make babies scream. "I mean it! No fucking in my cab."

"*Sí, señora*, no fornication in the vehicle. We'll save that for later."

STACCATO

Staccato

Soundtrack *"Normal Person," Arcade Fire*

As a teenager, Elias had spent hours in the Music Shack. It was his escape. And he knew Effie would love it just as much.

On the outside, it looked like a flea market. Records stacked two and three crates high filled plastic foldout tables.

On the inside though, the place was magic.

Effie covered her mouth as she surveyed the store.

Paul ducked out from under the counter and gave him a hearty handshake. "Elias, my main man, you here for the Fender?"

"Is she ready?"

"As ever." He pushed his John Lennon glasses back on his nose. "Who's this beautiful woman with you?"

Effie glanced over her shoulder. Once she realized he was talking about her, she strode toward him with her arms out. "I'm Effie, you sweet, sweet man."

Paul hugged her and wagged his brows at him behind her back.

She twirled around the store. "You own this place?"

"You a music lover?" Paul asked.

"I'm a music liver." She wrinkled her nose. "Wait, that came out weird. I'm not a liver. I live for music is what I meant to say." She reached out and caressed a curved instrument. "Is this a crumhorn?"

"It is," Paul said.

"I've never seen one up close before. Can I try it?"

"Cover this part with your lips and use your tongue to make a long hiss."

On the first try, she made it work.

He and Paul shared another look. "Where'd you find this one, Elias?"

"Picked her up in an alley."

She corrected him. "I picked *him* up in an alley." She wandered over to a shelf. "What's this?"

"That's a Xun."

"Looks like an egg. How do you play it?"

"Like a flute." He blew the instrument.

She tilted her ear toward the sound. "It's like a hummingbird."

"Oldest instrument in the world."

"Fascinating!" She clapped and wiggled. "What other cool stuff do you have?"

"Elias, why don't you go check out the guitar, while I kidnap your girlfriend."

If only she *were* his girlfriend.

Paul led Effie upstairs, and he drifted to the back office. His phone vibrated in his pocket. It was Gail again. She'd been texting non-stop since that morning. He closed his eyes and answered.

"Where the hell have you been?" Instead of waiting for an answer, she shot questions at him like a machine gun—one after the other, rapid-fire—pelting him in the gut. Tickets, passports, airline information, tour information, missed interviews. Instantly, her overbearing force sucked up his joy like a black hole. When she finally paused for a breath, he spoke.

"I've been writing songs," he said.

"Well? How's it going?"

"It's going."

"So they'll be done for the tour in three days?"

He rubbed his forehead. *The fucking tour.* He was not looking forward to being cramped on a bus for months, traveling like a zombie. As much as he loved music, he hated touring. Not to mention, live performances made him physically sick.

Twice, he'd asked her to cancel it, but she'd reiterated that almost all of his income came from concerts.

"If you don't tour, people will forget you. And I've got fifteen other bands ready to take your place."

He hated to admit it, but she was right. Gail was right about a lot of things. She knew the music business better than anyone. No one could deny she'd helped Urban get to the top. And even though sometimes it felt like he'd sold his soul to the lowest bidder, the salary made up for it.

It was shameful, but lately the money meant more than the music. Bands didn't last for more than a decade. Music tastes change. People change. Then what would he do for a living? Get a desk job?

With Urban's eventual demise ever-present, he'd socked away every last penny of his earnings. Except for his loft, the studio, and his basic living expenses, he lived like a pauper. He couldn't risk burning up his savings.

St. James made fun of him all the time. "Why don't you buy yourself an adult toy or travel or something? Spend some of your fortune, for Christ's sake."

Elias wasn't the only one in the band concerned about money. They'd all grown up poor on the lower-east side and had no desire to go back to that life.

For that reason, they didn't roll like rich rock stars. They didn't spend money on drugs and parties. They didn't trash hotels. Most of the time they didn't even stay in hotels. They rented cheap houses and ate in. They spent money on what mattered—their crew. They paid their roadies what they deserved, and because of that, their tours were always a success.

Making millions doing what he loved—it was what he'd always dreamed about. So why wasn't he happier?

"Who's the latest fuck?" Gail sniped.

"Who are you talking about?" He prayed it wasn't Effie.

"The blonde Pocahontas? There are pictures of you plastered all over *TMM* from last night."

Mierda, the photographer was from *Total Music Magazine,* or as his bassist referred to them, Total Music Motherfuckers.

The main reporter was this guy named Len Neal. He had a network of spies all over the world sending him trash. He hated Len so bad he couldn't even come up with a metaphor.

But a bad review from Len could ruin the band. In fact, he'd singlehandedly ruined *Nickelsmacked.* And lately, Len's shitty reviews had them dangerously teetering off the same cliff.

"Who is she?" his manager asked again.

"Nobody."

"You better not be fucking someone without a signed NDA. You don't want a repeat of that little groupie situation."

No, he sure didn't. Tina's fake pregnancy almost cost him his career.

"Make sure the label knows about the new songs before you leave," she said. "We'll need to update our royalty agreement."

He tugged at his collar, feeling suffocated all of a sudden. "Gail, I gotta blaze. Talk to you later." He hung up and loped up front.

Effie was peering down into a glass case. "Can I see it?"

Paul gave her a sly squint. "I don't know. Esmeralda's pretty special."

She clasped her hands. "Pretty please!"

Paul chuckled and pulled out what appeared to be a violin bow.

She gasped. "She's the most beautiful thing I've ever seen."

Elias kissed the back of her neck.

She spun around and kissed him back. "Look!" She showed him the bow. "It's made from mammoth tusk. And it's inscribed."

He examined the tiny lettering. "What does it say?"

"*Ton amour est ma musique*," Paul said. "'Your love is my music.' The maker was in love with the violinist. Try it out." He passed her an old violin.

It wasn't a song she played—it was more like an emotion. He felt it in his bones.

Paul seemed just as riveted. "Where'd you say you guys met?"

"Behind a dumpster." She winked at him.

Elias winked back. "What was that song you just played?"

"It wasn't a song—it was chaos." She turned to Paul. "How much for the bow?"

"For you?" He scratched his chin. "Three grand."

She coughed and handed it back. "Goodbye, Esmeralda. I'm afraid I can't afford magical bows."

Knowing full well he could afford to buy it for her, Paul shot him a questioning look over the rim of his glasses.

He tugged his earlobe. "We better get going. Later, man. I'll send Annie to pick up the guitar."

"Come back and visit me soon, Effie." Paul waved. "Next time, leave your boyfriend at home."

She beamed. "That would be great. I mean, visiting you again, not leaving my boyfriend."

My boyfriend. Why did those words sound so sweet?

"*Adios*, man. Don't let that one get away."

It was the second time that day someone had said that. And once again, the statement hollowed out his insides.

He had to let her get away. Life on the road made him piss-poor boyfriend material. And she didn't deserve that.

Outside the store, she hugged him and pressed her ear to his chest. "What's wrong?"

"Nothing."

"But your heartbeat. It's in sad mode."

This woman. He didn't even have to say anything. All he had to do was breathe and she understood everything.

With the end drawing near and the weight of the tour bearing down on him, he barely noticed the thing he tripped over.

She bent down and picked up the object. "Aw, it's a tiny nest. Must have fallen from up there. Poor birdies. Maybe you can put it back." She handed it to him.

He tucked it high up in the branches.

"My hero!" She batted her eyelashes and pretended to swoon.

She was so silly and cute. And so not his. "Effie, I need to tell you something."

She pressed her finger to his mouth. "Shhh. The pitch in your voice is off. Whatever you're about to tell me, I don't want to hear it." She let out a shaky breath and gave him a weak smile. "Can you spend the night again?"

One more night. Just one more. Then he'd leave her alone. "Thought you'd never ask."

CODA

Coda

"'How long is forever?' asked Alice.
'Sometimes, just one second,' said the White Rabbit."

Soundtrack *"Signal," SOHN*

Elias's heavy mood crowded the cab on the way back to her place. She wrung her sore wrists and watched the Brooklyn Bridge pass by in a blur. Something was wrong.

The two flights of stairs to her apartment felt like climbing Mt. Everest. Inside the loft, he took off his jacket and hung it over a chair.

"Should we order take-out?" she asked.

"I'm not hungry." He sat on the windowsill and stared out at the streetlight.

She sat next to him and took his hand. "Hi."

"Hi."

She rubbed her cheek on his scruff and breathed him in. "Elvis?"

"Yes, F-bomb?"

"Wanna play around?"

His smile flickered then dimmed.

She sat back and examined him. There was sorrow and regret in his gaze. He was about to tell her it was over. "That's not the way you're supposed to look when a girl asks you to make out."

"How do I look?"

"Like a sad pickle."

The corners of his mouth turned up slightly then flattened. "I'm leaving."

And there it was. "When?"

"In three days."

"For how long?"

"The summer."

"I can wait."

"Effie, I can't be your boyfriend."

She placed her hand over his Adam's apple, feeling his masculinity for the last time. It bobbed under her touch.

He turned his gaze back out the window. "I don't want to go."

"Don't."

He responded with a quiet exhale.

"Can we still make out?" Her question came out sounding desperate. She laughed as if it were no big deal.

A crease appeared between his brows.

"Might as well live it up while you're here."

That time he answered her with a kiss. A tender kiss. A chaste kiss.

But if this was their last night together then, dammit, she was going balls-out. She grabbed his face and turned that kiss into a frenzy of tongues and bites and moans and hair pulls. She made that kiss a metaphor for how she felt.

His mouth roamed down her neck to her breast. He raised her shirt and licked her nipple.

She pulled away. That's not what she wanted from him. Not

another one-night stand. He was more than that, and if she slept with him, he'd never have a reason to come back.

"I'm sorry, but you're leaving. And I—"

He squished his cheeks together and nodded. "How 'bout we write music instead?"

"That I can do."

The song they wrote told the story of their short time together in perfect harmony. And in a way, it was like making love.

At the end, they collapsed into bed together and kissed until the sun came up, until their lips were swollen and raw, until they finally crashed with their mouths still molded together.

The next morning, Elias quietly rose from her bed. It hurt to watch him put on his jacket. He opened his mouth to say something.

"Don't—" she said. "Don't say goodbye. Just tell me you'll see me later."

He smiled, but his eyes didn't. "*Chau*, F-bomb."

"Hasta la vista, Elvis."

For a full twenty minutes she watched her door, thinking he'd change his mind and come back.

He didn't.

INTERMEZZO

Intermezzo

"It's no use going back to yesterday, because I was a different person then."

Soundtrack *"Eating Hooks," Moderat*

The next day, a cold front blew freezing rain over the city. Ice encased the cherry blossoms outside Effie's window like glass boxes. Inside her apartment the radiator banged as if it were alive. She shivered next to it in the cotton sundress she hadn't removed from the day before.

The weekend flickered in her memory like a dream. The only sign it was real was the beard rash on her chin and the two dirty bowls in the sink with ramen stuck to the edges.

Now what?

This wasn't just a bad day. This was her life.

You don't have to feel this way, said her addiction, clawing at her.

But drugs wouldn't fill the void. Nothing would.

"There will be bad days," her therapist had told her, "when it feels like the world's against you."

"What do you do then?" Effie asked.

"Get up, dress up, show up, and never give up."

So that's exactly what she did. She got up, dressed up, and went out to find a job.

New York was saturated with violinists, as it turned out. Even a job playing at Sachs had fifty applicants ahead of her.

That meant she had to wait tables, which also meant working in an industry filled with drugs.

Quick cash, night hours, and rote tasks—the perfect job for an addict. She filled out applications at twenty-five restaurants to no avail.

At the twenty-sixth place, a greasy spoon near her loft, the owner took her to a booth in back and interviewed her on the spot.

It wasn't really an interview *per se*—it was more like a visual assault.

A dirty toothpick bobbed between the owner's lips as he violated every inch of her body with his snake-like eyes. He shifted the stick to the side of his mouth. "There's an apron and a pair of shorts in back. You can start now." His rubbery turkey neck jiggled as he spoke.

"Shorts? Really? It's cold outside."

"Want the job or not?" He pulled the toothpick out and pointed it at her like a weapon.

No lie, if he touched her with that thing, she'd probably shrivel up and die. "I wasn't prepared to work today. I'm not wearing the right shoes." She held up a heeled boot. "Sucks, because I could really use the cash."

"There's something else you could suck for cash." His cheeks coiled into red balls.

Was he smiling? Did he find that funny? A buried memory crawled out from the depths of her mind. Once, she'd smoked crack with a middle-aged married man for the price of a blowjob.

Afterward, she threw up in his lap, and the guy tossed her out on the street.

That was the last time she'd prostituted her body. She would never be that hard up again.

She gave him a sweet smile and swept everything off the table into his lap—the ketchup, mustard, relish, sweet-n-low packets, creamer, napkins, silverware, and water glasses—all of it.

He squealed like a woman and jumped out of the booth.

"Whoops," she said dryly then marched out with her chin high and her wallet even emptier. *Life may suck dick, but I don't.*

Outside, she blew fog on the window and drew a giant penis with her middle finger. The act wasn't nearly as satisfying as she'd thought it would be. She frowned at her reflection. *Well, that was fun. Where to next?*

Bed seemed like the only option at that point. So she huffed it back to her apartment. For the rest of the afternoon, she stared at the crack in her ceiling, praying for money to fall out of it.

And then someone knocked.

Elias.

She flung open the door and found major disappointment on the other side.

A skinny guy with a bike helmet held out a clipboard. "Sign this." He handed her a long box.

"What's is it?" She ripped it open and found the engraved bow inside. The card read: *A rare beauty for a rare beauty. Stay wild, F-bomb. Fondly, Elvis.*

She set down the package and threw her arms around the deliveryman.

He didn't hug her back. "Get off me, lady."

She squeezed him tighter. "Hug me. Please."

He patted her back. "You done yet?"

"A minute longer, please."

He peeled her off him.

"I don't have money for a tip."

He rolled his eyes then clacked down the stairs, mumbling about the "crazy bitches in New York."

The urge to get high hit again. She started to text Skip then decided against it. And her judgie sister didn't have the right shoulder to cry on.

No job. No boyfriend. No one to talk to.

But she had a violin and a magic bow. And that was something.

15

DISSONANCE

Dissonance

TOTAL MUSIC MAGAZINE

URBAN'S DUBLIN SHOW: A TOTAL BUZZKILL

By Len Neal

LAST NIGHT, *Urban kicked off their sold-out tour in Ireland. Hungry for the music that's inspired a generation, fans were sorely disappointed to hear the "same old shit."*

I'd say El Love was basically "going through the motions," but that would be too generous.

With all the technical failures last night, El Love's voice came out sounding like the cry of a cloistered and isolated soul, which is more or less what he's become.

Guess the woman spotted with him in New York didn't inspire any new music.

Bassist Cato Lawson didn't seem half as thrilled to be onstage as he was coming out of that gay bar last month.

Griffin Macchio played to the beat of a different drum last night. Or should I say he played the drum to a different beat—his timing was so off, the other musicians had to slow down to match his meter.

Another low point was when Indie rock diva, Missy Reed, had a fan thrown out for bringing a selfie stick.

The highlight of the night wasn't the music, but the little person next to me, wearing a unicorn horn glued to his forehead.

Rich (the unicorn dwarf) had this brilliant thing to say about the concert: "What happened to balls-out rock-n-roll? Now it's just artless fucking gobshites and bloviating flesh bags. My mammy would have fallen asleep at that show. What happened to crazy? I want somebody with a fucking drug habit."

Good point. Maybe Love should pick up a drug habit. Maybe then he'd write some new music.

In the meantime, if you've spent 150 Euros on a ticket, get your money back.

BELFAST, IRELAND

Soundtrack *"No Woman," Whitney*

CATO READ Len's review as if he were Morgan Freeman narrating *The Shawshank Redemption*. "Bet after Len finishes trashing musicians, he punishes himself with his mother's dildo." Cato slammed his laptop closed.

Missy chimed in. "At what age do music critics die?"

"They don't," Cato said. "They turn back into the primordial ooze from whence they came."

Hal, the band's hulkish bodyguard, added, "How does he live with himself? I have a good friend who's a little person. Great guy. Don't people have a sense of honor and dignity?" He wiped a tear from his eye.

Cato got up and patted the bodyguard's bald head. "Aw, big guy, wanna hug?"

Hal smacked his hand away. "Touch me again and I'll take out your teeth."

Cato, ever the shit-starter, poked Hal with his pinky finger. The bodyguard grabbed his wrist and flung him to the ground.

"Oh, it's on now!" Cato jumped to his feet. "Come on, motherfucker. Game on."

"Ta gueule!" The bus driver yelled from up front. "Je ne peux pas conduire ce putain d'autobus avec toi hurlant, comme ça."

"Nobody understands you, LeStrange," Cato said. "Speak Eeengleesh."

Instead, LeStrange swerved the bus and knocked the bassist on top of Annie, who screeched like a stuck pig.

"Shut the fuck up," Elias shouted. "The man's trying to drive. We've got a million dollars' worth of equipment on this bus. You guys gonna pay for it, if he wrecks this rig?"

Cato glared at him for an annoyingly long minute.

"What?"

"What. Is. Up. Yo. Ass?" he asked. "You been buggin' since we left New York. You need me to put Prozac in your smoothie or sumptin?"

He flopped back on his seat. "I don't like getting shitty reviews."

Griffin growled his assent. Since the tour started, that's all his drummer had been doing—growling, barking, and howling at the moon. That, and screwing every female within a ten-foot radius. Whatever was going on between him and his girlfriend wasn't helping their reviews at all. But as long he didn't break The Rules, that was his drummer's business, not his.

The Rules were like the band's Ten Commandments, except there were only four. And instead of being carved in stone, they were written into their contracts.

RULE 1: NO YOKO ONOS

Girlfriends, boyfriends, spouses, groupies, and random one-night stands—none of them were allowed on tour.

RULE 2: EVERYONE SIGNS AN NDA

Band members, and those in an intimate relationship with a band member, must sign a non-disclosure agreement. This was a recent addendum, created after his groupie fiasco.

RULE 3: NO FRATERNIZATION

Shitting where you ate caused drama. And he had first-hand experience to prove it. Long before they made it big, he and Missy had a fling. Things were tense back then, and though they had finally worked through everything, it had taken a serious toll on the band. In fact, she still held a grudge. It was subtle, no one spoke about it, but it was always the proverbial elephant in the room.

RULE 4: NO DRUGS OR ALCOHOL ON THE TOUR

The band was their job. And like a job, substance abuse wasn't allowed. Drugs didn't just ruin careers, they killed people. Including his mother.

Anyone caught breaking The Rules, would get kicked out of the band and lose their future song royalties.

In the band's seven years together, no one had ever broken The

Rules. He was convinced that was the reason for their long-term success.

So even though Griffin's wandering dick was affecting his soap opera of a relationship back home, as well as his performances, his drummer wasn't breaking The Rules. Still though, his emotions were getting in the way of his career.

Elias could relate. Ever since he'd left New York, he'd felt achy and weird—almost like he had a mild case of the flu. And it wasn't the bad reviews. It was Effie.

Everywhere he went she was with him. When he was performing, she was onstage next to him, adding chaos. On the road, she didn't leave his thoughts for a second. When he ate dinner, she was there, telling waitresses to 'fuck off' in Chinese. And when he went to sleep at night, she was curled against him with her head above his dick.

Except she wasn't there. And that was the problem.

Why didn't he get her number? He'd give anything to hear her smoky voice.

He rested his forehead against the window and watched the rain-blurred Irish countryside whizz past in slices of green. *Pickle green.*

He needed her. He needed help. He needed music.

From the overhead compartment, he pulled out his guitar and tried to work out the remaining lyrics to the songs they'd written. He played the chorus to "Chaos" a few times, but his mind kept drawing a blank. It didn't sound right. Not without the violin. Not without her.

Cato shuffled back and sat across from him.

"Go away," he grumbled.

"What? The black man can't sit in the back of the bus?"

He sighed. "What do you want?"

"I want to hear that song again."

He played the whole thing.

"That's tight. When'd you write that?"

"Last weekend," he said.

"I like it."

Missy sat across from him. "It's great," she said. "Doesn't sound like the stuff you usually write. Are we playing it on the tour?"

His immediate response should have been yes, but they were Effie's songs. And even though she'd given him permission to play them live, she also didn't have a clue who he was. Plus, he didn't want to play them—not without her. "I've got five new songs, but they're not mine." He set down his guitar.

"Fuck you mean they're not yours?" Cato said.

"Someone helped me write them."

Cato blinked then flapped his palms out. "Well? You gonna tell me who it is, or am I gonna have to Guantánamo Bay your ass?"

A wild woman. An enchantress. A dream. "Someone in New York."

"Songwriter?" Missy asked.

He picked up his guitar again. "Something like that."

Cato's burning scrutiny seared the side of his face.

"What, *pendejo*?"

"We've been playing the same old shit for a year and a half, and you finally write something new, now you're telling me we can't play it, because"—he cupped his ear—"say it again. Because somebody else wrote them?"

"We wrote them together."

"So pay the man. And be done with it. We're dying. If we don't get some new life . . ." He tweaked a nod, forcing him to fill in the blank.

"Woman," he said. "A woman wrote them."

"A woman?" Missy's question sounded like an accusation.

"Violin student from Juilliard." He hesitated briefly. "She can play anything, though. She's a genius."

"So? Students need green. Pay her for the songs and be done with it. Problem solved." Cato wiped his hands on an imaginary dishrag.

If he paid her off, she'd think he used her. And he didn't want to be another guy on her list of bad experiences. That weekend meant a lot to him. *She* meant a lot to him. And she deserved better than a payoff.

"They're her songs," he said. "Without her, they don't sound right. It's the way she plays them."

"There's violin in all of them?" Cato asked.

"Not all. She played the cello and the piano in two songs."

Missy's hand shot up. "Hold on. Are you saying I can't play the piano?"

"It's not the instrument. It's the way she plays."

Both his bandmates' faces broadcasted disbelief. He slumped down in his seat and fixed his gaze on the roof. What exactly was he trying to do? Convince them to hire her? Could he even do that? Bring her on tour? Would she do it? She might, if she were broke enough.

"So hire her, then," Cato said, reading his mind.

Missy tossed her mane and raised a smug chin. "We have enough musicians in this band."

Typical Missy response, he thought.

His keyboardist was one of the few women in the industry who wasn't a plastic pop singer, and that made her royalty in her fans eyes. And another cool female in the band could easily usurp her place on the throne.

Around other women she was catty, to say the least. She was especially unpleasant to the women he slept with. Her silent treatments were legendary. And when she was in a bad mood, the whole band suffered.

She'd never agree to let Effie play with them. Which sucked, because his mental health was at stake, not to mention his career.

Cato held an imaginary microphone in front of Missy. "Miss Reed, can you describe what it's like to go back on welfare after making it big in music?"

Her face paled. Missy grew up hungry. She still had issues with food. She never left anything on her plate. To her, it was a criminal offense to waste food.

They'd all been hungry back in the day, and none of them had any desire to return to that life.

Missy's bitchy attitude instantly dissolved and left her droopy and meek.

Cato slapped her slumped shoulders. "Our ship is sinking, boo. We need a life boat, quick."

She huffed. "How well do you know this girl?"

He shrugged. If he told the truth, that he'd only spent a weekend with Effie, she'd never go for it.

"What if she's a psycho? Or a drug addict? Or an axe murderer? Or what if we don't get along?"

No way Effie was a psycho druggie, but Missy had a point.

"Tell her it's a temporary gig until further notice," Cato said. "And make her sign a contract."

"What about our contracts?" Missy added. "Is she going to share song royalties like the rest of us?"

He hadn't thought of that. "That's her decision."

"Gail will have a shit fit if she doesn't," she said.

Gail. Another roadblock. "What if we make a new label for the songs?" he said. "Heart's been screwing us for years. How about we screw them over for a change?"

Cato tapped his temple. "Smart man. I like it. But what about your little friend?"

"She follows The Rules like us." Elias said. "If she breaks them, she's out, and the royalties go back to us."

Griffin made his way to the back. "Gail will never go for that shit."

"Her daddy might, though," Elias said.

Cato dove back in his seat. "'Kay, while I get my beauty sleep, you kids figure everything out."

A spark of excitement burned inside him. Bringing Effie on and making a new label was a brilliant idea. He should have done it years ago, back when he'd signed with Heart Records.

Since then, he'd spent over a million dollars in legal fees trying to get out from under them. But unless Heart proved to be grossly negligent, he was locked in for life. And since Urban was one of their biggest moneymakers, Heart was anything but negligent.

They flat out owned him.

But they didn't own Effie.

He whipped out his phone and texted his roommate for his boss's number.

After going back and forth with that *idiota de mierda*, Skip, he finally got her digits.

The minute he heard her voice, a slice of vividly blue sky appeared from out of the gray clouds.

RALLENTANDO

Rallentando

GLASGOW, SCOTLAND

Soundtrack *"Reflektor," Arcade Fire*

In an old nunnery outside of Glasgow, on the coast where several lochs merged, the band practiced the new songs. The secluded location and thick granite walls turned out to be the perfect location for the explosion about to take place.

Spontaneously adding new songs on a tour was akin to lighting a stick of dynamite—things were bound to blow up. Pulling off their shows was a gargantuan feat.

Urban's crew of twenty included the sound guys, stagehands, roadies, grips, lighting technicians, and hair and makeup. Their team ran Urban's shows like a machine. Dropping Effie 'the bombshell' into the production at the last minute was breaking the machine into a million tiny parts.

In the old days, all they did was get up on the stage and play. It wasn't the theatrical performance it was now. In fact, the planning for this production had been in the works for a year. And now they had to start from scratch.

Chip, the sound guy, spoke up. "I know nothing about violin acoustics."

"We'll cross that bridge when she gets here," Elias said. Effie was arriving in Edinburgh the following day. And they'd planned to introduce the new songs at the show that night.

"Is she going to string her own instrument?" another guy asked.

Que lío de mierda. What a mess. A stabbing ache took up permanent residency in his shoulder, and sleep was nothing but a distant memory.

Despite everything, deep in his core, he felt calm and peaceful. *This is right. I know it. I feel it.*

"We'll figure that out later," Elias said.

A door slammed shut, and a blur of red blasted into the space. Gail stomped toward him, her fancy shoes clomping on the wood floor. She crooked a finger, beckoning him to follow her outside like a puppy dog. "A word," she said.

He hated her alpha bitch act. "Here's fine."

She tore off her sunglasses and shot him a tight-jawed smile. "Sure. Here's fine. As long as you're comfy with me carving off your nuts in front of everyone."

Someone laughed then coughed.

"You hired that weekend blonde from New York? The one in the pictures? To play in the number one highest grossing band? Without telling me? Are you insane?" She dropped her bags with a bang. "Missy told me you didn't write the new songs."

Et tu, Missy? He shot his keyboardist a warning fire look— she'd better have a good explanation for stabbing him in the back.

"Effie and I wrote the songs together."

Gail snorted. "You don't have a clue, do you? You think all I do is run errands? There are unions involved. Payroll. Legal. The press. Licensing deals with Spotify and Pandora and iTunes. Call up your little fling and tell her you changed your mind. Maybe you can hook up after the tour."

Boiling heat flooded his head. He swept a stiff arm toward the door. "Everyone out except the band."

"Aw, I was about to order popcorn," Hal said.

"Out!" he shouted.

Hal and the crew scurried out of the room.

Elias motioned to an empty chair. "Have a seat, Gail. You must be tired after that long flight. Did you take the jet you bought with my money?"

Gail dropped her hard stance and vigorously rubbed an eyebrow. "I am a little tired."

Cato scooted a chair across the floor and sat in it backwards. Griffin set his drumsticks on the snare. Missy stood wired in the back. No one spoke a word. He allowed the silence to linger longer than necessary.

"How long have we been together, Gail?" He sat down and crossed an ankle over his knee. "Five years?"

"Almost six."

"That's right. Happy anniversary."

She didn't thank him.

"And in our almost six years together, have we ever let you dictate our music?"

She bolted up and shook her fist at him. "I'm looking out for your best interests."

"Our best interest would have been to scrap this tour. But since we're here, let's get something straight—I pay you to do a job. If I want your opinion, I'll ask. Is that clear?"

He directed the next speech to the band. "Effie is a professional musician and a songwriter. She's not a fling. Understood?"

The lie's impact hit him right after he said it. That meant he couldn't be with Effie out in the open. He'd be breaking The Rules. There was no way around it though. If they knew the truth, they'd never go for it. He'd just have to solve that problem later. After his managerial problem.

With the conviction of a television preacher, he asked them to take a blind leap of faith. "Our music needs to evolve or we die. Effie's the big bang."

He glared at Missy until she turned away.

Then he blazed out of there and ran down to the coastline. A freezing gust of wet wind bit his face, and a gong buoy clanged in the distance. An eerie orange moon backlit the clouds over the black loch, making them look like haunted . . . boobs.

A vision of Effie under the jungle gym entered his thoughts. He chuckled to himself, and just like that, the cutting wind turned into a tropical breeze.

REPRISE

Reprise

"She generally gave herself very good advice (though she very seldom followed it), and sometimes she scolded herself so severely as to bring tears to her eyes."

Soundtrack *"Welcome To Your Life," Grouplove*

"Do you believe in love at first sight?" Effie asked her sister on the phone.

"Are you high?" Callie asked.

"Just answer the question."

"Are you?"

"I told you, I'm clean. For good."

Her sister let out a loud breath. "Why are you asking this incredibly random question?"

"I met someone—"

"No," her sister shot out.

"No, what?"

"No, I don't believe in love at first sight. Not for you. You love everything at first sight, the postman, that gross guy at the gas station, that mustachioed woman at the store you hugged. Hi! I'm Effie! I do whatever feels good. I don't think. I just do—"

The airline announced her flight was boarding soon.

"Where are you?" Callie asked.

"JFK."

"Oh, shit."

In the background Walker shouted, "Jesus Christ on a cracker. Give me that damn phone."

Callie muttered a few obscenities then Walker hopped on the line. "Effie, darlin'. How are you?"

"Great," she said. "You?"

"In love and sh—poo. Pull over! Your sister should not be allowed to drive."

She chuckled. "Where are you guys?"

"Michigan. It's cold here. But we're snuggling up. That's it. Give me the keys, Blue."

A muffled struggle occurred then Callie came back, panting like a prank caller.

"What's that heavy breathing? Is Walker touching you?"

"I'm having an anxiety attack. Why. Are. You. At. The. Airport?"

Rewind to eight days ago.

Penniless, desperate, and on the edge of a dark hole, she had her phone out, ready to call her sister and beg for money for a flight home. At that precise moment, Elias called.

It was kismet.

She couldn't stop thinking about their weekend together. Did it really happen? Or was it a dream? And why did he show up only to leave a day later? What was the goddamn moral of the story?

Then an unrecognizable New York number flashed onscreen.

"F-bomb?"

"Elvis?"

"Hi," he said.

"Oh my gosh! I'm so happy to hear from you. I got your present. Thank you so much. Did Paul give it to you for free?"

"I'm glad," was all he said. But he was smiling. She heard it in the subtle lilt of his velvety voice.

"How'd you get my number? How are you? Where are you?"

"Scotland."

"Oh." It was so quiet on the other end she could hear her own heartbeat. "Are you there?"

"I need you." He cleared his throat. "I need a violinist. For our songs. Are you available?" He sounded weird. Impersonal.

"Is someone there?" she asked.

"Yes. I mean no. In the other room. The band." He paused. "Can you make it?"

"Make what?"

"The trip. Can you play with us?"

She flopped back on her bed and tried not to cry. "I'm sorry. I can't afford to—"

"I'll take care of everything," he said. "And I'll pay you, of course."

A logical person would have asked how that was possible when he didn't have a job. A logical person would have asked for more details. A logical person would have at least asked for his last name.

"Okay," she said.

"Thank God," he mumbled.

She counted to ten—a trick her counselor taught her to curb her cravings. What did this mean for her career? Was it a good idea to take a trip with a complete stranger?

"Actually, can I think about it?"

Dead air clogged the line.

"Elvis?"

"Yeah, I'm here. That's fine." He sounded disappointed. "You want to call me tomorrow?"

Outside her window, a ray of sun lit up the only blossom left on the cherry tree. *Another sign.* What did she have to lose? Nothing. "Never mind. I'll do it."

"You will?"

"Sure, why not? Scotland sounds way more fun than Brooklyn."

"How soon can you get here?"

"I don't know. There's the passport and—"

"My manager will take care of all that. Text me your email."

Manager? He probably meant Annie.

He rattled off a few details in a flat business-like tone, and during that time, she picked a cuticle until it bled. Something was off about the conversation. From what it sounded like, he wanted a violinist, not her. Which begged the question, why was he calling her, when surely there were other violinists in Scotland?

"Hey, Elvis?"

"Yeah."

"I missed you."

He didn't hesitate for a second. "I missed you, too."

And the axis righted itself again. Instead of droning on about boring business stuff, he talked about his tour so far—it hadn't been great—and she recounted what she'd been doing—mostly watching the grass grow in Central Park—and though the conversation was more friendly than romantic, she felt certain things would change the moment she landed in Scotland.

Another long stretch of silence passed. "Hello?"

"I have to run," he said. "My manager will be in touch." And then he hung up and the axis wobbled again.

She needed some advice. But from whom? She crossed her sister and Skip off the list. They'd just tell her she was crazy.

Just then, a card from the Music Shack fluttered off the gift box from Elias. Maybe Esmeralda really was magic?

Half an hour later, she met up with Paul.

"Can I ask you a question?" she said.

He pushed his glasses back on his nose. "Shoot."

"If someone you just met asked you to go on vacation for the summer, would you go?"

"You talking about Elias?"

"No, I'm asking for a friend."

His cheek twitched. "Uh-huh. So what are you"—he coughed into his fist—"what is *your friend* hoping to get out of this vacation?"

"She's not sure."

"If you don't have any expectations, then go."

That wasn't entirely true, but it was what she wanted to hear, so she high-fived him and said, "I'll have my friend send you a postcard from Europe."

"Tell Elias I said hi."

Fast forward to now.

"ARE YOU FUCKING KIDDING ME?" Callie cried. "You've met some loser in a band?"

"He's not a loser."

"You said he was unemployed."

"No, I said he doesn't have a job."

She groaned. "Check the thesaurus, little sister, because in my book that's the exact same thing. What's the name of this loser's band so I can look them up?"

She tapped her teeth. "Urban, I think. I can't remember."

"What the fuck? Urban? Jesus, you *are* high, aren't you?"

"Stop asking me that. I'm not high."

The enormous man next to her was staring. Earlier he'd taken off his shoes and propped his fungus-filled feet up on his suitcase. She picked up her luggage and moved out of earshot.

"What's his name?" Callie asked.

The boarding announcement blared over the loudspeaker. "Elias."

"Elias." Callie repeated. "Elias from Urban asked you to play in his band and you love him."

"I'm not sure about the love part, yet."

"Hey, Walker," her sister shouted. "Get a load of this. My sister's at the airport, boarding a flight for . . . Where the hell are you going, anyway?"

"Scotland."

Callie snorted. "She's boarding a flight for Scotland to play on tour with Urban, because she thinks she's in love with the lead singer—"

"El Love?" Walker asked.

"Elias Lovaro," she clarified. "Not . . . whatever he said."

"*Riiiight.*" Callie snorted again. "When did you meet him? And where?"

"At the ad show."

"What ad show?"

"Tell her to have fun," Walker said.

"Go sit in the back," Callie told him. "This is crazy, Effie. This isn't real, right?"

The airline called out her row. "I have to go."

"Stop. Don't do this, Effie. Don't go. It's bad for your recovery. Think of all the drugs—"

"He doesn't do drugs. I have to go."

"Wait!" Her sister sighed again. "If I hadn't met the man of my dreams aboard a giant silver dildo . . ." Another sigh. "Please, please be careful. I'm not talking about the drugs. Well, I am, but what I mean is, take care of your heart. It's precious. And vulnerable. Don't give it away to the first person who asks for it."

Too late. "I'll call you when I land." She hung up on her sister's fake sobs and found her seat, which unfortunately was right next to Fungus Feet.

She smiled at him though, because he was the last poo in her toilet, so-to-speak. After that flight, she was flushing her shitty life down the drain.

STACCATO

Staccato

EDINBURGH, SCOTLAND

"Down, down, down. Would the fall never come to an end? 'I wonder how many miles I've fallen by this time?' she said aloud."

Soundtrack *"Hoochie Coochie," Band of Skulls*

The hackney cab circled the parking lot and stopped in front of a giant soccer stadium. "I don't think this is it," Effie said to the driver. "This doesn't look like a club."

"You said Murrayfield, right?"

"But that's a stadium," she said. His band wouldn't play there.

"Murrayfield *is* a stadium."

She was too exhausted to argue. It felt like she'd been flying for days. For two hours she'd sat on the JFK tarmac. In London, customs flagged her bow for containing ivory. Then she spent two hours filling out forms and missed her connection to Scotland. And now this guy was trying to con her into getting out here.

The driver pointed to the marquee. "See, right there, it says Urban."

This is what she knew about Elias's band: nothing.

For the past week, she'd been running around preparing for the trip. She was a classical musician. She didn't know jack about indie rock.

They'd written acoustic songs so she figured they'd be playing in coffeehouses, not stadiums.

Her sister's voice echoed through her head. *You don't think. You just do.*

"Better hurry," the driver said. "They started at half past."

She clutched her violin case like a weapon. Twenty dollars—not Euros, dollars—was all she had left to her name. There was no turning around, no going back.

At the door, a bald man with a long white Hulk Hogan Fu Manchu blocked the entrance.

"Name?" he said.

She pulled out her passport. The music was so loud she had to shout. "Effie Murphy. I think I'm on the list?"

"Ah, Miss Murphy! You're late. I'm Hal, head of security. They only have two songs left. Let me take your case."

She gripped it like a vise. "I've got it. Thanks."

He eyed her suspiciously then darted down a dark tunnel. She ran after him. The music above vibrated the ceiling. He passed her a pair of earplugs then gestured to the stage.

She ducked behind a mountain of amplifiers and saw nothing but a towering arc of blue spotlights shooting beams into the dark-cherry sky.

Sonic booms blasted her bones. She moved behind the drummer's platform, where a shirtless sweaty man with back tattoos and neck-length sopping-wet hair banged on the drums so hard his muscles rippled to the beat.

On the keyboards in front of him, a woman with mousy brown hair sang background vocals.

Beside her, a lanky man with chocolate milk skin and big green eyes plucked his bass.

She snuck to the other side of the stage. A huge screen displayed a four-story high image of Elias to the screaming audience.

Her heart sped up to 180 BPM. *God,* he was gorgeous.

His voice flowed out like hot liquid. Like audio lava. Like a melted wax melody. He made love to his fans. And she wanted to back her ass up against him so he could play her just like he played that guitar.

They transitioned to the next song, and all at once she couldn't breathe. He was singing the song from the wedding that night— the sad Grace song.

Then he started dancing. *Dancing.* "I don't dance," he'd said. Bits of their conversation flurried around her like black crows. *I don't have a job. My place is a dump.*

The music faded out and all she heard was her pulse skyrocketing. Mr. Love-At-First-Sight would be singing *their* songs to sold-out crowds all over Europe.

You don't think. You just do.

She dropped her violin case.

The sound caught his attention, and he looked over his shoulder. When he saw her, he grinned like an idiot.

In return, she struck him down with a lightning glare and burned that smile right off his face.

FALSETTO

Falsetto

Soundtrack *"Apocrypha," Arcade Fire*

That brief glimpse of Effie had sent fire surging through his blood. He almost walked off the stage right then, but the fans demanded an encore. "Where is she?" he shouted to Hal.

Hal shrugged and pointed out the back door. "Went that way, I think."

A bunch of brats milled around in the hallway. The minute they spotted him, they were on him like hounds on a fox. Cell phone cameras flashed. Random people slapped him on the back. A labyrinth of limbs reached for him and screamed for his autograph. Women flashed boobs, begging him to sign their tits. Someone grabbed his crotch.

His skin was literally crawling with parasites. He couldn't move or do anything except plaster on a fake smile and pretend to enjoy the attention.

Where was she? He scanned the crowd. "Hal, get me out of here."

The bodyguard linebackered his way through the throngs and created an escape route. Near the dressing rooms, he found her.

She gripped her violin case with both hands and stared at the wall like she was in a trance.

He flew to her side and dragged her into the dressing room, locking the door behind him.

Either she was jet-lagged or shell-shocked. Whatever it was, she didn't seem happy to see him. She set her luggage on the floor and devoured the nails off her right hand. Nope, she definitely wasn't happy to see him.

Adrenaline still pounding through his veins, he twitched and paced the tiny room, trying to calm down enough to speak coherently. "How was your flight?" he asked.

"You lied." She still wouldn't look him in the eye.

"I did?"

"You didn't tell me you were some big rock star." She waved her arms in a circle.

"I hate that word."

She huffed and jammed her hands on her hips.

"I told you I was a musician."

"I thought you were in a garage band!"

"Look, that night . . . I just,"—he fisted the back of his hair— "I just wanted to be me, not El Love."

"When you asked if you could play our songs, you didn't tell me it was for a stadium full of people."

"But surely you looked us up when I asked you to tour with us?"

She dropped her gaze to the floor.

"You didn't Google us?"

"I didn't have time."

Thank God. That meant she hadn't read the trash on him either. "My manager sent you the contract. Didn't you read it?"

"She told me to have my lawyer look at it. I don't have money for a lawyer, Elias."

He lowered his brows. "So you haven't even read it?"

She ground her fists into her eye sockets. "I'm so stupid."

He stroked her cheek. "You are anything but stupid, *mi amor.*

Why don't you take a little nap on the sofa while we load up? You must be exhausted."

Someone pounded on the door. "Love, we need you out here." It was Cato. "You in there with that hot blonde?" He pounded on the door. "Oh, God, fuck me, El Love, fuck me harder." He knocked again. "Seriously, El, we need you."

"Give me five," he shouted back.

"Come on, man, you know you can't last that long."

He ground his jaw. "My bass player thinks he's funny."

A faint smile replaced her frown. "I'm sorry. I'm just . . . *overwhelmed*." A whoosh of air came out with the last word. She jumped and clapped. "You were so great, tonight. Your voice is amazing."

"It is?"

She rolled her eyes. "First you tell me you're a poor deadbeat, now you pretend to be Mr. Humble Shy Guy?"

He took three deep breaths before the next confession. "I am shy. Or I guess the new buzzword is introverted."

She let out a loud cackle and slapped his chest. "I didn't know you were a comedian, too."

"No, really. I don't enjoy performing live. It takes a lot out of me."

"Could have fooled me. Looks like you were born for the stage."

"It's not real," he said. "None of this is. It's just theater."

"My sister's an introvert. Crowds make her uncomfortable, too. Well, actually, *humans* make her uncomfortable."

For him, uncomfortable was putting it mildly. Crowds were torture. But he didn't tell her that.

Instead, he kissed her—lightly at first, just to test the waters.

The waters were smoking hot apparently, because she jumped up and wrapped her legs around his waist, then mauled his mouth, giving him an instant boner.

"I missed you so much," she said between kisses.

"Me, too," he said. "I'm so glad you're here."

They made out like long lost lovers until Cato hammered on the door again.

"*Andá a cagar, puto!*" Elias yelled. "I said I'd be out in a minute."

He set her down and tipped up her chin. "Before I go, I have to tell you something."

"Tell me later." She climbed up his body.

"No, Effie, *mi amor,* this is important. Since you didn't read the contract, you need to know about The Rules."

"The Rules?"

"You and me?" He pointed back and forth. "We can't be like this outside of this room."

"No, PDA, check." She kissed his hand.

"Not just in public. The band can't know either. We don't allow girlfriends on tour. And band members aren't allowed to hook up. We have to keep this a secret."

"I'm your girlfriend?"

His chest tightened. That was the most loaded question ever, and one he wasn't ready to answer.

"Who made up that stupid rule?"

"I did."

"Take it back, then."

"I can't."

She scratched her head. "This feels sketchy."

"I've got to load up." He bolted towards the door, eager to escape that conversational minefield. "We'll talk later."

If she stuck around after that.

VIBRATO

Vibrato

---

*"I wonder if I've been changed in the night? Let me think: was I the
same when I got up this morning? I almost think I can remember
feeling a little different. But if I'm not the same, the next question is
who in the world am I?"*

Soundtrack *"Strange Vacation," Quest for Fire*

An upper, a jolt, a little numbness, some extreme bliss—that's what
Effie needed. And it was there, in that stadium, somewhere. And
probably out in the open. She waited by the bathroom and
watched for grinding jaws. Waited and watched.

Roadies rushed around loading equipment into the truck.
Interviews, autographs, parties, schmoozing—it went on for hours.
Such was the life of the rich and famous. Such was the life of the
guy she'd known for forty-eight hours.

The smell of cigarette smoke wafted down the hall. She rushed
outside. A group of guys were smoking by the door.

"Can I get one of those?" she asked.

A guy with a grizzled beard shook one out of the pack and lit it for her.

After a long dizzying drag, she moved away from the group and leaned against the outside wall, sucking down drags with her shaky hand.

"See that chick Griffin was hammering backstage?" one of the crew said. "Didn't Love used to bang her? The one that claimed he was her baby daddy?"

"Tina," answered a skinny kid.

"Yeah, her." He whistled and took a swig of his beer. "Maybe when she's done with Griffin, she'll give me a hummer."

Another guy laughed. "Broads want pretty-boy rock stars, not ugly roadies."

"My dick's a pretty boy," said the skinny kid.

"I don't want to hear about your tiny dick."

While they sized up their penises, Effie smoked the cigarette all the way to the filter.

What am I doing here? Finding love, said her heart. *Getting paid,* said her mind. By the end of the summer, she'd be a whole lot less broke. She could easily afford another year of tuition and even pay her sister back.

Something felt wrong about the arrangement. Maybe Paul was right—she'd expected more from Elias, especially after traveling for a day and a half.

Elias popped outside right then. "There you are." He glanced over his shoulder to see if anyone was watching then gave her a quick kiss. "You smell like cigarettes. You don't smoke, do you?"

"Secondhand stink." She pointed to the roadies.

He frowned. "Wish they'd quit that shit."

He led her to a double-decker bus, where a short man with a captain's hat over his wild red curls kissed her on both cheeks. "*Bonsoir,*" he said.

She hugged the guy.

He didn't hug her back, which was weird considering he'd just kissed her.

"LeStrange is our driver," Elias said. "He's French. Nobody understands him."

"His name is LeStrange?"

"Eddie LeStrange," Elias confirmed.

The driver corrected his pronunciation. *"Non, ce n'est pas étrange, connard."*

She waved. "Hi, LeStrange."

The driver rolled his eyes and opened the door.

Big-screen TV, leather couches, kitchen and bathroom—boy, they traveled like rock stars. "Wow, sweet ride," she said.

Elias stowed her violin then plunked down across the aisle from her and closed his eyes.

The rest of the band stared at her. Well, more like glared at her. Especially the drummer.

With his Roman nose and fierce golden eyes, he was frightening and alluring—carnal and sexual—like a lion on the hunt.

The bassist sat at the other end, his big white grin and flashy green irises standing out on his dark skin. At least, he seemed happy to see her.

She smiled back.

He kept grinning.

She frowned.

He kept grinning.

And people think I'm weird, she thought.

The keyboardist next to the bassist saw the whole thing. With her delicate features, olive skin, sooty-colored hair, and tiny red frown, she reminded Effie of a mouse.

She waved at her. "Hi! I'm Effie."

Elias snapped open his eyes. "I'm sorry. I'm out of it. I didn't introduce you, did I? Everyone, this is Effie." He gestured to the front. "You already know Annie."

His mother didn't look up from her laptop.

Effie held back the urge yell *Jianren* to the woman.

"That's Griffin," he said, nodding at the drummer.

"Isn't a griffin one of those half-bird, half-lion thingies," she asked.

The bassist snorted. "More like a dirty rooster." He fanned his face. "Boy, you stank. You got this whole bus smelling like a cheap ho. Pew."

She snickered. No one else did. Especially not the drummer. "So that's your real name, then?" she asked. "Griffin?"

"His real name's Ralph," the bassist said. "Ralph Macchio."

"Like *The Karate Kid*?" she asked.

A violent red chemical reaction spread over Ralph's visage.

The bassist fell back in his seat, screaming and laughing and kicking his legs like a toddler having a tantrum.

Elias touched her hand. "He prefers Griffin."

She nodded. "Makes sense. I liked that movie though."

Elias cleared his throat and motioned to the bassist. "Cato here is the *puto de mierda* who kept interrupting us earlier."

"What does that mean?" she asked.

"Well-endowed," Cato said.

The keyboardist scoffed.

"And that's Missy," Elias said.

"Nice to meet you, Misty." Effie said. "So glad I'm not the only female here. Don't think I could handle all this testosterone by myself."

"*Missy*," she snapped. "Not Misty."

She slapped her forehead. "Oh, sorry. I'm terrible with names. Just ask Elvis." She giggle-snorted. It wasn't even funny, but she was delirious with exhaustion. Any minute now and she was going to start hallucinating.

Elias cleared his throat again.

"Ever tried lemon and honey for that?" Effie asked.

He coughed and continued the introductions. "Think you met Hal already. He's pretty much part of the band."

Elias rubbed his eyes. "I'm fried. Give me a minute to decompress."

"Go for it," she said. *I'll just be over here fending off the daggers from your band.* She dug out another lollipop from her backpack, and by the time she reached the gummy center, the bus pulled in front of a shack. *Was that where they were staying?*

"What the—?" Cato sprang to their side of the bus. "I'm gonna kill your mother, El."

"This place even have running water?" Griffin asked.

"I got a good deal from my cousin," Annie said. "Half off."

Elias popped his jaw but stayed quiet. He was different around everyone else than he was with her. Then again, how would she know?

Cato craned his neck. "Where are all the Hobbitses at?"

Hal guffawed. "It totally looks like the goddamned Shire."

"Maybe it's nice inside?" she said.

All eyes landed on her.

"Or not."

"I call the master." Missy yanked her suitcase down from the overhead compartment.

Annie found the key under the mat and stuck it in the lock. The door wouldn't budge.

Elias tried next and failed. He cursed in Spanish then banged his forehead against the door.

Hal raised his hand. "Volunteers to break into the Hobbit Hole?"

"Not it," everyone shouted but Effie. Once again, all eyes focused on her.

"Is this some kind of hazing thing?" she said. "If so, I don't want to be in your frat."

Everyone's gaze shifted to Cato. "Oh, I see." He threw his bag on the ground. "You want the black man to break in and take the heat for all you bitches."

Elias turned to her. "His dad's a locksmith. He can break into anything."

"Yeah, in New York," Cato clarified. "Not in the Shire."

"Hurry the hell up." Missy shivered. "I've gotta pee."

"Yeah, hurry." Hal rubbed his arms. "It's frickin' cold out here."

LeStrange grabbed his crotch. *"Mes testicules ont rampé à l'intérieur de moi pour garder au chaud."*

Everyone stared blankly at the driver.

"Think he said something about his testicles," Griffin said.

Cato shook his head then stomped back to the bus, mumbling about what a bunch of racists they all were. He took his sweet time and finally came back with a screwdriver and a flashlight. A second later, he sprung the lock.

Effie ran over and hugged him. "My hero."

"That's right." He pointed to himself. "Hear that, bitches? I'm the hero. H.E.R.O."

"Get the hell out of my way, hero." Missy bolted through the door and flicked on the light.

Hal screamed like a woman and covered his mouth.

"This place is a shit hole," Griffin said.

Annie surveyed the room. "This look like . . . *China*."

"China is a trash can?" LeStrange asked.

"Speak English," Cato said.

"That was English, no?" he said.

Cato huffed. "I can't understand a word you're saying."

"It smells like boiled anus in here," Hal said.

Effie plugged her nose and surveyed the scene. Piles of dirty dishes and overflowing trash bags crammed the kitchen. In the living room, a fire had burned a hole through the floor and something brown stained the couch.

"Did somebody give birth on that?" Cato asked.

"Qu'est-ce que c'est bordel?" LeStrange said.

Cato flopped out his arms dramatically. "English motherfucker!"

"One-goddamned-bathroom. One!" Griffin shouted from down the hallway. "And the water heater is the size of Hal's head."

Missy ran to the bathroom, holding her vagina. "Gross!" she shouted then ran out with fear in her eyes. "You don't want to know what I just flushed down the toilet."

"You got that right," Hal said.

They crept upstairs. The so-called master suite contained nothing but a full-sized mattress on the floor.

Rickety bunk beds filled the other two tiny rooms.

"Don't rich rock stars normally stay in five-star hotels?" Effie asked.

"Only three rooms?" Annie opened a random door. "Where's number four?"

"Think I found four," Griffin said from under the stairs.

Cato went back to investigate. "Is Harry Potter asleep in there?"

Elias gripped his cheeks and muffled an irritated sigh. "Hal, can you deal with the couch?"

"I did two tours in Iraq. I can handle sleeping on placenta."

"Missy and Annie, the master's all yours."

"Yippee," Missy said flatly.

Annie groaned. "She snores."

"I do not!"

"Cato and Griffin in one bunk." Elias pointed down the hall. "Effie can have the other. I'll sleep in Harry Potter's cupboard."

"You're too tall," Effie said. "I'll sleep in the cupboard."

"You're not sleeping in the cupboard."

"Why does she have to sleep in the cupboard?" Cato asked. "Sleep in the other bunk with Elias."

Elias's hazel gaze landed on her mouth. "You okay with that?"

"Yes!" She sounded a little too excited. "I mean as long as I get the top bunk."

"Deal," Elias said.

Everyone dragged themselves to their rooms, except Annie, who turned on the shower and shut the bathroom door.

"You better not use all the hot water." Griffin pounded on the door.

"Yeah," Cato shouted. "You gotta get that ho stank off before you get in bed."

"Piss off," Griffin said.

Elias closed the bedroom door and let out a long exhale. "Tell me you've got your underoos on." He wrapped his arms around her.

She batted her eyelashes. "Maybe."

He nibbled the shell of her ear, sending tingles between her legs. "Can I see them?" he asked.

"Maybe." She was getting good at this flirting thing.

He wiggled his brows and immediately ripped off his shirt and dropped his pants on the floor.

She covered her eyes "Whoa! I see you're not wearing your underoos. I thought you were shy."

"My dick's not shy. Now lemme see those undies." He gripped her hips.

She slapped his hands. "What about The Rules?"

"Fuck The Rules." He reached for her boobs.

She ducked away and waved a finger at him. "Naughty. Naughty."

He wet his lips and cracked his neck. "Can we at least sleep in the same bed?"

"Sure. Just don't touch me."

He smirked and waved a hand. "After you, then."

She climbed the ladder and scrunched up against the wall. He flicked off the light and lay beside her. The bed creaked and groaned.

"Think this thing's going to hold?" she asked.

He tangled his legs with hers. "I'm gonna fire Annie."

They broke out in a riot of giggles, making the bed wobble dangerously.

"I like this place," she said. "It's silly."

"Silly?"

"You're right, it's a sewer. I'm just happy to be here with you."

He lifted her hand to his mouth and kissed it. "Feel me smiling? I haven't smiled in two weeks," he said. "Not since I left you."

She traced the satin fabric of his lips and pressed her ear to his chest.

"I'm sorry." He ran his fingers through her hair.

"For what?"

"This mess."

"I'm used to messy."

He yawned. "Not me."

"Maybe you need more chaos in your life."

"Or less," he said and instantly fell asleep.

A minute later, they crashed to the floor.

Elias grabbed her leg. "You all right?"

"What happened?"

He crawled out and turned on the lamp.

Hal burst through the door with his gun cocked.

Like a ninja, Elias leapt behind the wreckage, hiding his naked body.

"What the hell happened in here?" Hal boomed.

"The bed broke," Effie said.

Hal scratched his shiny head. "Who was on the bottom?"

"Um . . ." She turned to Elias and winced.

Elias rubbed the corner of his mouth.

Hal ran his tongue over his teeth, gave them a curt nod, then backed out and closed the door.

Elias turned to Effie. "You okay?"

"Are my eyebrows stuck in the shock position?"

"We could have died," he said.

She collapsed in a fit of giggles.

He smiled down at her. "What's so funny?"

"Imagine the headlines." Effie squared her fingers. "'Rock star dies in tragic bunk bed accident.'"

"Don't call me that."

"Bunk bed?"

"No, rock star."

"How about cock star?"

"Hmm. I like it."

They cleared a spot on the floor and placed the mattresses on top.

She shuddered. "Seriously, you could have been crushed under there."

He held her hand. "I'm pretty tough."

"No kidding. What was that ninja move you pulled?"

"Learned that in 'Nam," he mused.

"Cock star. Ninja. You're full of surprises."

The wind whistled through the broken windowpane. She could tell by his breathing he hadn't fallen asleep yet.

"You worried about Hal telling everyone?" she asked. "Is that why you're so quiet?"

"I can't stop thinking about being inside you."

A gap of silence passed. "We don't even know each other."

"I know." He kissed her temple. "We'll start tomorrow."

RESONANCE

Resonance

Soundtrack *"Everybody Daylight," Brightblack Morning*

Elias opened his eyes the next morning and found Effie curled against him, her hair spread out like a silken blanket. *Finally.* Finally she was back in his arms.

Someone shrieked down the hallway.

Effie bolted upright. "What was that?"

"I don't know. Sounded like Cato."

She stretched. "Good morning!"

He smiled. *"Buenos días."*

She surveyed the room. "Wow, this place looks worse in the daylight."

"Yeah, let's get out of here."

They dressed quickly and made for the kitchen. Except for Cato, everyone else was packed and ready to go.

"About time." Griffin scratched his chest.

"Stop," Missy said. "You're making it worse."

"Making what worse?" Elias asked.

"Bed bugs. Fleas. Shit, I don't know." He lifted his shirt and showed the welts covering his torso.

Cato charged out of the bathroom with wild eyes. "I'm awake now, motherfuckers. Y'all hear me screaming? The hot water ran out right as I was rinsing the soap off my balls."

All of the guys groaned. All of the women giggled.

"Talk about a rude awakening," Hal said.

"No shit," Cato said.

"*Mierda*," Elias said. "Guess I'm not showering until the next place."

"I wouldn't recommend it," Cato said.

"Let's get out of this dump," Elias said.

Once they were on the highway, Elias grabbed his laptop and sat next to Effie. "We recorded the new songs during our practice sessions." He handed her his headphones. "I want to get your input."

She put them on and pressed play. While she listened, she twitched, scratched, wrung her wrists, rubbed her eyes, and bit her nails.

He pressed stop. "What's wrong?"

She wrinkled her nose. "Everything."

"You serious?"

A huge bullet list of problems poured out her mouth.

Cato leaned over the back of his seat. "What's wrong with the bassline?"

"Your rhythm isn't matching the drums," she said.

"Yo, Griffin," Cato said. "The violinist doesn't like your beats."

Griffin fired off a few rounds of heavy artillery into his video game enemy. "Oh yeah? Tell her I don't give a shit what she thinks."

"Tell Ralph he's a butthead," Effie shouted back.

"Butthead?" Cato stomped and cackled. "Burn."

Griffin threw the controller on the seat and barged back with murder in his eyes.

A staring contest began, Effie and Griffin fighting to the death. "You're inconsistent," she said. "And you play like a madman during the ballad and like an old man during the harder songs."

The veins on his drummer's arms pulsed as he squeezed and released his fists. "You know who you're talking to?"

She gave him a sweet smile. "Ralph Macchio?"

Adding more insult to injury, Cato kicked and pointed and laughed.

If she didn't stop busting their balls, they'd never listen. He touched her arm. "F-bomb?"

"Yes," she said, not breaking eye contact with the now irate Griffin.

"Instead of telling them, show us what you mean." He turned to Griffin and Cato. "Get your guitar and drum machine." He yelled up front. "Missy!"

Missy shot to the back. "What?"

"Grab your keyboard."

"Why?"

Effie started in. "Because it sounds like sh—"

He placed his hand on hers, shushing her before Missy kicked her ass. "Get your keyboard, *porfa*."

Missy frowned down at their hands then grabbed her instrument from the overhead bin.

Everyone gathered around Effie. She pressed play on the laptop. "Right there! Did you hear it? The timing is off. Pass me the drum thingy."

Griffin tightened his jaw and shoved it at her.

"I've never played one of these before," she said. "How does it work?"

Elias turned it on and gave her a set of drumsticks. "Just tap it like this."

"Oh, cool. Okay. Start the song." On the first try, she hammered out a perfectly synced beat. "Hear the difference?"

If Griffin didn't, he was going to send him to music school.

His drummer uncrossed his arms and gave her a slow deliberate nod. "Yeah, I hear it."

She clapped and cheered. "Yay! Okay next." She went over the changes with Cato then moved on to Missy.

"Your voice is flat," Effie told her. "And you keep hitting the wrong note." She shouldered Missy out of the way and played the tune herself.

Missy bored holes through the side of Effie's face. "You're telling us what to do, how do we know you don't suck?"

Effie's hand froze above the keys then slowly dropped to her side.

For the first time, Elias felt disconnected from his band. They acted like Effie threatened their survival, but it was she who would keep them from dying off.

"Effie," he said. "Show Missy what a terrible musician you are. Get out your violin."

"What do you want me to play?"

"Whatever you want."

"I'll play a classical piece then one of the new songs. How's that?"

He nodded. "Go ahead."

Annie and Hal wandered back for the show.

Her song made the hairs on the back of his neck stand up.

Someone sniffled.

"Dude," Cato said to Hal. "Are you crying?"

Hal wiped his face. "I'm a sensitive guy."

Next, she played the song they wrote. "This is where Missy's vocals come in." She sang the part with a hypnotically sexy voice. And when she finished, no one said a thing.

"I didn't know you could sing," Elias said.

She snorted. "I can't. You heard me, right? I'm terrible."

"No, girl," Cato said with a resigned sigh. "You can sing. And play bass. And drums. And keyboard. And write songs. You got that?" He snapped his fingers. "What's it called? Assburgers? You know, like *Rain Man*?"

Effie mumbled "asshole" under her breath then stuck another lollipop in her mouth.

"I'm just fucking wit' chew." Cato held out his knuckles for a fist bump.

She bumped him back with her sucker. "I was fucking with you as well."

Cato bent over and laughed. "You're all right, F-bomb."

Elias's tension drained away. Cato's approval meant everything. *One down. Two to go.*

Everyone else returned to their seats, leaving him and Effie alone in the back.

"Hi," she whispered.

"Hola."

She lowered her chin. "They don't really like me, do they?"

He pressed his finger on her mouth. "Shhh. You're fine. This is a big change. They'll warm up eventually." At least, he hoped they would. Otherwise, it was going to be a rough ride.

She perked up. "What should we do now?"

He leaned closer. "Get to know each other."

"What do you want to know?"

"All of your secrets," he whispered.

Her smile faded. "Let's save those for another day."

COUNTERPOINT

Counterpoint

Counterpoint

LIVERPOOL, ENGLAND

"O Mouse, do you know the way out of this pool? I am very tired of swimming about here, O Mouse!"

Soundtrack *"Four Seasons op.8," Vivaldi*

Through the open window in her practice room, Effie watched the kids across the street leap over the lawn sprinklers. Droplets of mist glistened off their bodies and shrieks of joy rang out each time the water blasted them. It must have felt so good, the cool water hitting their hot skin.

"She's just a kid, Elise," her father shouted. "Let her go outside and play."

"If she falls and breaks her hand, she'll ruin her career," her mother sniped back.

"Her career? She's six, for Christ's sake."

"Don't you think I know what's best for my own child?"

"Your child? Last I checked, it takes two to make a baby."

"I won't let you ruin her career like you ruined mine."

The sprinklers rotated over the slick grass. *Tshht, tshht, tshht.*

"Not a day goes by that I don't regret knocking you up. You want to be a single parent? Be my guest." The garage door slammed and her father's car zoomed past.

He didn't come back that night. Or ever again.

"Alice began to feel very uneasy: to be sure, she had not as yet had any dispute with the Queen, but she knew that it might happen any minute, 'and then,' thought she, 'what would become of me?'"

Soundtrack *"Chemical," Jack Garratt*

WHILE THE ADULTS—ELIAS and Gail—argued about her, Effie watched everyone play in the pool out back. Hal and Cato floated on rafts, and Annie swam from end-to-end like a frog. Missy dipped her toes in the water, and Griffin snoozed in the sun.

What she wouldn't give to be out there with them.

After they'd arrived in England, Gail Heart and her lackeys blasted through the mansion door like a red tempest and rained a shitstorm down on everyone.

With her perfectly coiffed black hair, artfully applied makeup, and tailored red suit, one might have mistaken Gail for a CEO rather than a band manager.

But when she opened her mouth, Gail morphed from a professional businesswoman into Queen Bitch.

Not once had Gail called her by name. Instead, she referred to her in third-person. "Tell the violinist the hairdresser is waiting upstairs to cut her mop."

"I'm right here," Effie said.

At first, she couldn't fathom what she'd done to deserve such treatment. They'd only known each other for half an hour. But once they sat down to discuss her contract, it became abundantly clear. Elias had gone around Gail and made his own label. And the woman blamed her.

"Who do you think you are?" Gail snapped at Elias. "Prince? You can't just make up another name in the middle of my tour."

He jabbed a thumb at his chest. "It's my tour. Besides, Effie's not in the band. She's a contract musician."

"A contract musician who's playing in my band, on the tour Heart Records funded." Gail punctuated every word with a slap on the glass table.

Elias sat back and smirked, clearly amused by Gail's frazzled state. "We wrote the songs outside of the label. They don't belong to you."

"Then you can forget about putting that twit onstage." Gail flicked a finger in her direction. "She fucks up, and it's Heart Records who's liable, not you."

He flipped to the end of the contract. "Page seven states the band is liable for anything that goes wrong."

Gail slapped the table. "That's not good enough. I need to see a return on my investment."

"My lawyer and I already spoke to your father about this," Elias said. "It's a done deal. Either you sign the contract or the tour ends here."

Gail's nostrils flared as if she were about to breath fire out of them and torch everything to the ground. "You went behind my back!"

"Your dad says 'hi,' by the way," Elias said.

The manager's silence lingered for a moment. Then she leaned forward and propped her chin on her folded hands. "Remember when I met you? You were playing in that shitty club in the meatpacking district?" She laughed a little. "You were so broke you had to duct tape the holes in your shoes."

She stood and shook a stiff finger at him. "Go behind my back again, and you'll be playing at redneck county fairs from here on out."

Elias shot up from his seat. "Get out."

"Struck a nerve, did I?" Gail leveled him with a glare. "Good." She stuffed the signed contract in her designer bag. "That twit so much as blinks the wrong way, and I will end you." Then she stormed out with her servants in tow.

The minute she left, Elias charged out the back door and left.

Heart racing and stomach churning, Effie sat glued to her chair, feeling like she'd just witnessed her own beheading. *I need to get wasted.*

She bolted up and tore through the kitchen, searching for something to get her high. But all she found were dishes and a few cans of soup.

"What are doing?"

She spun around and found Annie leaning against the doorway. "How long have you been there?"

"Not long. What were you looking for?"

"Aspirin." She rubbed her temples. "I have a headache."

"Come to my room," Annie said. "I fix pain."

Puh-lease. What antidote could this woman possibly have to cure the pain of addiction? "No thanks. I'm fine."

Annie narrowed her eyes as if she could see right through her bullshit.

With no other option in sight, Effie followed the woman to her room and sat on the bed.

"Your chi not flow," Annie said. "Your life-force is stuck."

Was it that obvious? She blasted out an irritated sigh. "Great. Just what I needed to hear."

Annie shut the blinds then snapped on a pair of rubber gloves. "Gail is a cunt."

"Did you just say the C word?"

"Gail's chi is also fucked," Annie said. "She needs to get laid.

Sex helps energy flow." She unwrapped a needle and held it above her face.

Effie warded her off with a pillow. "Nuh-uh. I'm not letting someone in a Hello Kitty bikini stick needles into my skull."

"Wha? My ass looks great in this suit. Now shut mouth and lie down."

"I don't trust you," Effie said.

"I don't trust you, either." Annie tapped a needle into her head.

A moment later, tears leaked down her face. "What's wrong with me?"

Annie dabbed a cool washcloth on her face. "Shhh. Be still. The chi is flowing."

All of a sudden, she felt weightless, as if she were floating in space. Forever passed, or maybe just a second, and Annie opened the shades.

Effie sat up. The needles were gone. So were her cravings. She wiggled her fingers. Her hands didn't hurt anymore. Neither did her neck.

"Feel better?" Annie asked.

"My arthritis is gone."

"You have a lot of bad chi." She tossed her gloves in the trash.

"Annie?'

"Hmm?"

"What do I do now?"

"Pfft. How should I know? I'm acupuncturist, not fortuneteller." She shook her head and mumbled something in Chinese.

Effie raised a brow. "What did you just say?"

Annie cracked a devious grin then waltzed out of the room.

23

DUET

Duet

Soundtrack *"Modern Man," Arcade Fire*

In a festering rage, Elias walked almost two miles to downtown Liverpool.

Gail had become the enemy.

When he'd started the band, he'd been so thrilled to be backed by a major label he didn't even blink an eye before he signed Heart's contract. But it wasn't long before he realized he'd not only signed away Urban's royalties, he'd also signed away his soul.

Heart Records owned him.

But they didn't own Effie.

Guilt gnawed on his conscience. *Poor Effie*. She was so innocent and naïve. During his meeting with Gail, she looked shell-shocked, like he'd slapped her in the face.

Thunderclouds boomed overhead, and the sky spat rain on the streets. On the corner, he ducked inside a teashop.

The aroma of dried tea leaves permeated the place, and light jazz played in the background. Faces aglow from their laptop screens, none of the patrons noticed him enter.

Silently, he cheered about not having to pose for a selfie with a stranger.

He ordered a cup of Earl Gray and settled on a tattered sofa in the back. As the rain poured outside, his anger dissipated into dread.

What if Gail was right? What if he'd made a horrible mistake? What if Effie was terrible onstage? Or worse, what if she ruined his career? His career meant everything.

An older couple straggled in from out of the rain. While the man ordered at the counter, the woman shook off her wet coat and sat at a table nearby. Later, the man sat next to her with two mugs.

The woman sipped her tea and smiled. "Mm, jasmine. How did you know that's what I wanted?"

"It's your favorite when it rains."

"What if it's sunny?"

"Mint."

"How did you know?"

He kissed her cheek. "After all these years of sleeping next to you, think I haven't been paying attention?"

The woman covered his hand with hers. "You know me better than I know myself, darling."

As Elias listened to their conversation, melancholy flooded him. He couldn't fathom what it would be like to be with someone long enough to memorize her drink preferences. In his world, long-term relationships didn't really exist, and those that did were an anomaly.

Crowds of people gathered around him every weekend, and yet, somehow he still felt lonely.

A worker turned the station to classical, and violin music floated out. He closed his eyes and listened to 'symphony of humanity'—spoons tinkling and rain spattering and light whispers of love-me-nots from the couple beside him. And soon, warm thoughts of Effie cleared away the clouds around his heart.

He pulled out his phone and texted her.

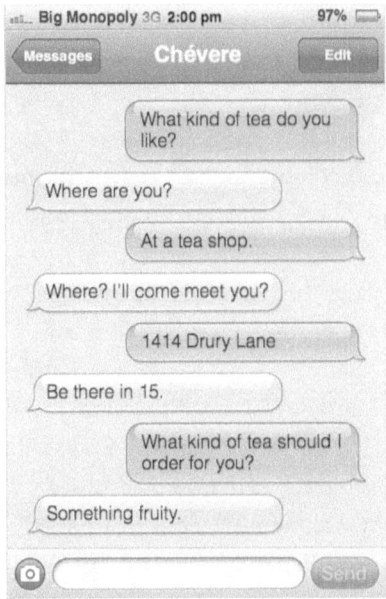

Not even ten minutes later, she skipped back to the sofa and sat next to him. "LeStrange dropped me off," she said. "Someone took a picture of me outside. They must have thought I was famous."

"You will be soon."

She snorted. "More like infamous."

He kissed the raindrops off her rosy cheeks and poured her a mug of raspberry tea.

She squeezed his leg. "That's delicious. What are you drinking?"

"Earl Grey."

"Hmm, I would have taken you for a chai lover."

"I'm a basic man with basic tastes."

She took another sip and set down her mug. "So, basic man, want to tell me why you left me alone with your crazy mother."

He coughed a laugh and set down his tea.

She squinted. "Think it's funny? Why'd you bring me here, anyway? So you could use me to get back at your manager?"

He lifted her hand to his lips. *"Flaquita,* you know why I brought you here."

"For your band."

"For me."

She didn't seem convinced. "Then why'd you leave? And why didn't you tell me where you were going? I was worried."

"You were?"

She snatched back her hand. "Duh! Just because I don't know you, doesn't mean I don't care. It's raining. You don't have a jacket."

He couldn't help but smile. Someone cared about him. *She* cared about him. *"Perdoname.* I'm sorry. I needed time to think. I'm used to solving problems on my own."

"Well, you're not alone now. So next time, tell me where you're going and when you'll be back, or I'll cut off your *cojónes.*" She snipped her fingers.

"I see you're learning Spanish."

"I'm serious."

He crossed his heart. *"Te prometo,* I won't leave without telling you again."

"Good." She wiped her hands and sat back. "Now what are we going to do about Gail?"

He tucked her under his arm and nuzzled her neck. *"We* are going to focus on the music. And I will take care of my manager. Once she hears you play, she'll leave us alone."

She didn't seem convinced. Frankly, he wasn't either.

"You better be right, *jefe.*"

He groaned. "First Annie, and now you. I'm not your boss."

"Yes, you are."

He wagged a finger. "No."

"Then what are you?"

"A cock star."

ESPRESSIVO

Espressivo

"'Mine is a long and a sad tale,' said the Mouse, turning to Alice, and sighing."

Soundtrack *"Burn the Witch," Radiohead*

The rehearsal sucked. It was all wrong. Everything. Now she understood, on a visceral level, Professor Frommer's reaction to her audition.

So far Urban had played the set list three times, and every time, her irritation swelled. The fourth time, she set down her violin and walked off the stage.

"Where's she going?" Cato asked.

"I need a minute." She grabbed her bag and jammed a lollipop in her mouth, then darted toward the opposite end of the field.

Elias jogged down the ramp and ran after her. "What's up?"

"Nothing." She crunched down hard on the candy.

"Stop for a sec." He hooked her elbow. "You okay?"

"I'm fine." She gave him a gritty smile.

"F-bomb?"

"It's offal," she blurted out.

He jerked back. "Awful?"

"No, *offal*, as in the remnants of a dead animal. It sounds terrible."

He pinched his lip and said nothing.

"I'm sorry. I know that was harsh."

Still no response.

She kept walking.

He caught up with her again. "Tell me how to fix it."

"Griffin's timing is still off. And Missy's not even trying. Cato's just messing around. You're overpowering everyone else."

He threaded his hands on top of his head and paced in a circle. "Let me talk to them first. And we'll go from there."

They trudged back through the weeds and climbed back onstage. Elias voiced Effie's complaints to the band. Immediately after, Griffin tossed his drumsticks at the amp, Cato yelled "fuck this shit" every other second, and Missy looked downright homicidal.

Effie hurried to the keyboard and played the song. The yelling stopped. "This part right here needs intensity. Hear the difference?"

They said nothing.

She hopped up and grabbed Cato's bass.

He swiped it back. "Girl, bye. You don't touch Shanequa."

"Just for a minute, please."

He handed over his instrument as carefully as he would hand over his penis.

She played the bassline. "Legato, not staccato."

"I don't speak Russian," he said.

"Smooth and flowing, not sharp and separated." She shoved it back in his hands and ran to the drums. "Get up," she told Griffin.

He gave her a look that said over his dead body.

"Griffin," Elias warned.

"She's not touching my kit."

"Fine, I'll clap the beat." She started at 70 BPM. "Now play with me."

He picked up a new set of sticks and banged on the drums.

"No, that's not right. You're off by a beat. Subtract one."

Finally, he got it right.

"That's great," she said, "but louder. This song is about heat and attraction and sex."

Griffin hammered harder.

She applauded his efforts then turned to the others. "Elias and Cato, here's where you come in."

After they started, she spoke to Missy. "Now sing."

The keyboardist's voice was as meek as a mouse.

"Come on!" Effie shouted. "More passion." She ran to the microphone and belted out the lyrics.

Missy backed away, shot her a stiff middle finger, and stomped off stage.

"Let her go," Elias said.

Effie ignored him and ran after her. "Stop, Missy. Talk to me."

Missy picked up her pace. "Fuck off."

"What is your problem?" Effie yelled.

Missy spun around and charged toward her. "My problem? MY PROBLEM! You're my problem. Who do you think you are? You have a weekend fling with Elias and suddenly your Yoko Ono ass is telling me what to do?"

How did she know about their fling?

An ungrounded amp buzzed in the background, providing the perfect soundtrack for the tension that sizzled between them.

"You're right," Effie said softly. "I'm sorry. This is the first time I've written anything besides classical music, and I'm nervous because so much is at stake."

"You act like I'm some amateur. I've been playing for fifteen years."

"It's not that you can't play, it's that you don't care."

Missy spun on her heel. "I don't have to put up with this shit."

Effie grabbed her shirt. "Want to know how I know that?"

Missy turned and gave her a mock bow. "Yes, please, enlighten me. Tell me what else I'm doing wrong."

"I'm cursed with extremely sensitive hearing. That's why I can pick up other instruments so easily." Effie pointed to the stage. "That amp is making me crazy. I can hear a lawnmower off in that field." She pointed up to the sky. "That plane sounds like it's flying right through my brain. I hear you breathing and insects flying and roadies' footsteps in the dirt." She covered her ears with her fists. "It's maddening."

Missy looked about as sympathetic as a serial killer.

Effie clenched her stomach. "If something's off-tune, I get sick to my stomach. If the tempo's off, I get this weird pain in my eye." She blinked one eye. "It's awful." And it was also the reason she'd turned to drugs—to numb the pain.

"I don't care about your stupid hearing."

"I can hear emotion. And you don't have any. The way you play sounds generic. It sounds like you don't want to be up there."

"Everything okay, Effie?" Elias yelled from the stage.

After his one-sided question, a flicker of sorrow flew across the keyboardist's face.

All at once, Effie understood everything—Missy was in love with Elias. That's why she didn't like her. Missy was jealous.

Unrequited love. The most painful love in the world.

Though Effie had never experienced it, she felt Missy's pain deep in her gut.

"How long have you been in love with him?" Effie whispered.

A flash of surprise went off in Missy's eyes. "What?"

"Does he know?" Effie asked.

Missy's brows bowed, her chin quivered, then a sob broke free. Effie hugged her. "I'm sorry."

Missy swatted the tears off her face. "I'm fine."

"No one means it when they say those words."

"I'm not in love with him anymore," Missy said. "I have a boyfriend."

"You do?" Then why the hell was she stuck on her man?

Missy nodded. "Sam."

"I take it you're not in love with Sam?"

"I love him, but in a different way. He's warm and affectionate and makes me laugh. But there's just no, I don't know, there's no"—she rubbed her fingers together—"fire I guess. He's too nice."

Effie tried not to roll her eyes. "He sounds like a beast."

"I know it sounds bitchy. The thing is, Sam would make a great husband and father, and I've always wanted to be a mom. And Elias isn't exactly marriage material. Even if he were into me, he doesn't want kids."

That information neither surprised her, nor changed her feelings for him. Marriage and kids didn't really matter to her.

Even though Missy's secret was out in the open, it still didn't solve the immediate problem.

"The way you feel right now?" Effie said. "Use it. Tell everyone how you feel through your music."

Missy slumped over and sighed. "I'll try."

Effie hugged her tightly, and that time, she hugged her back. "Missy?"

"Yeah?"

"Who's Yoko Ono?"

"Seriously?"

"Never mind. I'll look it up."

The next time around, Missy sang and played her heart out. And afterwards, her normally pinched mouth spread into a broad smile. Clearly, she'd experienced some sort of catharsis.

Urban practiced until midnight, and by the end, they sounded so good, Effie performed a cheerleader routine, which included a half-assed split jump.

Elias snuck up behind her after that and pressed his hard-on against her ass. "Later, I'm gonna make you do the splits across my face." He bit her earlobe. "Leave your door unlocked tonight."

RUBATO

Rubato

"Forgetting pain is convenient. Remembering it, agonizing. But recovering the truth is worth the suffering."

Soundtrack *"Fires," Band Of Skulls*

As promised, Elias rapped on her door later that night. She opened it, and he lunged for her, taking her face in his hands, and kicking the door shut behind him.

His husky voice sent a scorching shiver down her spine. He grabbed her ass and hoisted her against his erection. "Feel how much I want you."

She wanted him. *Oh God*, she wanted him. But it was too soon. She still wasn't sure. "Elias," she whispered. "I need to go slow."

He released his grip and set her down. Forehead creased with tension, he pinched his bottom lip for a moment. "I want to make you come—"

"Elias—"

"I don't mean sex. There are other things we can do." He

curled his fingers around her neck. "And after that, I want to bury my face in your hair and feel your bare skin against me while I sleep."

A soft squeak popped out of her.

He tore off his shirt and stepped out of his jeans. He was lean and hard—*everywhere*. He gave himself a leisurely tug then sat in a chair across from the bed. "Take off your clothes," he ordered. "Slowly."

"Elias—"

"Now." Though his command was gentle, his gaze was anything but.

She unbuttoned her top and shrugged it off her shoulders.

"Touch your breasts," he said. "Pinch your hard nipples." The evidence of his arousal bobbed in agreement.

She did as he asked, and a spasm of pleasure released liquid heat between her thighs.

Mouth tilted in a half grin, he rubbed the head of his cock through his fist. "Are you getting wet?"

She nodded.

"You like watching me?"

"Oh, yes."

"Take off those Hulk undies. I want to see for myself."

She stepped out of her clothes.

"Come closer. That's it. Spread yourself open so I can see how swollen and wet you are." He bit his lip and glanced up at her. "Rub that hard clit for me, make yourself wetter."

Her knees almost buckled the minute she touched herself. She gasped and closed her eyes, rocking against her hand.

"Watch me," he said. "Open your eyes."

As he worked his cock in his hand, flames hit her center.

"Put your finger in your pussy then let me suck it. I want to taste you."

"Oh my God. I can't stand up."

"Sit on my lap."

"I can't."

"You can and you will." He pulled her down sideways on top of him. "Now do as I asked."

She dipped her finger inside and held it out for him.

He rolled his tongue around it and sucked it clean, pressing his own finger into her mouth.

"That's it." He took hold of himself again. "Now fuck yourself, while I do the same."

Panting, she leaned back and spread one leg over the arm of the chair.

He latched onto her nipple.

An intense ripple of ecstasy rolled through her. She arched up into his mouth. "Feels good."

"That's it, *mi amor*. Come."

Come was an understatement. It was more like she exploded.

A guttural cry of masculine lust let loose, and he crashed his mouth against hers, sucking on her tongue, while he blasted cum on her belly.

Out of breath and limp, she collapsed back on his damp chest and ran her fingers over his nipples. "Wow, I needed that."

"Me, too." He kissed her again, then picked her up and carried her to bed. After that, he strutted into the bathroom, with a playful grin on his face, then came out a moment later and washed her belly and thighs with a warm washcloth.

This beautiful man was the perfect harmonic mixture of sweetness and masculinity.

A brief moment of panic consumed her—this wasn't going to last. Bliss never lasted—it disappeared in an instant.

But then he enveloped her in his warmth and swept his fingers over the curves of her shoulders, into the crook of her elbow, and around her wrist—his touch as light as butterfly wings—and she let go of her negative thoughts, and instead clung to the blissful moment.

He drew a line down her center and circled her belly button. "This is where you were given life."

A suppressed giggle burst out of her. "That tickles."

He smiled against her skin. "Your laugh is beautiful."

She lifted his chin. "You make me melt."

He gripped her hip, then rolled her over on her tummy and examined her side. "What's that horrible scar from?"

The memory of the wound shot like a bullet through her mind.

"You were almost there. Almost free from what you fear. You could have been cured. You could have forgotten."

EFFIE PLANNED her suicide much like a composer writes his own requiem.

When her father picked her up after her first visit to rehab, he wasn't at all happy to see her. There was no love or sympathy in his expression, nor any remorse from having neglected her.

As a matter of fact, he didn't look at her at all. Nor did he speak to her. He drove her back to his house in complete silence.

At his home, he treated her like a pest who'd invaded his house. She was no longer his kid apparently. The position had been taken over by his other two daughters, who weren't fucked-up junkies.

Instead, he and his new wife—a docile and doughy woman, the polar opposite of her mother—and their two kids who looked just like her, carried on with their lives as if she didn't exist.

In the mornings, her father made the girls pancakes then drove them to school. After school, he attended their soccer games and Girl Scout meetings. At night, he and his new family sat down for dinner and rehashed their day. He told stupid jokes and made them laugh. And at bedtime, he tucked his replacement daughters in bed and read them stories.

Throughout his daily family routine, Effie was invisible. No one asked her how her day went. She made her own food, usually a bowl of cereal, and ate by herself at the counter. Then she'd shuffle to her room and go back to sleep.

After a month there, a dark web of depression spun around her, and all she did was sleep.

When her landlords went on vacation that summer, she woke up long enough to plot her demise.

First, she hocked his wife's jewelry and bought an eight ball, a rubber tube, and a syringe, then drove out to the beach right before sunrise.

She snorted line after line under the pier, picturing how she'd look dead on the ocean—her hair spread out like a mermaid's, seaweed tangled in it—and her blue eyes pecked out by seagulls. But she'd have a peaceful smile on her face, because finally, she'd be free.

After snorting half the bag, she cooked a spoonful over a lit candle. When the sun rose, she loaded the syringe and stuck it in her arm, and after that, she'd planned to swim out to sea.

What she didn't plan on was a bunch of junkies stabbing her and making off with the drugs. She also didn't plan on bleeding to death on the beach. And she definitely didn't plan on Skip surfing that morning then finding her wasted body sprawled across the bloody sand.

"Jesus Christ, Effie! Oh, shit! Oh, shit! What have you done?"

She remembered greeting him with a smile. "Hi, Skip. Are you dead, too?"

Terrified that she'd croak before the ambulance arrived, he carried her to his car and sped to the hospital.

Three days later, she woke up and found a different needle in her arm, as well as a six-inch sutured gash above her kidney. She also found Skip at her bedside, weeping with his face buried in his hands.

This struck her as odd at the time. She barely knew her sister's best friend. Why did he care if she died? But through the haze of drugs and beeping machines, she realized he wasn't there for her —he was there for the broken version of Callie.

"How long have you been in love with my sister?" she asked him.

"Oh, thank God." He rushed to her side. "You're not brain dead."

She laughed. She laughed so hard she popped the stitches in her side.

A blind rage took over his torment. "You think this is funny? You think suicide is funny?"

It was her turn to cry next.

He plopped down in the chair across from her and sighed. "Forever," he said.

"What?"

"I've been in love with Callie since I met her."

"Why didn't you tell her?"

"Because obviously she doesn't feel the same way. And because she lives with an asshole in Chicago now. And because, believe it or not, I have a little dignity."

She reached out for his hand and gripped it tight.

He teared up again. "Please don't make me tell your sister I found you half dead."

She gave him a stiff smile. "It'll be our secret. All of it."

His normal stoicism returned. "I didn't tell the doctor you tried to off yourself, otherwise you'd be in an institution right now."

A spasm of pain punched her heart. "How did you know?"

He gave her a crushing sarcastic look. "You're lucky I showed up."

"I don't feel lucky."

He regarded her for a moment. "When's the next time you're gonna try this? And what if I don't get there in time? You're a fucking ticking bomb, Effie, an F-bomb."

She let go of his hand and curled up in the fetal position.

"What are we going to do with you?"

"I can't go back to rehab."

"You have to."

"It doesn't work."

"I talked to the shrink here. There's an experimental drug study in San Diego. It's a year-long program."

And who was going to pay for that? Not her family. "Did you tell my parents?"

He shook his head. "I've been sitting here with my thumbs up my ass, trying to figure out what to do if you made it out of a coma."

The heaviness of it all—it was so unbearable. And then her will to live slipped away, and she closed her eyes and gave in.

A sharp smack woke her up two days later. "Get up," Skip said. "I'm driving you to San Diego."

"When you can't look on the bright side, I will sit with you in the dark."

"Effie?" Elias said.

"Mm-hmm?"

"What happened here?" He traced the outline of her scar.

Feeling exposed all of a sudden, she scooted out from under him and buried herself under the blankets. At some point she'd have to reopen those wounds and let the pain spill out. But what if he didn't want a broken woman?

She'd have to give it to him in measured doses, build up his tolerance. Just give him little sips of her story at a time.

"I was mugged," she said.

He tore back the covers. "They hurt you?"

"I was stabbed."

His brows drew tight. "Jesus. When?"

"A few years ago. On the beach."

"What did they take?"

"Nothing really." Ironically, they'd saved her life. "Pretty ugly, isn't it?"

He turned her to her side and kissed the scar. "This reminds me that you're not a figment of my imagination. That you're real." Then he tucked her into his arms and surrounded her with his heat.

She swallowed a heavy sob. "Do you have scars?"

He stiffened behind her. "A few."

"Can I see?"

He let out a weighted breath and turned over. Tiny white scars covered his back. They were small, but deep, like holes.

She pressed her fingers along the seams. "Who did this to you?"

"My mother. My real mother."

"Oh my God. With what?"

"The heel of her tango shoe." He let out a papery laugh then flipped back over.

She felt his childhood pain in the center of her core, more so than her own. She snuggled up to his neck and tossed a leg over him. "My mother was a different sort of animal," she said. "She beat me with words."

He stroked her back and said nothing.

"How did we both end up with rotten mothers?"

"My mother doesn't matter." He paused for a long while. "I may have her blood in my body and her marks on my back, but she's not who I am. What happened yesterday won't happen tomorrow. I choose my destiny now, not her. The past is like an old record. You can play it over and over and make it the theme song of your life. Or you can seal it up in a box and burn it."

She kissed the spot behind his ear. "Have any extra napalm lying around?"

He exhaled a sad breathy laugh, squeezed her tight, and gave her a soft kiss. "*Soñá con los angelitos, mi vida.*"

"What does that mean?"

"Dream with the angels, my little life."

ENERGICO

Energico

"'How do you like the Queen?' said the mouse in a low voice. 'Not at all," said Alice: 'she's so extremely—" Just then she noticed the Queen was close behind her, listening.'"

Soundtrack *"Empty Room," Arcade Fire*

Through two-inch feathered false eyelashes, Effie stared at her horror-stricken (or rather whore-stricken) reflection in the mirror. "I look like a whore!" She swiveled the chair and shot daggers at the hair and makeup guy. "What did you do to me?"

"Honey, you look fabulous," Kyle said. "Wait until you see your outfit."

"What outfit?"

The woman who'd taken her measurements a few days prior held up a black leather bustier and boy-shorts, attached by straps. "I'm not wearing that."

"Queen Bitch's orders."

Apparently, she wasn't the only one who despised Gail. "Give it to me." She snatched it from him and slipped behind a screen panel set up at the other end of the room.

"Well?" Kyle asked.

"I look like I'm ready to strip in an S&M show. This is awful."

He flopped a pair of boots over the screen. "Don't forget these."

"I can't walk in those. No way."

"Those shoes cost more than you made in the last five years," Gail said on the other side of the screen.

Effie's ribs closed in around her lungs. She peered around the screen and found Gail in Kyle's chair. Had it not been for the manager's mocking smile and cold glare, one would have mistaken her for someone almost laid-back.

She stepped out from the screen. "How do you know what I made?"

Gail examined her blood-red nails. "Because you don't have any employment history, or housing records, or credit cards, or auto loans. In fact, according to our background check, you didn't exist until you enrolled in school last year." She propped her chin in her hand. "Who are you, Effie Murphy? I'm dying to find out."

Effie wiped a trickle of sweat off the back of her neck.

"Let's start with the basics, shall we? Like why you've never played violin anywhere before Juilliard. What were you doing before? Stripping?"

Her mouth fell open.

"I'm sorry what was that?" She cupped her ear. "I can't hear you."

"None of your business." She sounded more desperate than defiant.

Gail shot up. "You *are* my business."

"What does it matter?"

"This is my band. And if you've got secrets, I need to know."

Effie balled her hands into fists and said nothing.

Gail flashed a demonic smile and strode toward the door. "Don't worry. I'll find out. Get those boots on, and get your ass ready to play." Then she disappeared like a puff of red smoke.

Missy traipsed into the tent, wearing a modest black sheath dress. Her eyes bugged out. "Jesus, you look like Madonna."

Effie felt a massive breakdown coming on. She fanned her face and bit her tongue to keep it at bay.

"You okay?" The keyboardist seemed sincerely concerned.

And that just made it harder to stave off the tears. She slipped on both boots, straightened to her new five-foot-ten frame, and squared her shoulders. "I'm fine," she lied, then hobbled outside to find Elias.

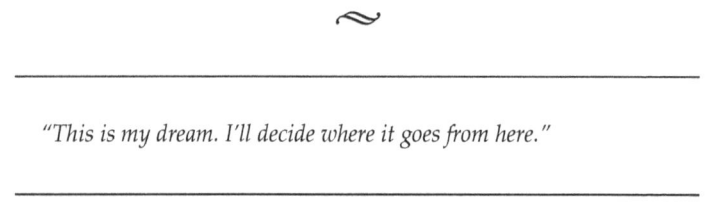

"This is my dream. I'll decide where it goes from here."

Soundtrack *"Dirty White Boots," Lenny Kravitz*

I CAN'T DO this sober. I can't play tonight. I should just pack up and go home.

She clomped over to the tour bus where Hal blocked the door. "Is Elias in there?"

"Whoa! Is that you, Effie?" He dipped his mirrored shades. "Holy Mol-ee. What'd they do to you?"

"Open the door."

"Can't. He's with Annie."

She grabbed his tit and twisted. "Open the door."

"Ow! Shit." He jumped out of the way.

In the back, Annie hovered over Elias's needle-covered face. "What's going on?" she asked.

He sat up and gave her a once-over. "What are you . . . *not* wearing?"

"Oh, just a little something Gail picked up," she said through her teeth. "You like?"

The needles in his temples jerked down with his brows. "No. What the fuck?"

She bit her trembling lip.

"Annie, take these things out. I need to talk to Effie for a minute."

His mother mumbled something in Chinese, took out the needles, and left the bus.

He crooked a finger. "Get over here, you sex kitten."

She sat down and caressed his forehead. "What's wrong? Do you have a headache?"

"I . . ." He swallowed and licked his dry lips. "I have stage fright."

"Why?" She took his clammy hand. "What are you nervous about? Me?"

"No. Yes. This show could make or break us."

"One show?"

He didn't answer.

"What's the worst that could happen?"

"Lots of things."

"Like what?"

"I split my pants once." He squinched one eye closed.

She slapped a hand over her mouth and snorted.

"The great leather pants incident of 2014," he said solemnly.

"I'm so sorry. It's not funny. Did anyone see?"

"Just the band."

"That's the only embarrassing thing that's ever happened to you?"

"That was enough to last a lifetime."

He split his pants? That's it? Her whole life was an embarrassment. Nothing was more humiliating than being an addict.

She needed a cigarette. "Know what we need?"

He pulled down her top and plucked her nipples. "Boobs?"

"Bob Ross."

"I like boobs better." He tried to kiss her, but ended up with a mouthful of stiff hair. "I'm not a fan of this vamp look. It's hot. But it's not you."

"I'd kiss you for saying that but I can't move my face."

"Take it off. You look better without all that junk."

"I'm sure your manager had her reasons for making me look like a ho."

His jaw clenched. "I'll talk to her."

"No, don't." The last thing she needed was to give Gail more ammunition. "Just leave it alone."

She jumped up and retrieved her phone. Once she found her favorite episode, she settled in the crook of his arm and pushed play.

Bob's fruity voice rang out. "It is my world," Bob said. "And everything in my world is happy."

"This is kinda weird," he said.

"Not doing it for you?"

"Not really."

She slid her hand over his crotch and caressed him until he stiffened. "I've heard endorphins help with anxiety."

"Is that right?" His mouth curled into a delicious smile.

She unzipped his pants. "Look at that rock star cock."

He lowered her bustier, freeing both nipples. "Oh, yeah?"

"Mm-hmm."

"Didn't we skip a base?"

"You can make it up to me later." With her feathered gaze anchored to his, she slid down to her knees then ran her tongue down his shaft. "Mm." He tasted so good. She kissed his swollen head then consumed him.

He pinched her nipples harder as she lowered her mouth. "That's it, suck my cock." He dropped his head back and groaned. "Stand up so I can touch your pussy."

She kicked a leg over his lap.

He ducked. "You almost took my eye out with your heel."

"Sorry."

"Bend over," he said. He slipped his hand under her shorts and ran a finger down her center.

A spasm of heat rushed straight to her clit. She closed her eyes and moaned.

"Continue your anxiety treatment, *por favor*." His voice was as smooth as his touch.

She licked the vein running down his length. "You taste so good."

He stuffed himself into her mouth and dove two fingers inside her. "*Guiero cogerte esa boca linda.*"

She stroked him faster, bobbing her head and circling her tongue.

He matched her pace and flicked her clit with his thumb, hitting the perfect spot.

Hal banged on the door. "Showtime."

"Be right out." Elias grunted and pumped faster. "I'm so close. Don't stop." His hand slapped against her pussy. "Can I come in your mouth?"

The dirty question sent a thousand vibrations straight to her vagina, and an orgasm ripped through her body.

At the same time, his heat blasted the back of her throat. And she swallowed every last drop as if it were the nectar of the gods. It was amazing how much she enjoyed getting him off.

Hal thumped the door again. "Now!"

"How do you feel now?" she asked.

Elias zipped up his pants and tongue kissed her. "Like a fucking rock star. How about you?"

She adjusted her leather shorts over her slick lips. "*Fantastico!*"

He grinned. "Let's go make some music."

"Elias?" She squeezed his hand. "What's it like out there?"

"Crazy. Fun. Once I get into it, anyway. It's addictive—the best high ever."

That terrible jittery sensation swept over her. "Elias?"

He wiped the corner of her mouth. "Yes, *flaquita?*"

"If you get scared, just think about me giving you head."

He kissed her neck. "I never stop thinking about you."

She hugged him tight. "Let's go make some music then."

TOTAL MUSIC MAGAZINE

URBAN'S INTOXICATING NEW VIOLINIST
By Len Neal

I'D ALL but buried Urban in the has-been stack, but after last night's Liverpool show, I'm putting them back on the best-fucking-band-ever shelf.

The show was like sculpted sonic art. I almost had an orgasm when they introduced their new songs.

They were loud and tight and intense, seamlessly transitioning into the next songs, whipping the crowd into a psychotic frenzy. People were practically herniating themselves to get up on stage.

Apparently, Love took my advice and found a new drug—violinist, Effie Murphy—and from the looks of it, he's hooked.

I don't blame him—Murphy's a bombshell. And her bubbly stage-banter was even hotter.

Later in the show, she broke the heel off her boot and joked that Love made her dance her boots off—and those boots weren't made for dancing—they were made for hookin'. Cato Lawson played a funky bassline to her boot striptease. At the end, she tossed them into the audience and shouted, "Dance your boots off!" then did a flying stage dive into the crowd.

According to several sources, Murphy and Love collaborated on the new songs. Believe me when I use this filthy cliché: they're a match made in heaven. Not only is their new material nothing short of brilliant, their performance together was like watching soft porn with a badass soundtrack. Her humorous I-don't-give-a-shit attitude combined with his cool charisma made for some serious drool-worthy cinema.

Forget what I said in the last review, hold onto those tickets everyone, because Urban's about to blow your mind.

27

ADAGIO
Adagio

LONDON, ENGLAND

"'Living backwards!' Alice repeated in great astonishment. 'I never heard of such a thing! But there's one great advantage, in that one's memory works both ways.'"

Soundtrack *"More Today Than Yesterday," Spiral Staircase*

In the middle of London, Effie spotted a giant silver dildo, its mirrored windows gleaming in the sun like a suit of armor. She snapped a picture and messaged it to Callie.

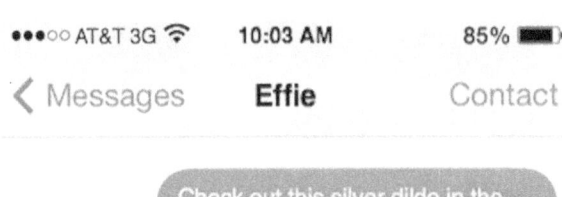

Her sister never replied. Probably because the size of the building paled in comparison to Hot Cock's real thing. She never shut up about the size of his penis.

Le Strange circled the London dildo then pulled up in front of their hotel. A mob greeted them, throwing themselves at the bus like zombies in need of human flesh.

"Don't stop. Go! Go!" Hal ordered LeStrange.

A crazy woman clung to the door as they drove away. LeStrange slammed on the brakes and she finally fell off.

"How are we going to get up to our room?" Effie asked.

"Through the restaurant," Hal said.

LeStrange parked, and Hal rushed them through the restaurant kitchen, toward the service elevator in the back.

Missy hugged herself, Griffin popped his jaw, Hal searched high and low for zombie fans, and Elias looked like he was about to crawl up the elevator shaft and escape. They acted like it was torture to be famous. They needed to loosen up and have fun.

"Oh, bugger!" Effie said in a British accent. "Wherever is the lift?"

They completely ignored her.

"I'm just taking a piss," she went on. "Come on! Laugh, you bunch of tossers!"

Everyone stared at her.

"She called you a masturbator, Cato," Griffin mumbled.

"Your mom's a masturbator," Cato retorted.

"My mom has ten kids. She doesn't have time for that," Griffin said.

Effie jumped back. "What! Ten kids! Holy fertility goddess. Doesn't she believe in birth control?"

"Don't talk about my mother."

She still couldn't believe it. "Which one were you?"

Missy answered for him. "He's the oldest and the only boy."

The Italian stallion flicked an annoyed glance at Missy. Elias coughed a laugh into his fist. The elevator door dinged. Annie pressed the top button, and the doors slid closed.

Inside, the same seventies' band her father used to listen to piped through the overhead speaker. She broke out into a dance routine, grooving her ass off, and singing along.

"What *are* you doing?" Missy asked.

"I love this song."

Elias's mouth twitched. The rest of them stared at her as if she were a deranged lunatic. She poked Cato's ribs. "Come on! Shake that money maker."

The bassist busted a groove, shaking his head, and caressing his body. He grabbed his crotch and ground down to the floor.

Hal sniggered.

She backed up against him and twerked.

"Oh hell naw," Cato backed away. "No female booty up against my groove thang."

She cracked up. "You must be gay if you don't want my booty." Truthfully, she had no booty whatsoever.

"Ding, ding, ding," Missy said.

She halted her performance. "Wait? You're gay?"

"Gay is such an outdated word," he said. "I prefer the term vagina-challenged."

"No way! Wow! I would have never guessed. You're so . . ."

The elevator dinged and everyone got out.

"I'm so what?"

She struggled to find the right term to describe his ultra-masculine sexual appeal. "Pimpish."

He stopped mid-stride and stared down at her. "I'll take that as a compliment."

"Please do," she said.

Cato shook his head and strutted down the hallway. The rest of them bolted to their rooms, including Elias.

This sneaking around crap was for the birds. She let out a heavy sigh and slid her card through the lock.

Inside, it was more like a palatial suite than a hotel room. Marble floors, gold drapes, a giant tub, and chandeliers. "Yippee," she cheered. "Now that's what I'm talking about. Real rock star accommodations."

She did a running leap onto the ginormous bed and jumped on it until it cracked. Not even a second later, someone knocked on the door to the adjoining suite. She froze. Had someone heard her?

"It's me," Elias said.

She ran to the door and swung it open. "Cheery-O."

He dragged her into his arms and fixed his fiery gaze on her mouth.

Throbbing heat waves rolled over her. "Hello, stranger," she cooed.

"*Hola, flaquita.*" He slid his lips against hers. "After sound check tonight, we're sneaking out. I'm taking you on a date." He pulled out his wallet and handed her a wad of cash. "Buy something nice to wear."

"Geez! How nice are we talking?"

"Very nice. Something that shows cleavage and ass."

"I will if you will."

"Not gonna happen."

"Hope you like snowsuits then."

"You could wear a clown suit and I'd still find you sexy as hell." He patted her bottom and swaggered back to his room. "Don't take too long. We have to leave in two hours."

"Wait, what are you going to do?"

"Introverted shit," he said.

"What does that entail?"

"Me time."

She blew him a kiss. "Have fun."

AFTER SOUND CHECK, they snuck back to the hotel and quickly changed. Elias tapped on the door. "You dressed?"

"Yes," she sang.

"Darn," he exploded through the door, a sly grin on his face. Then he took one look at her and his smile crumpled. "What the —?"

She spun around in her clown costume. "What do you think? Still think I'm sexy?"

"No."

She skipped to the bed, tripped on her big red shoes, righted herself, then held up his outfit.

He stared at it with terror in his eyes. "What's that?"

"Your costume."

"I'm not wearing that."

"*Sí, señor*." She dumped out all the costumes, wigs, facial wear, and silly hats she bought on the bed.

"No. No. No." He waved a scolding finger.

"Oh, come on! It'll be fun. Plus, no one will recognize you in this disguise. We can pretend it's Halloween. Now's your chance."

His mouth swooshed back and forth as he considered this.

"Put it on! Put it on!"

A short while later, they stood in line for the London Eye,

wearing rainbow afros, balls for noses, and polka-dot suits. She couldn't stop snickering.

"Shhh." He nudged her with an elbow. "Everyone's staring at us."

"Of course they are. We're wearing clown suits."

His giant red clown smile moved up an inch.

They made their way into the glass bubble. Rain pelted the capsule from outside. The guide handed her a bouquet of white daisies. "Compliments of"—she cleared her throat—"Pokey."

Effie clutched the bouquet to her chest. "Oh, Pokey! They're wonderful. Thank you."

His grin grew. "You're welcome, Humpy."

The guide left and soon they were rotating above the city an inch at a time.

Effie focused on the flowers rather than the view. They smelled like promises, and hope, and a little like rubber—she was still wearing the clown nose. Her eyes welled up.

He tilted her chin. "What's wrong?"

"It hurts."

"What hurts, *mi vida*?"

"My heart. It's exploding."

He frowned—which was a little freaky with a painted-on smile —and brushed the tears off her cheek with his thumb, turning his fingertip white. "Did I mess up? I've never bought flowers before. The daisies reminded me of you. I knew I should have bought roses."

She tried to hush him with a kiss, but their noses were in the way. She pulled off his then hers and tried again. "I love them."

He spat and stuck out his tongue. "That makeup tastes like paste."

She wiped it off. "Now try."

For half the ride they exchanged body-tingling makeup-smearing kisses. He unbuttoned her pompoms. "You're not wearing a bra."

"I don't like bras."

"Me, neither." He played with her breasts, alternating light feathery touches with panty-melting boob grabs. Then he bent down and outlined her painfully hard nipples with his tongue, sending goosebumps soaring over her skin.

"You're missing the show." He faced her toward the window and circled his arms around her from behind. One hand slid between her thighs and lightly circled her clit. "So warm and slick."

Below the Thames River seemed to flow faster while the city's lights grew brighter.

He pulled out his finger and sucked it clean. "Turn around so I can see you." He pushed down her underwear and dialed a heated stare between her legs.

Once again, he sank a finger inside, pumping it lazily to the point of torture.

"Bring me your penis," she commanded. "I need something to hold onto so I don't fall."

He snorted and unbuttoned his clown suit.

"You're not wearing underwear," she teased.

"I don't like them."

"Me, neither."

They stroked each other as languidly as the wheel turned, not building momentum until the very end.

Short breaths, juices sloshing, fabric swishing, and then an aria —a loud stream of beautiful Spanish curse words blasted out with his cum.

Orgasms—the most beautiful music in the world.

Though his clown smile had rubbed off, his real one was just as big.

She tugged her lobes. "My ears are still ringing. You were loud."

"It felt good."

His matter-of-fact tone made her laugh. "It sure did." An orgasm from Elias was the best high ever. Completely addictive.

A thought hit her. "What will we do when we have sex? We'll have to do it in a soundproof booth."

His eyes dimmed to sexual chocolate.

"What?" she asked.

"Just picturing you spread out on a mixing board."

"With all those knobs? Ouch."

"I'll lean you over it then."

She squinted. "Dirty Argentinian."

"*Quiero coger con vos toda la noche.*"

"What does that mean?" she asked.

"It's a secret."

The Ferris wheel stopped, and they left hand-in-hand, wearing bigger grins than when they'd arrived.

28

LEGATO

Legato

Soundtrack *"Wake Up," Arcade Fire*

The show that night was like foreplay. Elias's stage fright had all but vanished. All he had to do was focus on Effie—the way she smelled on his fingers as he gripped the microphone, the way she glided across the stage, playing violin like a goddess, the way she wound up the crowd, screaming "Dance your boots off!" to everyone.

Watching her dive off the stage and float over the crowd, laughing like crazy, made him grin like an idiot for one whole song.

They played four encores that night. Usually, he couldn't handle more than one. But that night he didn't stop. He *couldn't* stop. The music electrified him.

When they finally quit playing, he couldn't get to her fast enough, but backstage fans and reporters swarmed him like mad wasps. Someone squeezed his nuts and his sexual energy drained out of him like a flat tire.

"Hey, baby."

He bristled at the sickeningly familiar voice behind him.

"Tina."

She grinned up at him, her pupils huge from whatever drug she was on. If no one else had been there, he would have shoved her out of the way. But since that wasn't the case, he peeled her claws off his waist and lowered his voice. "I told you not to come to another show."

"Daddy says I can go wherever I want." She pushed out her bottom lip. "Are you still upset about losing our baby?"

"There was no baby."

She'd told everyone, he'd knocked her up. But he never took a chance with her. They'd only fucked twice. Both times he wore a condom. The first time he pulled out, and the second time, he didn't even come.

When he'd demanded a pregnancy test, conveniently, she had a miscarriage the next day. And when he didn't show adequate sympathy for her loss, she painted him as a cold-hearted asshole to *TMM*.

He could barely stand to look at her—she made him physically sick. "Stay away from me," he growled. "And stay away from Griffin, too."

She batted her mascara-caked eyelashes. "Jealous? We can always have a threesome. You can make a Tina sandwich." She stuck her tongue in his ear at the exact same time Effie popped out of the dressing room.

Mouth parted and forehead creased, Effie watched as Tina licked his neck. She clutched her chest as if she'd been shot, then burst through the back door.

The mob swallowed him up like quicksand. His muscles slackened and tightened at the same time. It was as if he'd been paralyzed. He couldn't move. Or think.

Finally, Hal came to the rescue and pulled Tina off him. Halfway out the door Gail blocked him. "*TMM* is here. They want an interview."

"Not now."

"Yes, now. It's Len Neal."

Len Neal controlled the music empire with his reviews. And for the last six months, he'd been singularly responsible for their dive in sales. Len could destroy a band with a few nasty words. And for the last six months, he'd been doing just that.

In the music industry, Len was a god. And he couldn't keep God waiting.

For a god, Len sure didn't look like one. In fact, with his green hoodie, bald head, and beak-like nose, he looked just like a turtle.

Len gave him a handshake and a back slap. "What up, dude?"

He gritted his teeth and lounged back on the sofa, mustering the will to stroke the turtle's ego.

"You were on fire tonight, dude." Len shot air pistols at him.

"You ought to know."

"Number one fan."

"Could have fooled me."

Len gestured surrender. "Hey, man, I just report the facts. My readers depend on me to tell the truth."

Bullshit. His "facts" were nothing more than his stupid opinions.

"So, what facts will you be reporting tonight?"

"You're back on top, man." He gave him the thumbs up. "I mean it. What changed? Is it that hot little blonde violinist? What's her name? Ellie?"

"Effie."

"Yeah, she's smokin.' You banging that?"

He planted both feet on the floor and gripped the sofa to keep from ripping out the reporter's throat. "Sounds like you need to get laid, Len."

"Dude, last night I fucked this married chick. Total MILF! Want her number?"

"You're a real player, Len." There was no mistaking the disgust in his tone.

"Right?" The critic tried to fist bump him and failed.

Annie appeared out of nowhere, wearing the cold glint of a

communist dictator in her glare. "This the man who insult my son?"

The reporter flinched back and blinked rapidly. "No shit? This is your mom?"

Elias stood. "I've got to blaze. Nice seeing you, Len," he lied.

"Any chance for an interview with Ellie?"

He turned back and stepped in an inch away from Len's face. "*Effie*. Her name is Effie. Not sure why you can't get it right, since you compared her performance to soft porn just a few days ago."

Len barked out a laugh. "Hey, man, I was just playing around. It's all about the entertainment, right?"

The reporter darted over to Cato. "Hey, bro!"

Cato stared down at the man with pure hatred on his face. "Never call a black man 'bro.' It's offensive."

While Cato schooled Len, Elias escaped out the back and found Effie talking to the roadies. As he moved closer, she hugged herself tighter.

He made intolerable small talk with the crew for a minute then made up an excuse to steal her away.

On the way to the bus, he leaned in and sniffed. "You smell like cigarettes."

"Do I?" She scratched her head. "The guys were smoking."

"Wish they'd quit that shit."

She scrounged for a lollipop in her backpack.

"Sugar's not good for you, you know."

Blue fury flamed in her eyes, and her lip curled up in a snarl. She brandished the sucker like a knife and jabbed it at him. "If I want candy, I will eat candy. Is that clear?"

He leaned back, his hands up in surrender. "*Sí, mami.*"

"And wipe that smile off your face."

"Yes, ma'am."

"Don't call me ma'am."

"Okay, *flaquita.*"

"And don't call me that, either."

He let her anger sizzle for a bit before he spoke. "I haven't been with her in a year."

She stared out the window, gnashing candy with tight jaws. "Who?"

"Effie, look at me." He tilted her chin toward him. "I wasn't a monk before we met."

"So you slept with her, then?"

"I'm not proud of it, but yes." He sat back and sighed. "Tina's trouble. She faked a pregnancy, and a big shitstorm followed. Then she tried to sue me for emotional damages. Unfortunately, her dad works for the label, so we'll probably run into her again."

She wrapped a lock of hair around her wrist. "But Griffin sleeps with her too."

"Griffin's kinda fucked up right now."

"He's not usually a whore?"

"No." He traced the inside of her thigh. "Women make up a huge percentage of our album sales. There will always be crazy women fans. Even Cato has to deal with them. We all do. I hate it, but it's part of the job. You just have to blow it off."

She rested her head against his shoulder. "I should have trusted you."

"If another man touched you like that—" He rubbed the back of his neck, the image too horrible. "I don't know what I'd do."

"Don't you trust me?"

"I don't trust men."

She rolled her eyes.

"I'm serious."

"Other men don't even cross my mind, Elias. You're the only one I see. The rest of the male species doesn't exist." She climbed into his lap. "That show was amazing."

He dragged her closer and licked the candied sweetness off her bottom lip.

She smashed her mouth against his.

Right then, Annie blasted onboard. "A-ha!" She pointed at her eyes then back at them. "I knew it! You think I can't see through the fog of your lies."

He gave her a warning look. "Annie—"

"Wha!" She zipped her lips. "I never saw face sucking. I hear nothing. I see nothing. I know nothing. No evil took place on this bus." Giggling like a fool, she scuttled off the bus.

A million knots formed in his shoulders. "*Mierda.*"

Effie, on the other hand, didn't seem the slightest bit upset. On the contrary, she beat the seat in front of her and did a little butt shimmy on his lap. "Your mom likes me."

"Of course she does."

"I thought she hated me." She cupped his cheeks and kissed him again.

He chuckled at her silliness. She was so full of life, *tan vivaz.* "*Me gustás mucho*, F-bomb."

"I like you, too, Elvis."

"Ah, you're learning." He pinched her glowing cheek. "Soon, I won't be able to whisper dirty secrets in your ear."

VIVACE

Vivace

CALAIS, FRANCE

Soundtrack *"Get Lucky," Daft Punk, Pharrell Williams and Nile Rodgers*

Urban ditched the other bus and took the train across the Chunnel from London to Calais, France, where LeStrange had his own operation.

"Where's the bus?" Elias asked.

LeStrange pointed to a bright pink double bus with the words Disco Bus painted in flowers on the side. *"Là-bas."*

Effie cheered. "Oh my God! It's amazing! It's like a Barbie camper."

Inside the bus, pink fur-covered sofa benches lined the sides, and a disco ball glittered over a stripper pole in the center. Dizzying strobe lights flashed along floorboard.

"Did you know about this, Annie?" Elias asked.

She shrugged.

He squinted. "You get off on this, don't you?"

Annie shot a finger off her hip. *"Lao ban,* disco king."

"Stop calling me boss. And don't call me disco king, either."

Hal waved a hand in front of his nose. "Is that patchouli?"

"Oui." LeStrange said, piling the luggage in the overhead compartments. *"C'est bon pour l'énergie sexuelle."*

"All I heard was sexual," Griffin said.

LeStrange pointed out a fruit and cheese plate in the mini-fridge. *"Il y a du fromage et des fruits au frigo."* He pushed a button on a panel across from the kitchen. *"Ce sont pour le système de son."*

"What'd he say?" asked Hal.

"No clue," Missy said.

LeStrange made his way back up front and started the engine. "A leetle musique *Française,* okay?"

"Speak English!" Cato plunked down in a furry seat.

"I don't want to hear French music," Griffin said.

The driver took that as a yes and blasted music through the speakers.

"Kickin' sound system at least," Griffin admitted.

"Is that Daft Punk?" Cato asked. "Shit, I forgot they were French. Turn it up, man."

LeStrange cranked it to eleven.

Hal bobbed his head and snapped to the beat. "I haven't heard this song in ages."

Cato and Missy sang along.

Effie danced around the pole, tossing her hair. "I've always wanted to do this," she said.

"Strip?" Elias asked.

"No, ride on a Barbie camper. This is like my childhood dream." She sang with the others and spun around the pole.

Dios, she was adorable.

Annie got up and did the robot dance next to Effie.

He almost gave himself whiplash laughing. The contagion spread rapidly. Missy snorted. Hal guffawed. Annie squealed. Effie

giggled. All of them, even moody-ass Griffin, broke out into
hysterics.

And soon Urban was on their way to Paris, speeding down the
highway in the Barbie Disco Bus, everyone singing and laughing
at the top of their lungs, like they were tripping on hallucinogenic
drugs.

30

IMPRESARIO

Impresario

DISNEYLAND, PARIS

Soundtrack *"Super Freak," Rick James*

The concert in Paris went off without a hitch, and since they had time to kill before they had to be in Belgium, he surprised Effie with tickets to Disneyland.

They dressed up in biker costumes and ran into Cato at the elevator. Head down and eyes on his phone, the bassist stepped on the elevator without noticing them.

Effie snorted.

Cato grabbed his heart. "Shit. Thought I was on here with a bunch of *Easy Rider* motherfuckers." He narrowed his eyes. "Why are you dressed up like Hell's Angels?"

Effie tossed her braid and adjusted her bandana. "So nobody recognizes us at Disneyland."

"I want to go to Disneyland. Hold up. Let me get my wallet. I'll go with you."

Elias shook his head and waved behind Cato's back. No way did he want Cato tagging along on their date.

But Effie ignored his distress signal. "Want to wear a costume?" she asked. "I've got more stuff back in my room."

"Let's see what you got."

An hour later, Rick James and a couple of bikers stood in line at Disneyland.

Cato punched him in the shoulder. "'Sup with you, old man? Why you so grumpy?" He called them "old man" and "old lady," claiming that's what motorcycle gangs did.

Grumpy wasn't the right word, more like furious. Until Rick "Cock-blocking" James showed up, Elias had planned to make out with Effie on the kiddie rides all day. On top of that, Cato would not stop singing "Super Freak."

"You feeling okay?" Effie asked him. "You're awfully quiet."

"He's super freakin' about the Temple of Doom," Cato said, sitting his ass between them on the ride.

It was hard to tell what Elias hated most about the Temple of Doom—Cato chanting "super freaky" every time they hit a deep slope, or his running commentary about the movie set. And since Effie hadn't seen the movie, Cato gladly filled her in on the plot during the Thunder Mountain ride.

"He fell into a pit of snakes?" she cried. "Then what?"

Cato told her on the next ride.

When an asteroid zoomed toward them during the *Armageddon* ride, Cato screamed melodramatically and made the little girl next to them cry. "Sorry for super freakin' out your kid," he told the parents.

After that, Cato bought monogrammed mouse ears for everyone—Grumpy for Elias, Bootsie for her, and Super Freak for himself.

Elias ditched the mouse ears on the next ride, and now, it was time to ditch the Super Freak.

The minute Cato excused himself for the bathroom, Elias

grabbed Effie and made a break for it, yelling "freedom!" like Mel Gibson in *Braveheart*.

She laughed. "Where to now, old man?"

He motioned to the Alice in Wonderland labyrinth. "Let's get lost in there."

On the way, he bought her a Mickey Mouse lollipop and kissed her freckled nose. "Let's hurry before Rick James catches up. We've got a lot of making out to do."

Inside the Queen of Heart's castle, they dry-humped each other in a dark corner until the Mad Hatter showed up and tapped his shoulder.

"Excusez-moi. Vous ne pouvez pas faire ça ici. You can't do that here."

"This is maddening," she said.

"Hop on, let's get out of here." He gave her a piggyback ride through the maze and finally found a secluded mushroom. He set her on top, next to the life-sized caterpillar, and stood between her legs. "With those braids, and that big lollipop, you look like a naughty Alice."

She winked and licked the sucker from top to bottom.

He growled and bit her neck. "Keep doing that and I'm going to have to take you right here on top of this mushroom, old lady."

She beamed. "I'm having the best time. Thank you for bringing me to Paris."

"Thank you, for existing."

Tears glistened in her eyes. "No one's ever thanked me for living before."

He stroked her cheek. "What's wrong, *mi vida*?"

"You make me feel..."

"Feel what?"

"That's it. You make me feel. I was numb before I met you."

Her kiss tasted like lollipops and happy tears.

"Well, well, what do we have here?"

Every muscle in Elias's body went rigid. "*Mierda.*"

Behind them, Cato grinned satanically underneath the giant

Cheshire Cat. "That's right, *mucho grande mierda*, motherfucker. You got some 'splaining to do, Lucy."

"Oh, no." Effie bit her knuckles and groaned.

Cato cupped his ear. "I'm sorry, what'd you say, Yoko Ono?"

"You gonna tell the others, man?" Elias asked.

Cato pushed his tongue against his cheek. "Nah, we cool."

"Sure about that?"

"We cool, I said." And that was the last time he mentioned it.

GLISSANDO

Glissando

Soundtrack *"She's The One," The Beta Band*

Forget music, romancing Effie had become Elias's new mission in life. Making her happy filled him with *machismo*. Around her, he felt stronger, taller, more sexual—like a panther on the hunt.

He couldn't wait to surprise her with a real life Candy Land.

The minute they arrived in Brussels, he snuck out and went to the famous candy store Pierre Marcolini.

Pink and purple flower vines climbed over the store's entrance, and colorful chocolate *Manneken Pis* statues filled the window displays. A chocolate kid, taking a chocolate piss—not exactly appetizing.

Inside the store, red and white swirled lollipops hung from the ceiling like balloons. Shelves of chocolate stuffed the store and bins full of rainbow-colored candy lined the middle. The sugary aroma of melted chocolate flooded his senses.

All of a sudden, he was a four-year-old boy again, making *Los Submarinos* with his mother in the kitchen. He sprinkled the dark powder into the steaming pot of milk while she stirred and hummed tango songs. Her hair was the same color as the dark chocolate she shaved into the milk. Back then he thought she was the most beautiful woman in the world.

Until she ruined herself.

He rubbed his chest, trying to deaden the dull pain the memory caused.

After he bought two enormous bags full of candy, he strolled down the street, whistling while he walked.

In a window display a block away, a sparkly ring caught his attention. The stone was the same color blue as Effie's eyes. A delicate silver setting surrounded the raw stone like tiny petals folding over a flower bud.

Without a second thought, he marched into the shop to buy it for her.

A woman in pigtails behind the counter lifted her goggles and shut off her blowtorch. Her eyes bugged out. "El Love?" She blabbered French nonsense for over a minute before realizing he couldn't understand a word. "My God, it is you. I can't believe you're in my store!"

He flashed her a smile. "Could you show me the blue ring out front?"

"Sure. Sure." She sprinted to the window and retrieved it.

"What is this stone?" he asked.

"Aquamarine."

He held it up to the light. "I've never seen anything like it. Did you design the setting?"

She clutched her chest and gushed more French. "*Oui*. I'm so glad you like it."

He pulled out his wallet. "I'll take it."

"*Mon Dieu!*" she cried. "You're getting engaged? But your fans will be so heartbroken."

Had he heard that right? "Engaged?"

She swooned and fanned her face. "I can't wait to tell my friends El Love is proposing with my ring."

He held up his hand. "*Esperá un momento*, did you say this is an engagement ring?"

She blinked. "*Mais, bien sûr.*

Her response hit him like an electric charge. "Can't it just be a normal ring? Why does it have to be an engagement ring?"

The jeweler jerked back as if he'd wounded her. Then she went on and on about her design and how it represented a merging of souls.

Whatever. No one tells Elias Lovaro what to do. So what if he wanted to give Effie a ring for the hell of it? Who said he had to get down on one knee?

He passed her his credit card.

The shopkeeper shrieked and rung him up. "This is so exciting. How long have you been together?"

"A while." Why didn't he tell her the truth? Maybe because no man in their right mind would buy a woman a ring so soon. "Actually." He laughed nervously. "Not long."

"Ah, c'est un coup de foudre?"

He shrugged.

"It means struck by lightning in English. But in French we say it to describe love at first sight." She smiled and handed him the bill.

His heart skipped a beat as he stared down at the total. Speaking of lightning, he'd just been struck by a twenty-five thousand dollar volt. *Dios mios*, what the hell was he thinking? He didn't even know her. They hadn't even had sex, yet.

He grabbed the ring out of the box, closed his eyes, and tried to kick start his logic. A million excited birds fluttered in his belly instead. He didn't have to give it to her right way. He could hold onto it until the right moment—like before their wedding.

An insane laugh burst out of him. "I've lost my mind. I've gone completely crazy." He twirled a finger next to his head. "*Loco!*"

The jeweler smiled and gave him a sympathetic nod. "Love makes everyone crazy."

ANDANTE

Andante

"Imagination is the only weapon in the war against reality."

Soundtrack *"Sacred Heart," The Civil Wars*

After the show in Paris that night, Elias snuck into Effie's room. "I have a surprise," he whispered.

"You do?" She leapt out of bed and did a split jump. "Goody, goody, gum drops!"

"Shh!" He pressed a finger over his smile. "Follow me."

They tiptoed down the hall like thieves, freezing every time the wooden floor creaked. "Cover your eyes," he said. "And don't peek." He led her inside his room. "Okay, now you can look."

Instant tears clogged her throat. A trail of fancy gift-wrapped chocolates, lollipops, and gummy bears led to the bed, where he'd fashioned a heart out of candied hearts.

"It's Candy Land," he said.

"It's . . . magical." She raised her nightie over her head and lay down buck-naked on the pile of candy. "Come here, Elvis."

He gave her a sly, sideways grin and crawled beside her.

She stroked him through the fabric of his pajamas. "I want you so bad," she murmured.

He grabbed her ass with both hands and hauled her over him. "I want to taste your sweetness," he said, then peeled her apart and licked a path down her center. "Mmm, you taste good."

He pinched her lips together and sucked and licked and massaged her into a frenzied state. Elias Lovaro clearly loved giving head. He savored the experience, drew it out, closed his eyes and moaned as if he were feasting on a gourmet meal. He was an oral sex aficionado—the God of Pussy Pleasure.

She grabbed his hair and bucked on top of him, ecstasy rippling through her core. And right as she was about to come, he lifted her up and lightly flicked his tongue, teasing her to the brink of madness.

Her clit throbbed as if it had its own heartbeat. "Oh my God!" She dropped back her head and cried out, "I can't take it anymore. This is torture."

He smiled then dove his tongue inside her.

She writhed and shook and begged him to do filthy things.

Then he raised her up again and leisurely pumped a finger inside her.

Panting and trembling, she reached back for his cock and stroked him, praying he'd pick up the pace.

He grunted and buried his head between her thighs again. "Fuck my face, *mi amor.*"

A thousand white stars exploded all at once, and she melted all over him.

Then he went back for seconds. "That's it, *flaquita,* come all over me again."

Elias Lovaro was the best high ever. He made her soul tingle.

Not once did he push her for sex. He made it clear that night was all about her.

Afterwards, they lay tangled up in a pile of candy, munching on chocolate and drawing on each other with licorice ropes.

He captured a bit of caramel off her lip and sucked his finger clean. "You have the biggest smile on your face."

"This is my happy place." She wiggled her toes. "Little squirrels live and play here."

"Bob Ross?" he asked.

"Yep."

"Total genius." He kissed her passionately. *"Estoy loco por vos, mi amor."*

"I don't know what that means, but it sounds beautiful."

"You're beautiful."

"I'm crazy about you, Elvis."

"Ha! That's what I just told you."

"In Spanish?"

"The exact same thing." He folded her into his arms and instantly fell asleep.

Later, she drifted off into Candy Land and dreamt she was Lolly and Elias was Lord Licorice, and close to the end of the game, she fell into the chocolate swamp and drowned.

CADENCE

Cadence

Soundtrack *"Some Sunsick Day," Morgan Delt*

The houseboat leaned dangerously to the left when they boarded. Inside, it smelled like a wet swimsuit stuck in a plastic bag for weeks.

"I said houseboat," Elias told Annie, "not a shipwreck."

"I had a coupon," she said.

"Of course you did," he said. And with the Amsterdam Festival that weekend, and every hotel booked solid, they were stuck on that sinking ship the whole weekend.

Elias stepped to the other side and the boat swayed with him.

"We're gonna die tonight," Cato said.

Griffin shouted from below deck. "There are no rooms down here, just bunk beds."

Elias turned to Annie with gritted teeth. "You!"

"Wha?"

He stabbed two fingers at her. "I'm onto you, old woman."

She stuck her nose in the air. "Ungrateful son."

Meanwhile, Effie had a ball pretending to be captain. She steered the big wooden wheel and talked on the broken CB radio. "We can cross another item off our bucket list."

"What do you mean?"

"Sailing."

"This isn't sailing."

"Sure it is." She flashed a sweet smile. "Just have to pretend."

He brushed his mouth against her ear. "Let's get out of here."

"Now?"

"I'll tell everyone I'm going for a run and then text you my location."

She tapped her nose and winked a few times. "Have fun on your run."

Thirty minutes later, an elderly woman, wearing a fanny pack and a shirt that said sexy grandma, sat next to him on the bench. The woman winked a blue eye at him. "How'd you like a little cougar action?"

"Effie?"

"What's up, stud? What do you think of my disguise?"

"I hate it."

She pushed out her bottom lip.

He pinched it then kissed her.

From under the bench, she pulled out a paper bag. "Go get changed, old man."

He peeked inside and groaned. "Oh, no."

She smiled and nodded. "Oh, yes. Come on. It'll be fun." She patted his leg. "Hurry, I've got another surprise for you."

"Can't wait," he said dryly.

A few minutes later, he walked out of the café, wearing plaid shorts with black socks, a grey mustache, and a baseball hat with a fake grey ponytail attached.

"Sexy." She hugged her stomach and laughed.

He shook his head and followed her to a tandem bicycle chained to a rack.

"Ready to ride this puppy?" She patted the seat.

"Is it safe?"

"Probably not. Front or back?"

He rubbed his chin. "Back, so I can watch your butt." He glanced down at her polyester pants and changed his mind. "On second thought."

"What? You don't like my britches?" She bent over and twerked in the middle of the street.

He just smiled and watched. Passersby probably thought she was convulsing.

"Saddle up, stud." She straddled the front seat.

"Maybe we should take a lesson first," he said, getting on the back.

"Pfft." She flopped a hand. "We've got this. But first we need a name for this bad boy." She stroked the silver frame. "How about Lightning?"

"*Perfecto.* On the count of three?" he asked.

She honked the bike horn three times. They pedaled a few wobbly feet then crashed into a garbage can.

"Whoops," she said. "Sorry, that was my fault." She got back on and honked the horn. "Ready?"

"Not really," he said.

They made it around the block then crashed again. He picked up the bike and held it steady. "Think we're getting the hang of it," he said. "Tour de France, here we come."

The third time was a charm. "We're doing it," she cheered. "We're riding a bike. Go team Love!"

Over the bridges, down the tulip-lined cobblestone streets, in front of the crooked cartoon buildings, and alongside the murky canals, they rode Lightning at warp speed. With the wind in his hair and the sun smiling down on his face—he felt like a balloon soaring above the clouds.

They ran over a bump and the gray bun in the back of her head bounced. "Whee!" She honked and waved at everyone.

"I'm crazy about you, F-bomb!" he shouted.

"I'm crazy about you, Elvis!" she shouted back.

After a while, they pulled over and parked. "I'm starving," she said. "Let's grab a bite at that place." She pointed to a coffeehouse.

"Unless you plan on being stoned for a week, I don't think you want to eat there."

"Oh? Ohhhh! Yeah, no."

"We can check it out if you want."

"No, no. I know how you feel about drugs."

"I don't care if other people smoke. I just don't want my band doing it. Drugs ruin too many careers." Including his mother's.

After he'd watched her waste away on heroin and parade her Johns around him night after night, he had no desire to use drugs, even recreationally. With a genetic predisposition for substance abuse, his stage fright, and an industry filled with "substances," he was bound to end up another statistic.

She stared off into the distance and pinched her neck.

"What's wrong?" he asked.

"Nothing. I'm fine. Let's go somewhere else."

They bought cheese and bread off a street vendor and picnicked with their feet hanging over a bridge. Later, they rode to the Red Light District.

"Let's go there." She honked and pointed to a neon flashing sign. "Sex-O-Rama. Yes!"

"I'm a hundred percent down with this idea," he said.

She *ooed* and *ahed* over the massive dildo collection. "I've never seen so many sex toys." She grabbed a basket and shoved a giant black dildo into it.

He pulled it out and examined it. "The Pounder? I may not be this big, but I'm pretty sure I can satisfy you."

"It's for Cato."

Thank God, because he didn't want that thing anywhere near her or him. He stuck a yellow butt plug in the basket.

"Who's that for?" she asked.

"Griffin. Maybe it'll help him get the stick out of his ass."

She tossed in a pair of Hello Kitty nipple clamps.

He raised a brow.

"For Annie."

"Ah."

They chose pink butt beads for Missy, a leopard-print cock ring for LeStrange, and a ball gag for Hal.

"What about us?" she said.

"I've got all the sex toys you need." He waved a hand over his hardening crotch.

A shy smile pushed up one blushing cheek. "Then we better get condoms."

"How soon do you want to try them out?" He clasped his hands in prayer. "Please say tonight."

"Soon." She spent a surprisingly long time selecting the perfect rubber for whenever "soon" was.

"Those are interesting," he lied.

"Well, I can't lose my good-sex virginity with ordinary condoms." She held up a package of French ticklers and glow-in-the-dark edible rubbers.

"Are you gonna eat those off me?"

"Maybe."

"Great." He motioned over his member again. "I'm not going to be able to ride that bike until this goes down."

"Maybe we should take a break up there." She pointed to a pink door up a flight of stairs that said *Live Sex Show*. Her brows wiggled. "Wanna?"

Watching her get all hot and bothered while strangers fucked on stage? "Yes, please. Two tickets," he told the clerk.

They sat in back of the theater, behind a lone Indian man and a bunch of frat boys.

"I smell popcorn." She sniffed the air. "Oh look, they have a popcorn machine. I'll be right back." She returned holding two bags of popcorn, which they ate whilst watching couples fuck onstage.

"This is kind of boring." She tossed a kernel in her mouth.

"It's just about over. He just came on her tits."

"Oh, yeah."

The couple pranced off the stage, and a naked woman came out and spread-eagled on a revolving platform. She lit a cigarette, blew out the smoke, and then put the filter between her legs.

Effie sat up and choked. "She's gonna burn her—oh my God, is she smoking a cigarette out of her vagina?"

"Looks that way."

Eyes wide, mouth open, and popcorn stuck to her face, she stared at the scene. "Does this turn you on?"

"Not in the slightest."

"Wanna go?"

"Thought you'd never ask."

Outside, he wheeled the bike off the sidewalk and she dumped the sex toys in the basket.

"Think that woman woke up one day and decided to do that for a living?" she asked.

"Maybe she was discovered."

"By like a sex-show talent scout?"

"It could happen." He sat on the bike and held it steady for her.

"Maybe if this rock star thing doesn't work out," she said. "I'll become a sex-show talent scout."

"Been there, done that."

She giggled, kissed his cheek, and hopped on.

They took the long way back to the shipwreck, laughing like kids, with the big black dildo flopping out of the basket like a toddler's arm.

DECEPTIVE CADENCE

Deceptive Cadence

"'I know what YOU'D like!' the Queen said good-naturedly, taking
a little box out of her pocket. 'Have a biscuit?'"

Soundtrack *"When I'm Small," Phantogram*

Backstage at the concert that night, Gail cornered Effie in the
dressing room. "Why aren't you wearing the outfit?"

"Because I'm wearing this." She twirled in her white sundress.

Gail looked as if she'd just inhaled raw sewage. "This isn't a
Phish show. You can't wear that."

"I don't know who that is, but I'll tell you what I'm not
wearing"—she pointed to the atrocity on the hanger—"that gold
onesie."

Kyle stepped a foot inside the room, saw Gail, then turned tail
and left.

Coward.

"What can I do for you, Gail?" Effie asked.

The manager sat on the dressing room table and folded her

manicured hands in her lap. "Did you know my father owns Heart Records?"

"I didn't."

"My grandparents escaped the Holocaust and came to the US with nothing, couldn't even afford to feed themselves. And now my father is one of the richest men in America."

"That's amazing," Effie said and meant it.

"Know how he got to be so rich?" She tapped her temple. "Intuition. All of Heart's bands make it to number one."

"Impressive."

"Urban was the first band I groomed for the stage when I started working for my father." She picked non-existent lint off her red suede pants. "He didn't think they'd amount to anything, but I had a gut feeling. 'Go, play with your little band,' he told me."

"Little band?"

"That's right. See, my father's a sexist pig. He didn't believe for one second I could turn a dive-bar band into the number one grossing band in history. In his eyes, women are useless."

This little therapy session couldn't be the manager's attempt to garner sympathy could it? If it was, she was doing a piss-poor job. "Guess you showed him."

"Elias would still be playing in bowling alleys if it weren't for me. I built his brand from scratch and made him a household name." Gail rose to her feet and wagged a finger. "And you, my little mystery, are off-brand."

Effie crossed her arms across her chest. "Maybe we should ask Elias how he feels."

"Don't bother. I already know you hold the purse strings now. You've got everyone fooled." She bent down and whispered, "Except me."

She nearly gagged on the scent of Gail's perfume. How could someone who smelled so good reek so bad?

Gail's lips pulled back over her fangs. "But I'm not about to tell my father that I can't control my"—she flashed finger quotes —"'little band.'"

"So that's it?" Effie asked. "That's why you're so mean? Because your father's a sexist pig?"

"Mean?" Gail snapped out an arid laugh. "I'm not mean. In fact, I brought you a little peace offering." She pulled out a gift-wrapped box from her bag and handed it to Effie. "Open it."

Effie shook the box. "What is it?" It was probably a bomb.

"Dutch lollipops." Gail gave her a cute wrinkly-nosed smile. "A little bird told me you're fond of them."

The polite 'thank you' she should have uttered got stuck in her throat.

The manager slung her designer bag around her shoulder and flitted toward the door in her spiky heels. "Wear whatever the fuck you want, Effie. If that is your real name."

Jesus, her real name? Did she honestly think Effie was some kind of criminal, traveling under an assumed identity? Money had made that woman insane.

Once the manager left, Effie's body ached as if Gail had somehow injected arthritis into her veins.

What she wouldn't give for a cigarette.

She tore open the box and bit into a lollipop. *Gah,* it tasted like chemical dog doo. Of course Gail would buy her shitsicles. But since there was nothing else, she devoured three more and stuffed the rest in her backpack.

Missy sidled up next to her. "You look pretty."

After having her ego shredded by Gail, the compliment sunk to the bottom of her gut like an anchor.

"What's wrong?"

"I just got attacked by your manager."

"God, I hate her," Missy said.

"Then why do you work with her?"

"Because she's a shark. No one messes with Gail."

The walls in the room throbbed with her head. Effie stood and stumbled.

"You okay?" Missy took her elbow.

"Think I need to eat something." She staggered to the tent out back, feeling dizzier with every step.

A caterer had set up a buffet for the band and crew. She caught a whiff of grilled meat and her stomach roiled. She wobbled over to a chair then everything turned fuzzy after that.

"If you cut your finger very deeply with a knife, it usually bleeds; if you drink from a bottle marked 'poison,' it is almost certain to disagree with you."

Soundtrack *"White Rabbit," Jefferson Airplane*

"Miss Murphy?" the caterer said. "Are you okay?"

"Hmm?"

"You've been standing in the same place for five minutes. You okay?"

She tugged her collar and wiped her forehead. "It's hot in here."

"It's only sixty degrees."

"I'm roasting."

She wandered over to a table and sat down across from Griffin.

He gripped his phone in one hand and buried his face in the other. "I can't eat. I can't sleep. I can't fucking play the drums. Please, Melody, *please* call me back. Please." He lowered his phone and stared down at it.

"Is Melody your girlfriend?" she asked.

He jerked his gaze up to hers. "What the fuck? Were you listening?"

She tilted her head. "You look sad. Are you sad? No wait, you look mad now." She fanned herself. "Geez. Who knew the

Netherlands would be such an oven." She wiped the sweat off her forehead with the end of the tablecloth.

Griffin gawked at her for another second then stood and left the tent.

Man, it was a kiln in there. She unbuttoned the top of her dress.

Hal strutted in, looked down at her chest, then back up to her eyes. "Uh, your shirt's, uh..." He flicked his fingers over his chest and made weird sounds.

"Speak up, man," she said. "I don't have all day."

His mustache lowered an inch with his frown. "Actually, you have five minutes," he said, turning back twice with a weird confused look on his face.

"Five minutes until what?" she shouted.

Griffin strode back into the tent. "What do you think, brainiac? Let's go."

The dark gray night slid through the tent door. How long had she been eating? Did she eat? She stood and fell back in her seat. Something wasn't right. Her head felt funny. And her limbs felt like jelly.

"You okay?" Griffin held out a hand.

"I'm fine," she lied. Because even though she could barely make out Griffin's face, Gail's speech rang clear in her head—if she failed, the band failed.

A second later, she stood onstage, in front of a field full of people. *How did she get up there?* She examined the fine mist clinging to her skin.

The crowd shouted.

She cringed and covered her ears. *What the hell was happening?* Who were all those people? Their faces were so flat, like stretched-out Silly Putty.

Someone touched her lower back and a voice boomed overhead. "You look amazing," the voice said. Elias belonged to the voice.

She touched his cheek to make sure he was real. "I miss you," she said.

"I just saw you in the caterer's tent."

"You did?"

He peeled her arms off him. "Showtime."

She swam under the laser beams, doing the backstroke to the beat. Music played in the distance. It sounded like violin. Her fingers glided down the frets. How did they move without her?

The field turned into a writhing orgy of color. She spun in a circle until the world spun with her. Someone stopped her. *A supernatural being. Elias.* No human could sing like that and look that good.

God, he was so perfect. Life was so perfect.

Voices echoed over the canyon. She grabbed the microphone. "Hello, beautiful people!" she shouted.

They responded with a roar.

Arms poked up from the orgy, flashing blue screens.

"For God's sake!" she screamed. "Put down your phones!"

A few screens went dark.

"I'll take off my clothes, if you do," she said. "We'll all take off our clothes and sing buck-naked. Right guys?"

Cato's mouth opened wide like the whale in *Moby Dick.*

More phones rose over the crowd. "Guess a naked woman on stage is just another day in Amsterdam, huh?" She slapped her thigh and chuckled. "I saw a woman smoke out of her vagina. Remember that, El?"

She shielded her eyes from the lights. Where was he? "Raise your hands if you know how to smoke out of your vagina."

Some guy screamed, "I do."

"You have a vagina, sir?"

Laughter rang out. *Beautiful, beautiful laughter.* Swirls of fabulousness rushed over her. "If I play violin with my vagina, will you put down your phones?"

"Yes!" screamed the crowd.

"All right," she said. "Put down your phones, then."

"What are you doing?" Elias said through a tight smile.

"Isn't this the most beautiful man you've ever seen? Aren't they all beautiful? Such pretty men. And Missy? I bet all the boys want to hump her." She put the microphone back on the stand and picked up her violin. "You guys ready?"

The crowd cheered.

"Okay, here it goes." She slid the violin under her dress then pulled it out. "Nope, I still see phones. Sorry."

"Dude, shut up," Cato stage-whispered.

"Caaaaaaatooooh. I love you. Oh my gosh, I got you something today." She ran offstage and came back with the huge black dildo. "Surprise."

Cato threw it over his shoulder, and Griffin picked it up and started drumming with it. *Such a funny guy.*

A sea of hands waved. "Catch me!" She dove into the sea, and the beautiful, flat-faced people passed her around. "Let me down. I need to dance."

She wrung the sweat out of her hair and performed the ideal cheerleader routine. She even did the splits. "Ow," she said to no one. "That hurt." Even though, it felt like she'd torn her groin, she laughed and laughed and laughed.

For three days, she danced. At least that's what it felt like.

And then all the joy fled and chills and nausea swamped her.

She weaved toward the stage. On the way, a flashlight blasted her vision.

"What is she on?" someone asked.

"I'm high on life," she said then threw up on someone's boots.

PIANISSIMO

Pianissimo

"'I only hope the boat won't tipple over!' she said to herself."

Soundtrack *"Deep Blue," Arcade Fire*

Twenty-four hours after the concert, Effie came to.

All night and into the next day, Elias practiced dumping her. She'd shredded his heart into tiny pieces and made a fool out of him. And she'd lied. And it was over.

While she remained comatose for the last day, visions of his wasted mother played over and over again in his mind. The horror and hatred and humiliation from his childhood crawled up from the basement and haunted him—men barging into his room at night while he hid in the closet, his mother's abuse when she hadn't had her fix, begging for money to eat.

Then one day it finally stopped. After school, he found his mother dead on his bed. He'd never forgotten the relief he felt at that moment. Nor the dread that set in afterward.

If the authorities had found out he was an orphan, he'd have ended up in a worse situation, in an institution, or jail.

So he stayed in his apartment for a month with her rotting corpse until the smell became unbearable.

Then he packed up what little he had and went to school. He hid in the library supply closet until everyone had left for the day.

For one year, he lived in the library, ate the food from the cafeteria, bathed in the locker room, washed his clothes in the mop sink, and didn't tell a soul.

And then Jun, a janitor at the school, discovered his hideout one night after a water main break.

Jun couldn't speak English, but his wife Annie could.

Annie arrived that night at the school and convinced Elias to come to their house so Jun wouldn't lose his job.

After that, with what little money they had, Jun and Annie fed Elias and treated him like the child they weren't allowed to have in China.

Since then, his life had taken a dramatic turn for the better. And yet, here he was, in front of this woman, feeling like the same troubled little boy back in Chinatown.

Effie sat up and glanced around the boat. "Where am I?"

He didn't answer.

She pulled her knees to her chest. "I feel like I've been hit by a truck."

"What'd you take, anyway?"

A line puckered between her brows. "Take? What do you mean? When?"

The innocent virginal look on her face made him sick. "Before you did your little comedy routine onstage. What were you on?"

She gripped her forehead. "I wasn't on anything."

He dropped his head back. "Jesus! What a liar."

She stumbled out of bed, still in her white dress from the night before. "I'm not lying! I'm clean. I don't take drugs. Please, Elias, listen to me." She reached for him.

He brushed her off like dead skin and waltzed out the door. "Pack up your shit. You're going home."

GRAVE

Grave

---

*"'When you have to turn into a chrysalis—you will some day, you
know—and then after that into a butterfly, I should think you'll feel
it a little queer, won't you?'*
    'Not a bit,' said the Caterpillar."

Soundtrack *"Miss You," Alabama Shakes*

Nobody ever believes a druggie. Doesn't matter how long you've
been clean and sober, because you won't be for long. People look
at you differently when you're a drug addict. Or rather, they *don't*
look at you. They avoid looking at you. You disgust them.

That's how her mother looked at her when she kicked her out of
the house. That's how her father looked at her when he picked her up
from rehab. That's how her ex-roommate's parents looked at her when
they kicked her out of their guesthouse. That's how people on the
street looked at her when she begged for money to buy more drugs.

And that's how Elias had just looked at her.

Like she was filth.

For a second, she'd almost believed him.

Coke, meth, crack, uppers, those were her drugs of choice. They'd numbed her sensitivity just enough to deal with the world. But it wasn't coke that had stolen the last twenty-four hours of her life. It was something else.

Bits and pieces of the concert came back together, blurs of color and people, instances of dancing with the crowd, feeling so good, then so bad.

But nothing felt as bad as having Elias look at her like a drug addict . . . when she wasn't one.

Callie answered her call immediately.

She burst out crying and couldn't stop to tell her why.

"Dammit, what's wrong?" Callie said.

She blurted out half the story—the rest was still a mystery.

"Effie." That's all her sister said. Her name. That's it.

She could almost see the pity and disgust on her sister's face. That '*look.*'

A torrent of tears rushed out. Nobody believed her, not even her sister. "Say something," she cried.

Silence bled between them then Callie blew out a long breath.

"Stop with the disappointed little sighs!" Effie shouted.

"What do you want me to do?" Callie snapped.

"I don't know. I think someone drugged me."

"Who?"

"I don't know."

"Did you drink something? Eat something?"

"Nothing except water and candy."

"What kind of candy was it?"

Red fumes billowed in the back of her brain. *Gail.* Gail did this to her. Gail's shitsicles. "His manager did it."

"The Evil Cuntress?"

Effie nodded into the phone. "She gave me lollipops the night of the concert."

"Like, pot lollipops? We found some of those in Walker's grandmother's house."

"No, they were different. Chemical tasting."

Her sister asked Walker a muffled question then came back on. "Hot Cock says it sounds like a Mollypop."

"Don't call me that in front of your sister," Walker said in the background.

"I don't think my sister gives a shit about your pet name right now."

Effie couldn't help but chuckle.

"You have any left?" Callie asked.

She grabbed her bag and sifted through a mountain of condoms and dick soaps. Two lollipops lay at the bottom of her sack. "Yes."

"Can you take them to the police or something?"

"How do I prove it?" Gail would never admit the truth. And the more shit she stirred up, the worse it would get. "Cal?" She was so dehydrated it hurt to swallow. "I haven't told Elias the truth. About me."

"Why not?"

"Because, he wouldn't," a sob fell out. "He wouldn't love me."

"Oh, Effie," her voice cracked. "Do you really believe that? It's all or nothing, babe. Warts and all. Remember when you told me that about Hot Cock?"

"Blue!" Walker shouted.

"I signed a contract that said I wouldn't drink or take drugs," she said.

"So what? Didn't you also sign something about not hooking up with band members? What's his deal, anyway? What band doesn't do drugs?"

"I'm not in the mood to play games right now," Effie said. "I need advice. What do I do?"

"I don't know. You sure he's the one? Maybe he's just Mr. Sexbridge?"

"What?"

"You know, the bridge between screwing and love? Mr. Make-Me-Feel-Good-Right-Now."

"We haven't had sex."

"Are you kidding me? How could you keep your hands off that man? You've seen him, right?"

"We're taking it slow."

Callie coughed. "Impressive. Few women have that kind of restraint. I certainly don't."

"What am I going to do, Cal?"

"Tell him about the candy. If he doesn't believe you, then fuck him."

Effie picked the scar on her side. "And the other stuff?"

"That's up to you, but I wouldn't wait too long."

The clock ticked on the bedside table and rain smacked the window. Effie sobbed in silence. "I'm scared."

"I'm scared for you," Callie said. "But if it doesn't work out, there are a million other rock stars in the sea."

"You sound like Skip."

"*Ugh.* You're right. That was an asshole thing to say. Okay, Walker's feeling me up. Update me as soon as you can. But not for an hour."

"Two," Walker said.

"Two. Be safe. Be brave. Call me if you need help. I love you."

Sure she does, she thought. Her sister didn't believe her anymore than Elias did.

Time crawled as dark clouds drizzled rain into her mind. She'd forgotten what hangovers were like—the depression, the fatigue, the humiliation.

Laughter rang out from above.

She tiptoed up the stairs and peeked over the railing. Annie and LeStrange were making out in the kitchen. She cleared her throat.

Annie screeched.

LeStrange clutched his chest. "*Putain!* You scare da *sheet* out of me."

She hung her head. "I'm sorry." *For everything.*

Annie squinted. "Thought you'd be gone, sneaky girl."

"Where's Elias?" she said. "I need to talk to him."

Annie lifted her pointy chin. "He won't talk to a druggie."

"I'm not a druggie!" she shouted. "Gail gave me laced lollipops."

"Wha!" Annie cried.

Effie told them story. "I don't remember what happened after that."

Annie played a video from the concert. Effie watched five minutes then begged her to turn it off. No wonder Elias hated her. The world probably hated her.

Rain beat the windows and the boat rocked. She covered her mouth and tried not to barf.

After a long silence, Annie spoke. "Elias lost his mother to drugs."

She snapped back her head. "What?"

Annie nodded. "My husband Jun found him sleeping at school. He lived there for a year after she died. When we brought him home, he didn't talk for months." She shook her head. "Very sad scared little boy. For Elias, love equals pain. He runs from it."

This was the most tragic news ever. Effie burst into tears.

Annie's eyes welled up. "He's different with you. You light up his darkness." She tipped her hands like a scale. "He is yin, and you are yang. You are good for him."

"No, I'm not," she whispered.

Annie pulled her hand away and brushed her hair off her face. "You are blind. Open your eyes. Maybe you see what I see." She made for the stairs. "I go get my needles."

LeStrange's gaze followed Annie until she disappeared below deck.

His red brows pinched together, and he gave her a sad smile. "*Ça va, chérie?* You look, *crevé.* I make you *du café* and a *croque-monsieur.*"

She wrung her wrists. "I'm not hungry."

LeStrange studied her for a moment then folded his hands across his belly. "Things like this *s'enfuir.*" He flapped his arms. "*Sheet* fly away like bird."

She shook her head. "The 'sheet' is not flying away, LeStrange."

"*Si.*" He tapped his temple. "*Tu vois,* I am older, *donc beaucoup plus intelligent.* I'm smarter."

"You mean wiser?"

"Yes. Yes. Dat's it." He trotted over to the kitchen and pulled out a pan. "I fought the *guerre* in Afghanistan. When I came home, my wife live with another man, and my children hate me. I was a *piece-of-sheet.* Drank too much. Smoked too much. Then I got the cancer. I say to myself, of course you get the cancer, LeStrange, life is *de la merde.*"

He leaned on the counter. "Then I meet 'dis happy woman at zee hospital. I ask how she could be like that, with tubes shooting poison in her arms?"

"She tell me, 'Life is funny, LeStrange,' she say. 'Laugh!' He lit the gas stove and slapped a skillet on top. "So I laugh more, and I beat the cancer."

The pan sizzled and smoked behind the counter, and the scent of fried bread floated around the boat.

LeStrange continued. "Now, I have a job I love. I repair my relationship with my children." He pointed down the stairs. "I meet a beautiful woman and hear a great band every night. I am a lucky man. But if you had told me 'dat five years ago, I would have laughed in your face."

Effie shuffled to the kitchen and hugged him. "I wish you were my father."

He hugged her back with such tenderness she broke down again.

Annie appeared with her acupuncture kit and told her to lie on the sofa. A short while later, everyone except Elias returned.

"Where's El?" Cato asked.

Annie frowned and shook her head.

He sat beside Effie on the couch. "You okay?"

"I'm so sorry about the dildo."

"I'm not." He grinned. "That thing is awesome."

"But now everybody knows you're gay."

"Griffin must be gay too, since you gave him a butt plug."

"I did?"

"You said it matched his eyes."

She gripped her forehead. "Oh, God."

He placed a mammoth hand on her shin. "I don't care if the whole world finds out I'm gay. But the record label cares and so does my family. Besides what happens in my bed is nobody's business."

"Don't you want to meet someone?"

His broad smile slid into a frown. "I don't really think two kids and a white picket fence are in my future. I'm on the road all the time. Hell, I'm lucky to get laid once in a black moon."

She took his hand. "You'll meet someone special soon. Someone who loves you and doesn't mind traveling."

"No Yoko Ono's on tour, remember?"

She groaned. "I don't want to hear that name ever again."

His expression grew serious. "Annie said El kicked you out."

A sound burst out from her that sounded like an animal dying. "He told me to pack up my things."

He nodded. "El ever mention his real mom?"

"No, but Annie told me a little."

Cato told her a little more—about the abuse, and her overdose, and a few other things, but by then his voice had morphed into thunder, and all she heard was doom and gloom.

But a sliver of hope remained, that one day someone would love her no matter what.

That hope, that feeling, that unconditional love—it inspired her to be a better person, someone who could attract that kind of love.

And now, after celebrating two years of sobriety, she could say, without a doubt, that love was more important than drugs.

Friendship, family, music, love, they were all within reach, as long as Elias let her back in.

CONSONANCE

Consonance

"But she went on all the same, shedding gallons of tears, until there was a large pool all around her, about four inches deep and reaching half down the hall."

Soundtrack *"Mama's Gun,"* Glass Animals

Elias wandered around in the dark rain for hours. The crooked shops and bicycle racks and cobblestone streets sunk into his chest like a knife. He wanted to cry. He never cried. Not even when his mother died.

Waterlogged and stiff, he returned to the houseboat hours later, praying and dreading Effie wouldn't be there.

But she was.

On the couch, she lay crumpled in a frail ball next to Cato, her face swollen and red from crying.

If only he could hold her one more time.

He erased the warmth from his expression and replaced it with ice. "Why is she still here?"

Effie burst into tears.

Cato rose to his feet. "F-bomb has something to tell you."

He slammed the door. "I'm not interested. She made a fool out of me."

"She didn't make a fool out of you," Griffin shot back. "Len gave us a great review. Everyone loved the show."

"Now you're defending her?" Elias said

Griffin charged over to him. "Ease up and go talk to her before I plant my fist in your face."

He stomped down to the belly of the boat.

Effie trailed behind him, whimpering, and sat on the floor, limp as a wilted flower.

Back stiff and fists clenched, he stood as far away from her as he could get.

"I didn't take drugs," she said. "Not intentionally. Gail laced my lollipops."

"She what?"

"With MDMA. Molly. She gave me a box of them." She shuffled over to her backpack and pulled them out. "She told me it was a peace offering after we argued about the onesie. I was so mad I ate three of them. I should have known bet—"

"*Qué carajo!*" He tore off his wet jacket and flung it against the wall. "Why?"

She pounded her fists against her head. "I don't know. I've been wracking my brain. The only thing I can come up with is the song royalties."

He slid down the wall and collapsed on the floor. It was too much. "Did you call the police?"

"What are they going to do? It's not like she raped me."

He wrenched his phone from his pocket. "I'm going to kill her."

She knelt in front of him. "No, Elias. If you accuse her, she'll demand a drug test, and I'll fail it. Which puts me in breach of contract. And if you don't finish the tour, she'll sic her lawyers on you."

She clutched her elbows and sat back on her heels. "We have to pretend nothing happened, or we'll both end up screwed."

He crushed her in a hug so hard she gasped. "I'm so sorry, *mi amor*. Please forgive me. I should have—Gail—I will end her."

Her body trembled in his arms.

"Please don't cry." He squeezed her harder. "I'll fix this, I promise."

"She's a crooked tree," she said with a brittle laugh. "She belongs in Washington."

"Bob Ross?"

She nodded.

"How can you joke about this?"

"Humor's the only emotion I have left."

He rubbed his brow. "I'm such a prick."

"Annie told me about your mom." She started to say something then stopped.

He banged his head back against the wall. "She shouldn't have done that."

"Why not?"

"My mother doesn't matter."

She lifted a scolding brow. "That's the stupidest thing you've ever said. Of course she matters."

The boat creaked and swayed, but Elias stayed silent.

"Well, someday, I hope you share your story with me. And someday, maybe I'll tell you mine. But right now, I need to know, do I have to hop the next flight to New York?"

He jerked up. "No! You're not leaving."

She slumped over and heaved out a weighted breath.

He tipped up her chin and fell into her sad blue eyes. "Do you forgive me, *mi vida*?"

She pressed her soft lips against his and brought him back to life.

"Don't go," he murmured. "Don't ever go."

"I won't," she said. "Besides, we're not done with our bucket list."

DE CAPO

De Capo

> "'Yes, but then I HAD done the things I was punished for,' said Alice: 'that makes all the difference.'
>
> 'But if you HADN'T done them,' the Queen said, 'that would have been better still; better, and better, and better!' Her voice went higher with each 'better,' till it got quite to a squeak at last."

Soundtrack *"Insensatez," Antonio Carlos Jobim*

To make their concert in Madrid on time, they had to drive for twenty-four hours straight. A whole day of eight people jammed together in a small space.

No one seemed particularly bothered by this. Annie played mahjong. Cato slept most of the time. El read books and listened to music. Hal sketched. Missy knitted. Griffin killed people in his video game. Everyone found refuge in their hobbies, content with their solitude.

Except Effie. She was anything but content.

With the events in Amsterdam weighing heavily on her

conscience, for miles and miles, all she could do was replay her past. Which part of her history did Elias need to know?

If it were up to her, none of it. But if Elias grew up with a drug addict mother, he needed to know. And if she didn't tell him, someone else would. And that pill would be a lot less bitter to swallow if it came from her.

∿

ACT I—OVERTURE

"First, she dreamed about little Alice herself, and once again the tiny hands were clasped upon her knee, and the bright eager eyes were looking up into hers—she could hear the very tones of her voice..."

AT AGE THREE, Effie and her twin, accompanied their pianist mother to the music store. While Callie tore everything off the shelves and ran around destroying the store, Effie admired a pretty instrument perched on a shelf. She plucked the strings and the most beautiful sound spilled out—like a breeze blowing through a crack in the window, or like crickets in the nighttime, or bird wings in flight.

The gorgeous melody muffled her mother's bleating, screeching, and scolding, as well as her sister's banging, stomping, and screaming.

The woman at the counter, who looked like an actress on *Sesame Street*, recognized a potential sale and sidled up to her. "That's a violin," she said in a condescending baby voice. "Let me show you how to play it." The saleslady tucked the instrument under her chin and ran a stick across the strings. What flowed out sounded even better than before.

"Can I try?" Effie switched the instrument to her other side, because it felt more comfortable, then imitated what the woman had done.

After that, she never watched *Sesame Street* again because practicing her instrument was more important. Nor would she ever play the violin left-handed again.

ACT II—ENSEMBLE

"'Oh, how I long to run away from normal days,' thought Alice. 'I want to run wild with my imagination.'"

FROM THE AGE of six until the age of nine, Effie and Callie's lives were mapped out in advance. In fact, their mother wrote their routine on the kitchen chalkboard in white paint.

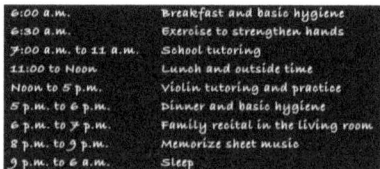

THE SCHEDULE WAS TBD on the weekends, because they were usually traveling and performing in recitals.

The strict routine didn't bother Effie at the time, because she and her sister were a team. And everyone knows misery is more fun with someone else.

Unlike Effie though, Callie was allowed to try a range of

instruments. But when her sister's musical giftedness never appeared, Greta focused solely on Effie.

Her mom put a second mortgage on the house and bought her an outrageously expensive violin from one of her German relatives.

"I don't want it," Effie told her. What if she accidentally dropped it? Then what? Would they end up homeless?

"Don't be ridiculous," her mother said. "A violin is as important as a violinist. Our lives are dependent upon your success now. You cannot fail."

By that point, their parents were divorced, so Greta Murphy devoted her life to making her child prodigy daughter into the next star. And if Effie dared deny her mother that role, there was hell to pay.

"Don't eat with your left hand," her mother would say at the dinner table. "You are no longer left-handed in this house."

"If I catch you playing with your sister again, you'll lose your outside privileges."

Her sister became such a distraction that Greta let Callie attend public school just to get her out of the house.

The night before her sister's first day of school, Effie snuck into her sister's room and stole a brand new box of crayons out of her backpack. Once Effie had broken every one of them in half, she then threw away the box and went back to bed.

ACT III–SOLO

"'What a curious feeling!' said Alice. 'I must be shutting up like a telescope!'"

"YOUR DAUGHTER EXHIBITS a few symptoms of ADHD," the first doctor said. "But most teenagers do. Exercise and a little fresh air should do wonders for her attention span."

The next shrink wrote a prescription for Ritalin without asking a single question. He also prescribed pain medicine to help with her stiff arms and neck.

Both pills helped her cope with her mother and made for a blissful barrier, which quickly dissolved once the doctor refused to renew either one.

∾

ACT IV—RITORNELLO

"Luckily for Alice, the little magic bottle had now had its full effect, and she grew no larger: still, it was very uncomfortable, and, as there seemed to be no sort of chance of her ever getting out of the room again, no wonder she felt unhappy."

"I NEED THE COMPETITION, or I'll never improve," Effie told her mother one night at dinner. The truth was, since she'd weaned herself off the drugs, she couldn't care less about violin. "At the School of the Performing Arts, I'll excel. I promise, Mother, it's the best thing for my career."

That fall, at the age of seventeen, Effie escaped her mother's regime and spent her senior year in a different sort of internment camp—high school.

For ages, she'd longed for a normal life, with normal friends, and normal teenaged problems, but once she started school, she soon found out she was far too abnormal to have that kind of life.

Socially awkward and culturally unaware, she repelled the cool kids, as well as the uncool kids. No one wanted to hang out with a loser who couldn't comprehend basic teenage trivia, like what brand names were in fashion, what TV shows to watch, and which parties to attend. She was a helpless mess.

No one spoke to her for months, until one afternoon, a popular boy from the drama program sat beside her in the cafeteria. His first words to her were: "You're weird." Then he said, "Wanna get high?"

Unlike her controlling mother, Brandon's wealthy parents neglected him. Instead of showering him with attention, they threw money at him. Nannies replaced his parents when he was a baby, video games replaced them during his elementary school years, and drugs replaced them during high school.

And with his parents' endless supply of money, Brandon supplied an endless amount of drugs.

Regularly, he and Effie skipped school and went back to his place in Malibu, where he lived alone because his parents lived on an island somewhere.

The first time they tried to have sex, Brandon was so high he couldn't get it up. The second time, he got it up, but couldn't come. The third time, he came so fast she didn't even realize what happened. The fourth time, they opted for a line of coke instead of a roll in the hay. After that, Brandon admitted he was asexual, most likely because of his antidepressants and drug and alcohol abuse.

Yet, he still made Effie his arm candy, and as long as he supplied the nose candy, she didn't mind.

Brandon wasn't her boyfriend or even her friend, really. He was more like a drug buddy, or a partner in crime. But at the time, he was all she had.

～

ACT V—ENCORE

"Imagination is the only weapon in the war against reality."

DESPITE BOMBING HER AUDITION, Effie received a full-ride scholarship to Juilliard at the end of her senior year, most likely because her mother knew the head of the violin department from her days as a concert pianist back in Germany.

"I want to take a break from school," Effie announced after she opened the school letter. "I'll go next year."

"Don't be absurd," Greta said. "You're going, and that's final."

"I'm eighteen. You can't tell me what to do."

"As long as you live in my house, I can."

Before their argument, Effie had done a fat line of blow off her hand in the bathroom, so without considering the consequences of her actions, she told her mother: "I'm moving the fuck out."

That night, she moved in with Brandon, where she stayed for the next four years.

In high school, Brandon focused on drama, and after high school, he thrived on it.

Even with his parents' Hollywood connections, he couldn't land a bit part. He'd developed a reputation for showing up on the set high or drunk, or worse, not showing up at all. Not to mention, his acting was so over-the-top, even soap operas wouldn't hire him for bit parts. He couldn't win over anyone in LA.

Instead, he became a sycophant, a back-slapper, and a parasite. He glommed on to anyone with a modicum of popularity or fame. He lived for the spotlight. It didn't matter if they were B, C, D, or Z-list celebrities, as long as they flicked a look in his direction, he was happy.

Because his parents paid for everything she did, including the drugs, she never questioned him. And he demanded nothing in return, not even sex, just her attendance at parties. Rather than stroking his cock for drugs, she stroked his ego.

Her new daily routine no longer included violin. Instead, she slept until noon, did a bump on the way to her waitress job, snorted up in the bathroom during her shift, and then came home and partied with Brandon until the wee hours of the morning.

Sometimes they danced all night at raves. Other nights, they went to sex parties and spent the night doing drugs, fucking random people, and never having orgasms.

Occasionally, they went skiing in Aspen and stayed in his parents' cabin or jetted off to the Caribbean to stay in his parents' island home when they weren't there.

With his parents' credit cards, Brandon bought her clothes at high-end boutiques and meals at swanky restaurants and massages at his elite country club. They lived like rich hedonists.

But even with all that money at her disposal, she'd never felt so empty. If money and drugs didn't make her happy, what was the point?

Then Brandon started dabbling in heroin. She had absolutely no interest in killing herself at the time. So instead, she watched him slowly fade away.

Eventually, his parents showed up one random night for an intervention and told him it was rehab or bust. He chose bust. And his parents brutally cut off their drug supply.

After that, they moved in with another rich Hollywood brat, as well as twenty other junkies, and started a life of petty crime. That's when she'd stolen her sister's ID and drained her savings.

Brandon broke into his parents' house and loaded up a moving van full of everything he could hock for drugs.

He'd also threatened to steal her violin from her mother's house, but she told him her mother had already sold it.

That instrument was the only thing tethering her to a drug-free future. Because she would quit tomorrow.

And the next day. And the next day after that.

But then the next day became the next month, and then the next year.

There weren't many salvageable memories from that time in her life. But a few cobwebs remained in the attic. For instance, she could still smell crack cooking and feel her body rotting away like it was yesterday.

Many times, when she was high, she'd composed symphonies in her head, but she'd never cared enough to write them down. The only thing she cared about back then was the instant zap of dopamine.

It wasn't long before Brandon became a vegetable. During that time, she wandered around Hollywood, begging for money. Once she had enough to buy a few candy bars and a couple of rocks, she'd hightail it back to the house, or over to the beach, and spend the rest of her day high as a kite.

One day, the police busted her for loitering and found her crack pipe. She'd already smoked everything, so they couldn't haul her in for possession. Instead, they called her father, and he hauled her into rehab the next day.

In rehab, she went through the harrowing stages of withdrawal then spent the rest of her three months in endless group therapy sessions with the other fuck-ups. After they shared their sob stories, they shared their drug connections.

And then she moved in with her father.

ACT VI—FUGATO

"And in our darkest hour before my final rhyme, she will come back home to Wonderland, and turn back the hands of time."

WITH SKIP'S GENEROUS HELP, she entered the experimental drug program in San Diego.

For six months, she'd lived in a private facility, where she received daily drug injections and attended cognitive therapy sessions.

Counselors also taught her basic life skills, like how to open a bank account and get a job.

After that, she lived in the clinic's halfway house for another six months and attended weekly therapy.

No one ever mentioned whether she'd received the placebo drug or not. It was possible. But in her mind, it was the therapy that had helped the most.

Though her therapist had uncovered a lot of issues, many she opted to bury instead. For instance, she never confronted her parents. Why bother? They didn't care.

Also, she never told Callie how much she resented her. There were two daughters in that household, and one of them was tortured, while the other one went surfing all day.

But since Callie had more or less forgiven her for stealing her life savings, and because she was the only family she had left, she never brought it up.

"'It's no use talking about it,' Alice said, looking up at the house and pretending it was arguing with her. 'I'm not going in again yet. I know I should go through the Looking-glass again—back into the old room—and there'd be the end of all my adventures!'"

WHICH OF THESE scenes should she divulge to Elias first? Was it better to go backwards, or forwards, or just sprinkle little anecdotes here and there? After twelve hours of thinking about it, she decided the best way to tell him was through music.

So she took out her music journal and let the story bleed out of her pen onto the staff lines.

When she'd finished Act I, Elias plopped down next to her. "What are you writing?" he asked.

"A symphony, I think."

"Can I see?"

She passed him her notebook.

"How do you write for all these instruments?"

"I don't know."

He shook his head. "You're gifted."

She slammed her journal shut.

"Did I say something wrong?"

"I don't like being labeled any more than you like being called a rock star."

His brows lowered. "But why? It's a compliment."

"Because it separates me from normalcy."

He scooted closer. "What do you mean?"

In vivid detail, she described Act I. At the end, Elias grabbed her hand and brought it to his lap. "Go on," he said. "I'm listening."

She took a deep breath and continued. "I won my first violin competition, then the second, then the third. After that, my mother became one of those beauty pageant moms you hear about, dragging me all over the place, forcing me to practice until my body ached. I just wanted to be a kid."

"You don't like playing violin?"

She shrugged. "It's the only thing I'm good at."

"You sell yourself short." He massaged her hands. "What about your father?"

Act II came next. "My dad left when I was six and married another woman. They had two daughters together. He wanted nothing to do with me after that."

Then she recited Act III and select bits of Act IV. "When my mom finally let me go to school, everyone made fun of me and said I was autistic. They called me 'Special Effie." She put finger quotes around the phrase.

"But you are special," he said.

"They thought I was mentally disabled."

"Ridiculous."

"But it's true. I hear things others don't. And feel things others don't. I'm not normal."

"What's normal? Is anyone normal? Normal is boring. I don't like boring. And you, *mi vida*, are anything but boring."

He gave her a reassuring smile. "People made fun of me in school, too. For being shy."

"Who cares if you're shy?"

"It's not normal."

"You seem normal to me."

"And you seem normal to me."

"Maybe we're both abnormal," she said.

"Absolutely. We're both freaks."

"Super freaks?"

"*Ay!*" He gripped his forehead. "Never say that again."

She rested her cheek against his shoulder. "I'm crazy about you, Elvis."

"I'm crazy about you, too, F-bomb."

BEL CANTO

Bel Canto

MADRID, SPAIN

"It would be so nice if something made sense for a change."

Soundtrack *"Desperada," B-Tribe*

At sunset, it was still a hundred degrees in Madrid. Giant mushroom-shaped shade structures sprouted up around the music festival and showered mist upon the melting masses, giving everyone an oily glow.

While Elias dealt with the sound guy, Effie watched a Spanish musician play on the side stage. It was a small band, only a DJ and a guitarist, but their sound was immense. Sensual and erotic.

A burning desire for sex engulfed her. If Elias were there, she would have given up her good-sex virginity right there out in the open.

Yeah, right. Like that would ever happen. He wouldn't even kiss her in front of Annie, let alone a huge crowd.

A bunch of loud Americans shoved next to her and destroyed the moment.

In the center, stood Tina, Elias's groupie. She snorted blow from a plastic bullet then passed it around the circle.

After everyone did a line, they swigged from a flask, then lit up a joint.

"Know what's better than this song?" one of them bleated. "This song for four hours!"

"Does anyone want this weed? I've got too much," said another.

A guy with a t-shirt wrapped around his head yelled out, "I feel like dancing! I want to dance!"

The dumbass was already dancing.

As she listened to their asinine conversations, hot shame swelled inside. She probably used to sound like that, like a complete moron.

"I'm a hundred percent about to vomit right now," Tina said. "But after that, I'm down for Urban."

Her friend blasted out a laugh. "You mean you're *going down* on Urban."

"How am I going to smuggle a shit-load of beer under this tutu?" asked her friend in a tutu.

No one answered. No one listened. They just babbled and spoke over each other and made noise—loud, fucked-up, noisy nonsense.

"Look, it's her."

Tina swirled around and stared right at her.

Effie bit back the urge to roll her eyes and waved.

Tina turned up her nose. "Let's go find Elias."

Then the clique swam through the mob and disappeared.

Someone kissed the back of her neck. She spun around and found Elias.

"Señorita." He brushed his mouth against her ear. "Are you by yourself?"

She clasped his hands and wrapped them around her. "Not anymore."

He swayed to the music behind her.

"Isn't that guy an amazing guitarist?" she said.

He stilled and said nothing.

"Can you play Flamenco like that?" she asked.

He moved to her side and glowered at the stage. "Never tried."

"He's so good." She circled her hips to the rhythm and raised her arms to the sky. "This song is so sexy."

He dragged her in for a greedy kiss. *"Voy a devorarte,"* he murmured against her mouth. "I'm gonna eat you up."

"Aren't you worried someone will see us?"

"No." His tone was gruff and definitive.

"What about the band? Or Gail?"

He loosened his grip and stepped back. "We should go. We're on in a half-hour."

She hung her head and sighed. Tina could molest him in public, but his own girlfriend couldn't? What kind of madness was that?

"You okay?" he asked.

"I'm fine," she lied.

FORTISSIMO

Fortissimo

"'We must burn the house down!' said the Rabbit."

Soundtrack *"Ready to Start,"* Arcade Fire

Bubbles floated in the breeze, beach balls bounced overhead, and the crowd belted out Urban's songs by heart.

Effie spread her arms and yelled out to the crowd in Spanish, "Dance your boobs off!"

Oh, no, thought Elias. Earlier, she'd asked him how to say 'boots' in Spanish. He'd jokingly told her the word for 'boobs' instead.

Silly woman.

Urban played the next song and women started ripping off their bras and flinging them on stage—dancing their boobs off. Elias ducked a leopard print one and kept playing.

Fireworks shot out of the stage and rained brilliant sparks over the fans. Effie dove into the crowd and sailed over everyone's heads, and kept sailing and sailing and sailing, all the way to the back. In the distance, she struggled to get down, but fans kept tossing her.

Where the fuck was Hal? Elias glanced down in the pit. Hal cowered on the ground, his arms over his head.

Elias motioned to Cato to play a filler riff. Then he jumped off the stage and pushed through the crowd.

He grabbed the guy holding her and yanked him back. Effie dropped into his arms, looking frantic.

"You okay?" he asked.

"Yeah."

They ran back to the stage. When they played "Chaos," things spun out of control.

Fans burst past the other security guards and rushed the stage. Instead of underwear, people hurled bottles and beach balls at them.

Elias sliced a finger across his throat and the band bolted backstage.

Blood seeped from a gash on Griffin's forehead. "Fuck, man. That was insane."

"Where the hell is Hal?" Missy screeched.

Good question. Where the hell was their bodyguard? Elias sprinted out to the tour bus.

Hal was curled in a ball in back, shivering.

"What happened?"

Hal flinched and turned, his eyes brimming with tears. "Is it over?"

"Yeah, man, show's over. What's going on?"

He rubbed his arm. "Fucking fireworks. Thought I was back in Iraq."

"Flashback?"

The bodyguard violently wiped the tears from his face. "Think you can talk to Gail and make sure that doesn't happen again?"

Elias scrubbed his hand down his face. "Yeah. No problem."

Hal stared down at his feet. "I let you down."

"No, our country let *you* down. I know the VA's not doing dick.

When we get back, we'll find you some real help." He clapped his shoulder. "In the meantime, I'll send Annie back. I'm sure she has some sort of Chinese voodoo for PTSD."

"Yeah, okay," Hal said.

Elias made his way up front.

"Hey, El?"

"Yeah?"

"Don't tell anyone, okay?"

"We're family," Elias said. "Just be real. Nobody's gonna dis you for losing your shit."

Hal nodded. "Thanks."

One problem solved, and another to go. He bolted off the bus and searched for Effie. He found her deep in conversation with the *pelotudo* from earlier—the "amazing guitarist" she couldn't stop staring at.

She giggled and twisted her hair and the guitarist bent down and whispered something in her ear.

He stalked up to them, threw an arm around her, and shot the *pelotudo* a touch-her-again-and-you-die glare. "What's so funny?"

"El Love." The guy tried to shake his hand and failed. "*Que pasa, tio*? Julio Esperanza. Nice to meet you. My band played before yours. Mustang?"

He shrugged. "Never heard of them."

Effie punched his shoulder. "We watched them earlier. Don't you remember?"

"I was too focused on kissing you." And without removing his glare off the *pelotudo*, he kissed her with lots of tongue.

"Ah, you are lovers?" Julio gave him a you-sly-dog look then stepped back a foot. "I am jealous. It's hard to find a beautiful, talented woman who can handle the road."

"She handles my road just fine." Elias cupped her cheek and kissed it.

"I'm having a party tonight at *mi casa*," Julio said. "You're welcome to stay with me. I have a guesthouse and a pool. *Habrá música y baile y tapas*—"

"Thanks," Elias said. "But we already have a place."

Julio saluted him and headed in the other direction. "Change your mind, I gave your girlfriend my number."

Elias waited until the asshole was out of earshot. "That *pelotudo* gave you his number?"

"His name is Julio, not"—she flicked her wrist—"whatever you said." She shot him a sideways glance. "Griffin's looking at us, you know?"

He dropped his arm and stepped back.

She ground her fists into her eye sockets.

"What's wrong?" he asked.

Out of nowhere, Tina appeared and slithered her arms around his waist. "Hey, baby," she cooed.

Effie's mouth dropped opened then pursed tight. A slice of blue ice blasted through her narrowed gaze and hit him right in the gut. Nostrils flaring and chin in the air, she spun on her heel and marched away.

He pried Tina's limbs off. "Get the fuck away from me."

"Aw, someone's in a bad mood. Want me to make you feel better?" She poked her tongue inside her cheek, faking a blowjob.

He scoffed and shook his head. "Classy." He bent down and whispered in her ear. "Come near me again, and I'll slap a restraining order on you."

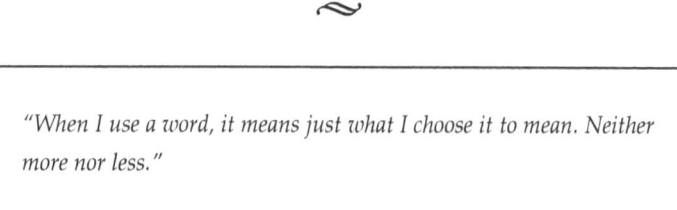

"When I use a word, it means just what I choose it to mean. Neither more nor less."

Soundtrack *"Without Walls," Chill De Lucia*

WHEN HE BOARDED THE BUS, Effie refused to look at him. Instead, she rubbed Hal's shoulders, offering quiet support.

Elias slammed his guitar in the overhead bin and plopped down in a seat.

Annie fed directions to LeStrange, and the bus pulled out and wound through the crooked streets of Madrid.

The ten-minute drive dragged on for hours as he sat helplessly bound to his seat, unable to speak to Effie in private.

LeStrange circled a residential area three times then finally stopped in front of a gate. The driver rubbed his chin. *"Ce n'est pas ici."*

"What's going on? Where's the pad?" Cato asked

LeStrange bounded off the bus and returned a moment later. He wiggled his fingers. "Fire."

"Speak English, man," Cato said.

LeStrange growled at him and pointed outside. "Go see."

Everyone tumbled off the bus and surveyed the property. Or what was left of it. Nothing but a pile of ashes remained.

"Is that our rental?" Missy asked.

Annie held up a picture of a house with the same gate.

"Was our rental," Cato answered.

Elias gritted his teeth and spun toward her. *"¡Qué lo parió! ¡Qué chanta!* I'm sick of this bullshit, Annie!"

She raised her hands. "I didn't know!"

"Did you call first?"

She winced and shrugged.

"Fuck," Griffin said to the sky. "I'm so tired and hungry I can't see straight."

"I can't sleep on this damn bus again," Cato whined.

"Moi, non plus," Le Strange said.

"Now what?" Missy asked.

"We can stay at Julio's house," Effie suggested cheerfully.

Elias clenched his fists. "We are not staying at Julio's house."

"Who's Julio?" Cato asked.

"I met him at the show," Effie told him. "He's super nice. He has a guesthouse and a pool. And he's having a party."

"Sign me up," Cato said and headed back to the bus.

"Count me in, too," Missy said.

Everyone else voiced their approval, and soon they were on their way to the *pelotudo's* house.

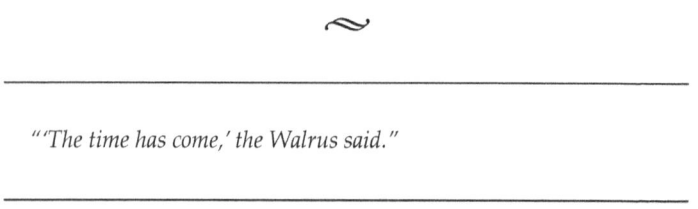

"'The time has come,' the Walrus said."

Soundtrack *"Sultanas De MerKaillo,"* Ojos de Brujo

THE PELOTUDO GREETED them at the gate of his mansion, dressed in white linen pants with no shirt. He was the perfect host, charming, warm, welcoming—and a complete *pelotudo*.

"Make yourselves comfortable," Julio said. "Then join us out by the pool."

"Your crib is awesome," Cato said. *"Gracias,* man."

"My pleasure," Julio said. "The women here love you."

Cato's smile wavered, but of course the *pelotudo* didn't notice.

Everyone showered and changed and headed out to the party. Fifty or so people gathered around Julio's pool. A DJ spun beats while a chef prepared tapas in the outdoor kitchen.

The *pelotudo* kissed Effie's hand. "Ready for your lessons?"

Elias ground his jaw. "What lessons?"

"She wants me to teach her Flamenco." Julio told him that in Spanish like were best friends.

They were not best friends.

Julio motioned to a makeshift stage on his patio. "Join us. You might learn something."

That fucker could suck his dick. And he told him that with a smile. *"Chupámela, pelotudo."*

Julio laughed.

"What did you say to him?" Effie asked.

"Nada."

The *pelotudo* gave her a guitar then strung his over his shoulder. "The trick is the rhythm." He slapped a beat on the side and motioned for her to do the same.

After ten minutes, she played as well as the *pelotudo* "Thanks Julio." Effie handed back his guitar. "Think I got it now."

The *pelotudo* squared his jaw and stopped smiling, butt-hurt because a woman was better than him.

Elias rolled his eyes and took her arm. "Let's get out of here."

They strolled over to a hidden spot behind the trees. While the *pelotudo's* music played in the background, Elias danced her around the lawn.

"I don't even have to put my feet down," she said. "How did you learn to dance like this?"

He dipped her over his arm. "My mother and father were tango dancers."

She let out a giddy yelp and bounced back up.

He kissed her long and hard.

She moaned in his mouth.

All at once, he had to have her. He threw her over his shoulder and dashed to the guesthouse.

"Where are we going?"

"To bed."

In the guesthouse, he dropped her on the bed and kicked the door shut.

She bit her knuckle and smiled.

"God, you're beautiful." He tore open her dress and latched onto a nipple. "*Tenés los ojos más lindos del mundo.*"

She whimpered and wrapped her legs around him.

"*Qué linda,*" he murmured. "*Sos divina.*"

"I love it when you talk dirty.

"I didn't say anything dirty." He smirked. "Yet."

"What are you waiting for?" She ground her pelvis against him. "Get crackin'!"

He dipped his finger into her slick heat. "*Tu concha está mojada.*"

"That's more like it."

Pre-cum oozed from the tip of his cock. *Dios*, he wanted to slide into home so fucking bad. He couldn't wait to feel her pussy quiver around him.

He doubled the effort. Mouth, tongue, both hands, he used them all and made her pussy a wet juicy mess.

She squirmed and moaned and clamped down on his fingers.

He nibbled her clit. "Feel good?"

"Don't talk. Don't talk. I'm almost there. Oh, God." She arched her back, scrunched her face, and held her breath.

"That's it, come for me, baby."

She grabbed his head and ground her mound against his mouth. "I'm coming. Sooooo hard."

He unzipped his jeans and pressed his cock against her entrance, dying to feel her come on his dick.

"Wait." She panted. "Condom."

"Fuck!" he shouted. "Where are the ones you bought in Amsterdam?"

"They're on the bus!"

"Fuck!" He rolled off her and tried not to shout.

Effie stared at the ceiling, rolling her lips between her teeth. Music and laughter grew louder outside their window.

He propped himself on an elbow and studied her. The post orgasm glow wasn't there. He caressed her cheek. "I'm sorry. I didn't mean to yell at you."

She faced him. "Can I ask you something? Why do want to sleep with me?"

"Is this a trick question? Because I want to make love to you."

"But do you?"

"Do I what?"

"Love me?"

He pinched the bridge of his nose. *Dios*, he wanted to say yes, he really did, but she was holding a gun to his head. It cheapened the moment. "I don't know," he said.

"You don't?"

"Why are you asking me now?"

She sat up and folded her arms around her knees. "I'm tired of sneaking around."

"You want me to tell the band I'm breaking my own rules?"

"Yes."

He closed his eyes and tried to imagine the outcome. Missy would throw a fit. Griffin would beat his ass for not letting Melody come on tour. And the press would have a field day at their expense.

But it seemed like she had one foot out the door. And he didn't want to lose her.

He scratched his scruff then let out a long sigh. "Okay. I'll tell them tomorrow."

"Don't you want to know if I love you?"

"Do you?"

She cupped his face. "With every ounce of my soul."

Right then, his heart split in two, and he handed half to her.

He pushed her down and rolled between her thighs. "*Te amo,* Effie. I love you, too."

She shoved him off. "Let's get some sleep."

"I really do love you. I didn't just say it to have sex with you."

She rubbed her lips for a moment then nodded. "Tell the others tomorrow, and we'll pick up where we left off."

He kept trying. "I'm serious. I love you."

"The thing is," she said softly, "you don't really know me."

Exhaustion slammed into him, and his eyelids grew as heavy as the conversation. "I love you. You love me. What else do I need to know?"

She shut off the light and snuggled up against him. A minute later, she whispered, "Everything."

"Sometimes I believe as many as six impossible things before breakfast."

EFFIE CURLED against him and purred in her sleep. He smiled at the wetness on his bicep. She'd drooled on him, and he was fucking happy about it. He was definitely whipped.

He examined the curve of her ear lobe, the violin rash under her chin, the freckles on her nose, and with a clear, unwavering calmness, he knew he loved her for sure. And after last night, he couldn't just tell her that, he had to prove it.

He eased his arm out from under her then quickly dressed and rushed downstairs. Everyone was already at the kitchen table with plates of fresh bread, fruit, and big cups of latte in front of them.

"Any more coffee?" he asked.

Hal threw a pointed look to a carafe on the counter. "In the pot."

Elias poured himself a mug and sat down in an empty seat.

Cato was in the midst of telling the band about the hot Spaniard he made out with at the party.

"Too short for you," Annie said.

"Did I ask you, woman?"

"He has to wear high heels to kiss you," she said.

"Maybe he can borrow those hideous boots Gail made Effie wear," Missy said.

"Those are long gone," Griffin said.

Elias chuckled.

Everyone quieted down and stared at him.

"Effie still asleep?" Hal asked. "We've got to get a move on soon."

Elias scratched his chin, inhaled, exhaled, sucked in another breath, then blurted out, "Effie and I are together."

Cato stopped peeling his banana, but otherwise no one seemed fazed by the news.

LeStrange looked at his watch. "Thirty minutes, we go."

"Did you hear me?" he said a little louder. "Effie's my girlfriend."

"No shit," Griffin said.

Missy brushed the crumbs off her lap and stood.

"It doesn't bother anyone that I'm breaking The Rules?"

"Nobody cares about your stupid rules," Annie said.

He rubbed his forehead. "How long have all of you known?"

Missy rolled her eyes. "Since you invited her to play with us."

"Not me," Cato said. "I found out at Disneyland. Then again my *straightdar* is broke to shit. I can't tell who's straight, who's gay, or who's fucking who." He shook his head.

Did Elias wake up in an alternate universe? "So none of you are pissed?"

"Oh, I'm pissed, all right," Cato said. "But when I find Mr. Right, you better believe he'll be riding the Disco Bus with all of us."

Elias turned to his drummer. "What about Melody? You want to bring her?" He prayed like hell the answer was no. Riding with them would be like riding with a reality show.

Griffin stared out the window and said nothing.

Elias prodded him again. "Ralph?"

"We're on a break."

"No, *you* on a break," Cato said. "She done."

"Leave him alone," Missy said.

For a brief second, Griffin's angry expression collapsed into a lost, hollow stare. Then he shot out of his seat and stormed off.

"You're an asshole," Missy told Cato.

"No, he's an asshole. Fucking everything in sight. No wonder she dumped him."

Missy chucked a wadded-up napkin at Cato's head. "He didn't cheat on her before she broke up with him."

"Time to go," LeStrange said.

Everyone rose from the table and went to pack their things.

Elias stared down at his coffee. This whole time everyone knew and said nothing. He felt like a fucking idiot.

Hal sat next to him and folded his arms across his massive chest. "Let me give you a piece of advice, lover boy," he said. "You better start treating Effie like a girlfriend soon, or she's gonna dump your ass." He held up a finger where a white line had replaced his wedding ring. "Trust me. Wise up and start romancing her." Hal scooted out his chair. "Buy her some candles or something. Women eat that shit up."

A big, bald, divorced bodyguard had just given him relationship advice. Elias really was living in an alternate universe.

CRESCENDO

Crescendo

LISBON, PORTUGAL

"The sun was shining on the sea, shining with all his might. He did his very best to make the billows smooth and bright. And this was odd, because it was the middle of the night."

Soundtrack *"Nem as Paredes Confesso,"* Amália Rodrigues
Soundtrack *"Se Ao Menos Houvesse Um Dia,"* Camane

Bob Ross would have loved Lisbon. With its bright red roofs and smiling, happy people, and tiny winding streets, the city looked just like a PBS painting.

Lisbon turned out to be her favorite stop on the tour, not so much because of the picturesque scenery, but more because Elias did something spectacular at the show that night.

Urban's fans placed El Love on a pedestal, as if he were a god and not a man who battled stage fright. His inability to interact with the crowd came across as cockiness, like he was too good for mere mortals. His onstage persona was nothing like the real man though.

But the real man came out that night. After the last number on their set list, Elias gripped the microphone with a shaky hand, stammered for a second, then licked his lips and spoke softly to the crowd. "This song is for Effie. It's called 'Euphoria.'"

Then with his coppery eyes anchored to hers, he sang a love song and announced to the world they were together.

Happy tears flowed down her face as she floated over the cliffs of Lisbon in a bubble of love, feeling euphoric.

And after the show, her handsome lover whisked her off in a limo to spend the night in a tree house.

Lit candles flickered inside the cozy room and the ocean breeze blew fluffed out the mosquito netting around like gauzy sails.

Portuguese music played softly in the background, accompanied by the ocean waves, and the crickets, and the sound of her heart, drumming a crescendo beat.

They took off their clothes and stretched out in bed. "I'm in heaven," she said.

"You *are* my heaven." He kissed her. "I love you, F-bomb."

A runaway tear slid down her cheek. "I love you, too, Elvis."

He drew circles around her nipples, and then explored the rest of her body, plucking and playing and probing his way down between her thighs.

His stubble grazed her skin as he feasted on her. She shifted so they could feed on one another. Slurping and moaning and sucking—they made their own sexual symphony.

"I need to be inside you." He rolled on one of her French tickler condoms, fighting a grin. "Sit on me and wrap your legs around me."

She should have known he wasn't a missionary man. Elias Lovaro was too passionate for ordinary sex.

She let out a breathy laugh as she slid down his length. With him inside her, she'd finally been put back together. Elias was the missing piece.

He moved inside her just like he danced—slow, sensual, and staccato.

She cried out for more, and for him to fuck her harder and deeper and faster.

He flipped her over on her back and lifted her leg over his shoulder. His hips slapped against hers in a slow circle.

They kept their gazes sealed together, and the energy between them could have ignited a missile.

He smiled and kissed her. "*Te amo*, Effie." Their tongues met and danced to the same rhythm as their bodies.

She squeezed him tightly inside her.

He growled and bit her neck, then backed up to his knees and rubbed her clit while he slid in and out.

She thrashed and cried out like a wild animal.

"I feel you clenching around me." He grunted and rooted deeper.

She arched into him and sang out like an opera star when the climax hit.

A second later, his abs flexed, and his head dropped back, and he gritted his teeth, and groaned a bunch of Spanish dirty words, then pulled out, tore off the condom, and spilled his seed on her skin.

Watching him come triggered another electric spasm inside her.

Afterwards, he collapsed on top of her and murmured, "*Te amo*," between kisses.

"I love you, too," she said.

She closed her eyes and memorized every glorious detail—their slick skin melded together, the erotic scent of hot sex, their winded breaths, the waves outside, her heartbeat, his heartbeat, the beard burn on her chin, and the pain in her cheeks from smiling so much. It was a forever memory, one she could unpack in the future, to cheer her up on a gloomy day.

"I'm not a virgin anymore!" she shouted. "You popped my good-sex cherry."

He laughed. "You're welcome."

"*De nada.*" She winked.

They giggled and kissed and hugged and tangled their legs and wiggled their toes. She felt like a kid again. An older kid. One old enough to have sex. Okay, maybe not a kid.

She lifted her wet hair off her shoulders. "Whew! It's hot."

"Let's go for a swim," he said.

"Yay!"

They dashed down to the ocean, completely nude, howling like children, and acting like they'd just pulled off the ultimate prank.

They floated on their backs, holding hands and staring up at the moon and stars, not saying anything, but feeling absolutely everything.

"This looks like a Bob Ross painting," he said.

"No worries. No cares," she quoted Bob. "Just floating and waiting for the wind to blow you around."

He chuckled. "Tell me another one."

"We don't need to set the sky on fire. A little glow will do just fine."

"Guy's a prophet."

"Totally."

ALLEGRO

Allegro

SIERRA NEVADAS, SPAIN

"'It sounds like a horse,' Alice thought to herself. And an extremely small voice, close to her ear, said, 'You might make a joke on that—something about 'horse' and 'hoarse,' you know.'"

Soundtrack *"Road to Nowhere," Talking Heads*

"Not good," LeStrange said before they left the next day. "*Zere* is a strike and zee highways are blockaded. We must take zee back way to Cannes through *L'Espagne*. It will take much longer."

This fazed no one until the air conditioning crapped out midway there, and the bus heated to a blistering ninety degrees inside.

Elias was still high off of making love with Effie and didn't complain once. But everyone else whined and moaned and bitched endlessly.

LeStrange stripped down to his bikini underwear, and not long after, everyone else in the band sported nothing but skivvies, including Hal and Annie.

Cato raised a judgmental brow at Effie's underwear. "Spiderman?"

"Stop staring at her," Elias snapped.

"Don't tell me what to do," Cato shot back.

"Shut up," Missy cried.

"Yeah, shut-the-fuck-up," Hal chimed in.

Two seconds of silence passed, then Cato slapped his hand on his chest and screamed at the sky. "I'm dying. I'm being baked to death. Oh, *lawd*. Help me, Jesus. Save me!"

"Shut-the-fuck-up!" everyone shouted at once.

"We've got to pull over," Cato whined, "before we kill each other."

Without warning, the bus blasted out black smoke then choked, squawked, and died—at the base of the Spanish Sierra Nevadas—in the mountains—in the middle of nowhere.

"I didn't mean stop here," Cato shouted.

LeStrange turned over the engine and pumped the gas. More black smoke poured out. The driver took off his captain's hat and stood in the aisle. "How you say, *'piece-of-sheet'* bus broke,' in English?"

"Think you got it, dude," Griffin mumbled.

LeStrange slapped his hat back on, slipped on his flip-flops, and flapped outside. *"Putain de merde!"* he shouted. *"Qu'est ce que c'est bordel?"* After a considerable amount of banging, he flapped back onboard, gripping a wiggling hose in his hand like a snake. *"Eh, ban,* slight problem. Le bus is *baisée."*

"The bus is fucked?" Missy said.

LeStrange pointed at her and nodded. *"Exactamente."*

"You have another one, right?" Griffin asked.

"Negative. But I make a call."

Ten minutes later, after shouting in French on the phone, LeStrange crept up the aisle again. "Bad problem," he said. "Zee mechanic truck is stuck on zee highway from zee strike." He held up the hose. "But is easy repair with new hose, and Granada is only five kilometers from here."

"Speak English, motherfucker!" Cato yelled.

"Three miles," Hal said. "That's not far."

"And how you gonna get three miles?" Cato asked.

"*Eh, ban,* we walk," LeStrange said.

Cato threw his arms back dramatically. "What the —? Somebody translate for this motherfucker."

"I'll go," Effie said, slipping her sundress back on. "Better than roasting on the bus."

"I'm down," Elias said.

"We can all go," she said. "It'll be fun."

"*We* aren't doing anything." Cato waved. "Bye, have fun."

"Hell with it," Hal said. "I'll go too. I need the exercise anyway."

For some odd reason, no one else wanted to take part in a boiling 5K across a mountain desert.

Cato snapped his fingers. "Chop, chop. Hurry up now, before I melt."

LeStrange flung the hose over his shoulder and they started off down the road.

Above, the blue mountain range jutted up toward the sky, and below the brown-scorched earth sizzled under their feet.

Nothing was alive out there. Even birds weren't flying overhead.

About a mile down the road, Effie tapped the driver's shoulder. "Um, LeStrange?" She winced at his underwear. "Your pants."

The driver smacked his hat against his thigh. "Ah, *sheet.*"

"Oh fuck. Great!" Hal threw up his hands. "Somebody's going to shoot us out here."

"Dude, chill," Elias said. "This isn't the Gulf."

LeStrange cursed in French, then continued flapping down the road with his underwear creeping up his ass.

After a while, Hal whistled a cheery tune.

"Willie Nelson?" LeStrange guessed.

"That's right!" Hal chuckled. "'On the Road Again.' Ever heard of that game show *Name that Tune*? You could be a contestant."

"Chante une autre."

Hal whistled the Talking Heads.

"Road to Nowhere," LeStrange shouted.

The bodyguard burst into song. "We're on a road to nowhere!"

LeStrange cracked an imaginary whip. "Ha! Ha!"

"You're a good singer, Hal." Effie said.

"My mother was an opera singer."

"No kidding?"

And with no prodding necessary, the bodyguard sang the entire Act 1 of *Rigoletto*, which made the next mile feel like light years.

Effie applauded wildly at the end and bounced a little faster down the road in her sundress. Even in the dusty, hot-as-fuck mountain desert, she looked like a goddess.

"Isn't she the most beautiful woman you've ever seen?" Elias said.

"Aw, that's cute," Hal said.

She looked over her shoulder and blew him a kiss.

A little further down the road Effie shouted, "Look, ponies!"

Elias squinted one sweat-stung eye at the dozen horses grazing in a corral. On the shack next to it a sign read: *Los Gitanos Horse Riding Adventures.*

"Isn't riding a horse on your list?" Elias asked her.

She clapped. "Yes!"

LeStrange shook his head. "*Mauvaise idée, les gars.*"

They ignored him and entered the paddock.

Elias waved at two crusty old guys and greeted them in Spanish.

In return, they glared at LeStrange's balls.

He asked them about the horses.

They glared at LeStrange's balls.

Next, he let the money talk for him and handed over an obscene amount of cash.

Suddenly, they understood every word.

LeStrange whispered behind his hand. "No good. Gypsies. *Gitanos*. Thieves. Bad idea."

They could be serial killers for all he cared, as long as they had horses for his girl to ride. He asked them a few questions.

The Gypsies shrugged and pointed to the horses.

"Guess we just pick a horse and go," Elias said.

Effie skipped to a dappled gray mare with a white mop-like mane and petted its velvet nose. "This one's mine."

Clueless as to the makeup of a good horse, Elias chose the one next to hers.

"Dat guy." Hal lumbered toward a huge black horse sequestered from the others. "A badass horse for a badass bodyguard. What's your name, big fella?"

It whinnied and snorted and pawed the ground.

"No! No! No!" The Gypsies waved their arms frantically.

Hal ignored them. "I'll just call you *Señor* Badass." He stuck a foot in the stirrup.

The horse dragged him to the side by the foot.

"Whoa, boy! Whoa."

The crusty Gypsies covered their mouths.

Hal threw himself on the beast's back as if he were scaling a wall during a military exercise.

The horse reared.

"Yeah!" he shouted. "Badass!"

Effie perched in her saddle, whispering sweet things in the animal's ear.

After carefully watching the Gypsies, Elias mounted his steed. Once astride, he broadened his shoulders and sniffed the air. *Powerful.* That's how he felt up there. Like a knight headed into battle. He should buy a horse and ride it frequently with his fair maiden.

LeStrange jumped and jumped, then finally hoisted himself up on the horse and grabbed the reins. "Ride 'em, cowboy," he said in his silly French accent, grinning ear-to-ear.

The Gypsies wanted nothing to do with LeStrange, so he was forced to lean over and untie his own horse.

Soon after, they all clopped down the road.

LeStrange cawed like a crow. "*Mes couilles.*"

No translation needed—men only made sounds like that when their balls were being smashed.

"Ask them when we can run," Effie said.

Before he even posed the question, she took off galloping down the road.

The Gypsies shouted something unintelligible and thunder approached from behind. A woman screamed bloody murder. Or at least it sounded like a woman.

It turned out to be Hal on a runaway horse. He clung to the horse's neck, ricocheting side-to-side, wailing like a banshee.

"*Putain,*" LeStrange mumbled.

Slack-jawed and wide-eyed, Elias watched the scene unfold like a movie. "*La puta madre.*"

Hal shrieked again.

"*Ay! La puta madre!*" What should he do? He didn't know how to ride a horse! He jabbed his heels in the horse's side, and miraculously, the animal's gear shifted to full-speed.

With the hot wind blowing hair in his eyes and the cloud of dust they kicked up, he could barely make out the shape of their horses in the distance.

Effie's horse reared, and then her flowery dress floated like a sail in the breeze, and she fell to the ground with a thud.

Elias jumped off his horse and ran over to her. Her body convulsed in the brush. One thought struck terror in him: *If she dies, I'll die.*

A split-second before hurling himself on the ground to perform CPR, he stopped short. She wasn't convulsing. Well, she was, but from laughter, not injury.

Weeds in her hair and dress around her waist, she laughed so hard only gasps came out.

"I thought you were dead," he said.

She grabbed her crotch and squealed. "I'm gonna pee!"

Meanwhile, Hal was still riding in his own personal rodeo. His horse bucked and kicked, yet somehow he stayed on and rode it like a bronco, the whole time shrieking, "No, Badass, no!"

Elias searched high and low for—*who knows?*—a weapon maybe? What the hell did horses eat?

On a hunch, he grabbed a handful of weeds and waved them like a white flag of surrender a few feet in front of Badass.

Foaming at the mouth and nostrils flaring, Badass finally stopped bucking. The horse gave Elias a wild-eyed, villainous look, grabbed the grass, and reared again.

LeStrange trotted up, grunting every time his balls hit the saddle. "Gypsies. No good."

The no-good Gypsies arrived on the scene. They scurried around the animal with their arms blocking their heads. One captured the reins and the horse finally settled.

Hal slid down, shaking and crying, snot running out of his nose.

One Gypsy pointed at Hal's horse then at Effie's and poked a finger through a hole in his fist. "*El Semental.*"

Animal husbandry ignorant, it took a moment before Elias finally caught on. "Ohhh!" he said. "*El Semental!* Hal's horse is a stallion?" He mimicked the fucking sign back to the Gypsies.

They nodded frantically. "*Sí, sí!* Stallion."

Effie dusted herself off. "Hal! You tamed the black stallion!"

Tamed was a humongous stretch, but the bodyguard stopped crying and puffed up his chest. "I did, didn't I?"

With one sweet sentence, she'd transformed Hal from a weepy man-child into a gallant knight.

Elias pulled a weed out of her hair and kissed her dried-out, dirt-speckled lips. Her blue eyes, more brilliant than the bright Spanish sky, blinked in surprise.

She jumped into his arms and attacked his mouth. "That was so much fun."

"Wild woman," he said.

"I can't believe we're riding horses! In Spain." She smothered him with kisses again. "Thank you. Thank you. Thank you."

After the dust literally settled, they got back on their saddles. One Gypsy rode Badass back to the corral, and Effie rode in front of him so Hal could take her horse.

As he breathed in her wild, weedy hair, a scary burning sensation crowded his chest. Since childhood, he'd stuffed his feelings in a locked box, and suddenly that box was wide open and overflowing with emotion.

In a little more than a month, he'd fallen in love, and in a little less than twenty-four hours, after he'd just made love to her for the first time, she could have died.

For an instant, he seriously considered fleeing over the Sierra Nevadas on the back of Badass the black stallion.

A little while later, they arrived in Granada, bought a hose, and hitched a ride in the back of someone's truck to the bus.

Soon after, they were on their way to France.

As Effie snoozed against his shoulder, he thought about how boring his life had been before her. She made everything a wild adventure.

FERMATA

Fermata

CANNES, FRANCE

"The Red Queen drew herself up rather stiffly, and said, 'Queens never make bargains.'"

Soundtrack *"Genesis," Justice*

The band didn't make it to Cannes until thirty minutes before the concert started. Luckily, the road crew had arrived before them and sound-checked their equipment.

On the way there, Gail had sent Elias a flurry of frantic texts. From the way his jaw popped every time his phone vibrated, Effie could tell he was arguing with his manager.

The instant the band barged through the stage doors, Gail attacked him. "Well, well. Look who finally made it. Do you have any fucking idea what I've been going through with these French fucks? They were about to fine you for being late. I told you not to hire your stupid mother as an assistant."

An older man with tight curly hair and the same features as Gail, hand blocked her. "Shut up."

The manager shrank back like a whipped puppy.

Elias nodded to the guy. "Mr. Heart."

Gail's infamous father barely acknowledged his client.

Right then, Kyle, the hairdresser, showed up and dragged Effie back to the dressing room.

"*Ugh*! What the hell is in your hair?" He yanked the brush through her hair. "It's a rat's nest."

She raised a hand. "Shh! I'm trying to listen."

Elias's soft voice was too low to hear, but Gail's was loud and clear.

"That's ridiculous," Gail sniped. "I didn't drug her."

Mr. Heart mumbled something, then Gail shouted again. "She's lying. You're making up shit so you can break the contract."

Elias said something again.

"Not my problem," Gail sneered. "She signed the deal. Oh, and by the way, hope she signed the NDA, because I'm not bailing your ass out again when she drags your name through the mud."

"What's an NDA?" Effie asked Kyle.

"Non-disclosure agreement. Heart's way of keeping a lid on the gossip. Everyone in the band and crew signed one. I heard a rumor that anyone who screws a band member has to sign one, too."

"I never signed one," she said.

"So it's true? You're with El?" He clapped a hand over his mouth and squealed. "Are you in love? Or should I say, is Love in you?"

She tore the brush from his hand and hit him with it.

Kyle lifted a shaped brow. "Better not let that secret out, or Queen Bitch will have your head."

"It's not a secret anymore."

Mr. Heart bellowed, "The violinist signs the NDA or doesn't go on tonight."

Effie jumped out of the chair and ran out to the hallway. "Where is it?" she said.

They stared at her.

"The NDA. Give it to me. I'll sign it now."

"Effie . . ." Elias held her back.

Gail yanked a document and a pen out of her purse and shoved it at her.

Elias ripped the agreement out of her hand. "Effie, don't. You don't have to sign this. I trust you."

She tore it back, signed the paper, and threw it in the manager's face. "I'm not a fling." She turned to Mr. Heart. "And my name is Effie."

Mr. Heart scoffed then turned to his daughter. "I knew you'd fuck this up. Control your client, or you're done."

Heart turned to Elias. "Think you can handle an autograph for the Mayor of Cannes. He's pretty pissed off."

Elias nodded and followed Mr. Heart down the hallway.

Gail stood completely still, holding her stomach like she'd just been stabbed.

For an instant, Effie felt sorry for her. "Fathers can be real assholes sometimes," she said with tremendous sympathy in her tone.

Gail's wounded expression vanished. "What?"

"Don't let your dad get you down."

The manager's steely eyes welled up. "I haven't been laid in six years. Six-goddamned-years. Not since I took Urban on as a client. I have busted my ass to the bone, making them what they are today. And you come in out of nowhere"—she fluttered her hands—"and destroy everything I've worked for." She let loose a roar.

The nearby crew stopped and stared.

"You, little girl"—she jabbed a finger at her chest—"are going down." She shot her wicked smile, then like a forest fire, streaked down the hall, her red coat flapping behind her.

Bile burned the back of her throat, and she stood paralyzed, watching her future blow out the back door.

44

ROCOCO

Rococo

"'You,' he said, 'are a terribly real thing in a terribly false world, and that, I believe is why you are in so much pain.'"

Soundtrack *"Rococo," Arcade Fire*

The concert in Rome turned out to be a shitshow. Literally. Italian pigeons had roosted in the outdoor amphitheater's rafters and pooped all over him during the show.

Then Effie stage dived onto the asphalt and split open her knee and sprained her shoulder.

At the hospital later, she'd refused pain medicine, for some ridiculous reason, and suffered in silence all the way back to the rental. The only good to come out of the visit was the birth control prescription and the negative STD results.

He was so looking forward to making her feel better with his bare cock. And they had the whole place to themselves

Annie and LeStrange had rented a private room. Missy's boyfriend had flown in for the weekend. And Cato was out at the gay bars. Even Hal was out with a woman he'd met at the concert. That left Griffin, and he had to be out boning some Italian *mina*.

But as it turned out, his drummer was not out boning someone —he was in the kitchen, boning Tina in the ass.

They would have been blissfully unaware of that fact, had Tina not been wasted out of her mind and shouting, "Fuck my ass harder, drummer boy!"

Elias slammed the door, but they kept going at it. He took off a shoe and tossed it like a warning flare into the kitchen. Unfortunately, it bounced off the counter and hit Tina in the face.

Then they stopped screwing, and the real fun began.

Tina accused him of assault and threatened to call the police. And now, Effie was in the kitchen, talking her down from the ledge.

"You can't keep doing this," she told Tina. "This lifestyle—the drugs, the random men—you'll just end up hating yourself."

Tina sniffled. "I know. I just get so lonely."

"You can always talk to me," Effie said.

His girlfriend was offering that psycho her friendship? *Me estás jodiendo!* He charged into the room. "Time to go, Tina. I'll call you a car."

The groupie glowered at him with makeup-smeared eyes. "You insensitive pig." She turned to Effie. "He was awful to me. Does he abuse you, too?"

Effie's brows shot up. Then calmly and succinctly, she told her to get the hell out. "Now."

Tina looked as if she'd just been slapped. She stopped blubbering and grabbed her shit.

He tried not to smile.

At the door, Effie schooled her again, "You accuse my boyfriend of something like that again, and I will sic a lawyer on your ass so fast your head will spin." She slammed the door and stomped back into the room, blue eyes blazing with fire. "I will cut that bitch if she ever shows her face around me again."

She vaulted into the kitchen and jabbed her finger into Griffin's chest. "You! Stop screwing around on your girlfriend with that"— she hissed at the ceiling—"Ugh! Just stop it!"

Griffin's jaw tightened. "I'm not cheating on my girlfriend."

"What happened to Melody?" Elias asked.

"She broke up with me."

Effie's hands flew to her hips. "I'm not surprised, you big cheater."

"I didn't cheat on her!" He dragged a hand through his hair. "She broke up with me before the tour."

"Eh, you'll get back together," Elias said. "You always do."

Griffin blew out a heavy breath then slumped over the counter. "Nah, man, Melody wants kids."

There wasn't much else he could say. Kids were a deal-breaker for his drummer. After Griffin's father died, he'd helped raise his nine sisters. He didn't want children because he'd already reared nine.

Effie hugged him. "I'm so sorry. You really loved her, didn't you?"

Griffin bit his lip and nodded. "She was my best friend. I can't sleep. I can't eat. I don't know how I can live without her." He hung his head. "But I don't want kids. I just . . . can't."

She hugged him tighter.

Griffin released a tortured sob, then clung to her, and silently wept in her arms.

Right then, Elias knew he had to marry her.

COLORATURA

Coloratura

Soundtrack *"Let it Be Me," Ray LaMontagne*

Elias took Annie to breakfast the next morning while Effie slept in.

His mother dipped her biscotti in a bowl of café and chatted about the places LeStrange had taken her the day before.

"So, you and LeStrange, huh?" He smiled and waggled his brows.

Annie turned bright red and downed her coffee like a shot.

"Well?" he asked.

Her lips pursed over a smile, then she burst out giggling. "He's so nice."

"I'm so happy you're moving on and letting go of Jun. It's time."

Her smile flattened. "I let go of Jun a long time ago."

He gave her a quizzical look. "What do you mean?"

"Jun was a good man, but I didn't love him. We were friends. Good friends. But I didn't choose him, my parents did. I choose LeStrange."

He patted her hand. "He seems like a great guy, Mom."

A serene smile passed over her. Then she brushed the crumbs off the table and folded her hands on top. "What you want to talk about?"

The bells chimed on top of the cathedral, and the pigeons cooed and flapped away.

"I need you to cancel the concert in Geneva."

"Why?"

"Effie needs time to heal her shoulder." He paused for a beat. "And I want to take her to Austria for the weekend. It's her birthday and I"—he closed his eyes—"I want to ask her to marry me."

Annie burst into tears. "I've been waiting and waiting for this day." She dabbed her cheek with a napkin. "You've been so lost and unhappy, ever since you came to us, running away from love."

"No, Ma, I haven't been running. I just never met the right woman. Effie is different."

She sat back and studied him.

"What?" he said.

"Did you tell her about you mother?" Annie asked.

"Not really."

"Why not?"

He reached for a napkin and tore it to shreds. "Because . . . I don't know."

"Tell me about her."

"There's not much to tell." He rubbed his eyes. "After my father died, she started drinking. One night, she got wasted and broke her ankle. The doctor got her hooked on OxyContin, and she never danced again. When the drugs ran out, she switched to heroin." *Then she became an abusive whore,* he didn't say. "Then she overdosed. End of story."

"Was she ever a good mother?"

He thought back to that time when his father was still alive, dancing sandwiched between them at Christmas. "Before the drugs, yes." He let out a breath that felt like it'd been trapped in his lungs for twenty years.

Annie sat up a little straighter. "So, you have a ring?"

He nodded. "Can you help me arrange a few things? I don't want Effie to get suspicious."

"What about Gail?"

"I don't give a shit about Gail."

She winced. "She's going to freak-the-fuck out."

"Yeah, well I don't care. She's been threatening Effie."

"Did Effie tell you that?"

"No, Kyle did."

"Why didn't she say something?"

He threw a piece of biscotti to the pigeons. They fought over the crumbs like fat, gray savages. "I don't know."

"*Érzi,*" she said carefully. "People have many phases in life. Like the moon, sometimes they grow dark before they become full."

"Is that one of those Tao proverbs Jun used to torture me with?"

"Shut mouth and listen. Effie doesn't talk about herself. Have you noticed?"

This was glaringly true. Except for a few bits and pieces, he didn't know much about her at all. "That doesn't matter."

"But maybe it *does* matter."

He rubbed his aching temples. "What are you trying to say?"

"If you love someone, you must love all of them. Even the dark parts—the craters of the moon."

The moon analogy was wearing thin "Effie doesn't have any dark parts."

"That you can see."

He dug out his wallet. "Let's head back. I want to be there when she wakes up."

Annie placed her hand on his. "You only move a little brick and let a crack of light in." She swept a hand across the table, sending her mug crashing to the ground. "Break down the fucking wall and let all of her in—light and dark."

He threw up his hands. "*Qué carajo*! My heart *is* open. Why do you think I'm asking her to marry me?"

She shook her head and mumbled in Chinese. "Stupid boy."

GRANDIOSO

Grandioso

"'It's a poor sort of memory that only works backwards,' said the White Queen to Alice."

Soundtrack *"Salut d'Amour, Op. 12," Edward Elga, Yo-Yo Ma, Kathryn Stott*

With its blue lakes and rivers and bright green valleys, Salzburg looked just like a fairytale land. The city's castles and spires pointed toward the heavens much like surrounding Alps. Classical music wafted out from open windows. And people picnicked in parks next to symphonies. It was a magical place.

Salzburg was also where Mozart grew up. He was the one composer she most identified with. Child prodigy? Check. Violinist? Check. Domineering parent? Check. Drug addict? Check.

Other than his gender, the only other difference was she'd never composed a whole symphony.

Elias had booked a room in a castle for the weekend to celebrate her birthday. He was the most wonderful man ever. And he was all hers.

That afternoon, she danced in the garden and sang *The Sound of Music* (terribly).

Elias watched her with a big grin on his face.

She leapt into his arms. "I love you more than air."

He chuckled. "In my language, we call soulmates our *medias naranjas*—our half oranges." He cupped the back of her neck. "*Sos mi media naranja, mi cielo.* You are my half orange."

She closed her eyes and listened to the sound of love. Romantic love. Soulmate love. Birds soaring and swans paddling. Trees rustling and flowers blooming. The sound of his hand stroking her tear-stained cheek. And the sound of his heartbeat in sync with hers.

"*Flaquita?*"

"Yes, lover?" she said without opening her eyes.

"Still with me?"

"Always."

Afterwards, the complete orange strolled hand-in-hand together, back to the castle and made soulmate love for the rest of the afternoon.

"Alice looked at it with great curiosity. 'I see you're admiring my little box,' the Knight said."

Soundtrack *"Die Entfuhrung aus dem Serail," Wolfgang Amadeus Mozart*

THEY NAPPED UNTIL SUNDOWN. When Elias woke up, he didn't look the slightest bit refreshed. His olive skin had paled to a sickly green.

"What's wrong, baby?" She touched his forehead. It was a million degrees. "You have a fever."

"I'm fine."

She snorted. There was that word again—*fine*. "You are not fine. Just rest. We don't have to be anywhere."

"Actually, I have something special planned for tonight. Go look in the closet."

She ran over and whipped open the door. Draped on a hanger was a blue lace gown, covered in plastic. She clapped her hands over her mouth. "You bought me a fairy princess dress?" She spit-leaped her way back to the bed and smothered his clammy face with kisses. "It's beautiful. I'll wear it when you're not sick."

"I'm fine," he said. "After a shower, I'll be good as new." He weaved toward the bathroom and turned on the faucet. "Get dressed. I'll be out in a sec."

Surely, he wouldn't go out if he were seriously ill, she told herself. The man was an adult. He had to know his own body's limitations.

She danced over to the mirror and held up the dress. For a second she didn't recognize herself. *Is that happy person, me?* She took a step closer and stumbled over Elias's pants. When she picked them up, a velvet ring box fell out of his pocket.

Her heartbeat shot up to 200 BPM. He was going to ask her to marry him. *Oh, no!* It was too soon.

In a panic, she grabbed the phone and ran out to the balcony.

Callie answered on the first ring. "Happy birthday—"

She cut her off. "Elias is asking me to marry him tonight."

A long stretch of silence poured through the phone.

"What am I going to do?" Effie said. "I haven't told him everything. If I tell him now, it's—"

"It's what?"

"Over."

"You really believe that?" Callie asked.

She answered with a sob.

"I need to meet this guy," her sister said. "He sounds like a total fuck-wad."

"He's not a fuck-wad."

"This is your first relationship. Therefore, your judgment is severely impaired."

She closed the balcony door. "Shut up, and tell me what to do."

"I can't."

"You can and you will."

"No, assface, I can't. Find your own way out of this rabbit hole. But if it were me . . ."

"Go on."

"Shit, I don't know. What I do know is I wasted way too much time not opening up to Hot Cock."

Walker groaned in the background. "Don't call me that in front of your sister."

Callie blew him off. "Anyway, if I'd been real with him from the get-go, we could have gotten down to business a lot sooner."

"Amen," Walker said.

The shower shut off.

"He's coming. I have to go." She hung up and ran back inside.

She stuffed the ring back in his pocket right as he opened the door.

He shivered and hugged himself. "You're not dressed?"

"Sure you're feeling okay?" Please say no. I'm not ready.

He slapped her butt. "Hurry up. I've got a big surprised planned for tonight."

Her stomach churned. She had a big surprise for him too.

ACCELERANDO

Accelerando

Soundtrack *"Die Immer lacht," Stereoact, Kerstin Ott*

In the balmy summer night, dressed in a tailored black suit, Elias shivered and sweated at the same time. He was freezing and burning. His hair hurt, and his stomach was on fire. And he hadn't even made it through dinner, let alone the concert and the proposal.

He wasn't going to make it. Effie was the only thing keeping him alive.

He smiled as he watched her roam through the Mozart Museum with childlike wonder, touching stuff that said 'Don't touch.' She pressed her face against the glass case containing the composer's violin and stared at it for five minutes.

The museum director, an ancient man with a cane, hobbled up to her. "Your boyfriend tells me you're a violinist."

"Not really," she said.

He pointed his cane at her case. "Is that your violin? That's an unusual case. Did it come with it?"

She nodded.

"Would you mind showing me your instrument?"

She shrugged and lifted it from the case.

He put on a pair of white gloves and examined the inside. "Where did you get this?"

"My mother gave it to me," she said.

"Your mother was German?" the director asked.

"Yes," she said.

That was the first time she'd mentioned her mother. Elias thought maybe her mother had died or something.

"Remarkable. The Nazis destroyed the maker's workshop. As far as I know, you have the only one of its kind. Few works of art survived that terrible era." He handed the instrument back to her. "Would you consider selling it to the museum?"

"No, I don't—" She waved her hands. "I . . . I can't."

The director nodded and gave her his card. "Think it over, and if you change your mind, call me."

"Okay, yeah, sure."

"Ah, your dinner has arrived. I'll let you enjoy your meal in privacy. *Guten abend.*" The director bowed and limped away.

While the caterers piled food in front of him, his Elias's vision blurred, and his stomach tightened. He covered his mouth and rushed to the bathroom.

After heaving his guts out, he cleaned himself off, then staggered back to the table.

Effie touched his forehead. "Oh, Elias. Let's go home."

"Eat up. The concert's in fifteen minutes." He tried to smile, but it was too much effort. He swallowed a belch and puffed out his cheeks.

She threw her napkin on the table. "That's it. We're leaving."

"But my surprise . . ."

"Forget your surprise! Now get your butt up." She wrapped his arm around her shoulder. "Lean on me, so you don't fall."

They wobbled outside, where the horse and carriage he'd hired awaited them.

"Is that ours?" she asked.

"You didn't think I'd take you to see Mozart on a Moped, did you?"

She blinked away her tears. "I can't believe you did all of this."

He kissed her hand. "I'd do anything for you."

She wiped her face. "Let's take it back to the castle."

He was too weak to protest.

Halfway there, a horse let out a steaming pile of shit. The scent punched him in the gut, and he hung his head over the edge and threw up.

Effie held back his hair. "Oh, baby. I'm so sorry you're sick."

"I'm fine," he groaned then threw up again.

No way could he ask her to marry him with vomit on his face. After the tour, he'd plan something even more romantic.

That is, if he didn't die later.

PRESTO

Presto

MUNICH, GERMANY

"And Alice began to remember that she was a pawn, and that it would soon be time for her to move."

Soundtrack *"Hailin' From the Edge," Apparat*

Despite Elias's terrible condition, there was no way they could cancel another show. Not only did they lose millions in revenue canceling the concert in Geneva, the Swiss also slapped them with a heavy fine.

She waited as long as she could then rented a car and drove them to Munich.

The whole time, he lay in the back, vomiting into a trash bag.

At the base of the Bavarian Alps, in a villa just outside the city, they rejoined the band, or rather, what was left of them. Everyone except Cato had been hit with the same plague.

She put Elias in bed and tended to the others. Twice, Hal cried for his mother. Griffin passed out on the bathroom floor in front of the toilet. Missy curled up in her bed and didn't move. Even Annie, the band's nursemaid, was a pale and sickly mess.

"I've got to get out of here," Cato said. "I can't take the smell."

Elias let out a hoarse moan. "Take Effie. I don't want her to see me this way."

"I'm not leaving you," she said.

"Go have fun," he croaked.

"Only for a little while," she said.

On their way out the door, Elias stumbled out of bed. "Where are you going?"

Cato had begged her to go dancing at a gay club, but she didn't tell Elias that. He worried too much about his friend's reputation. "Shopping. Then we'll come back. Right Cato?"

He scratched the back of his neck. "Yep. Just gonna check out the mall or wherever-the-fuck they buy shit here."

"Take Hal," Elias moaned.

"Dude, Hal's dead," Cato replied.

"Go back to bed," she told him. "We'll be fine." At least that's what she'd thought.

Half an hour later, they sauntered into Munich's hottest gay club. Tall, half-dressed blond men crowded around the bar. German house music pulsed hard beats, and lasers shot neon lights on everyone's faces.

"Are we in paradise?" Cato shouted.

"I'm the only woman here," Effie shouted back.

He surveyed the club. "I'm the only black guy here."

"Should we go?"

"Hell, no." He pointed to the bar. "Mind if I get a drink?"

She gave him a little shove. "Go get 'em, cowboy."

"You're not going to tell Elias?"

She zipped her lips. "Your secret's safe with me."

"Want anything?"

"Yeah, I want to see you dancing with that blond stallion over there." She threw a glance at a stunning man who looked like a centerfold in an Arian gay male magazine.

Cato rolled his shoulders back and put on a sexy smirk. "I'm going in. Wish me luck."

She blew him a kiss. "Meet you on the dance floor."

He swaggered over to the bar. The model guy checked him out from head to toe, and a minute later, they had their arms around each other.

She headed out to the testosterone-laden dance floor and stationed herself in the middle of a bunch of sweaty bare-chested men. Then she proceeded to dance her ass off. We're talking hair-whipping, tit-jiggling, twerking, aerobicizing, twirling around, split jumping, moonwalking, and just generally getting the fuck on down. She owned that dance floor. She was in love, baby, and she was celebrating.

But after an hour of boogieing, she started missing her sickly lover.

Sweat-soaked and tired, she searched everywhere for Cato, but he was nowhere to be found. *He probably went home with the Arian model*, she told herself.

She wandered out to the street, scratching her head. Did cabs just roll up to the curb like they did in New York?

Right then, someone shouted "faggot" then "nigger" in German.

Fear shot through her veins. *Cato!*

She ran to the back of the club and found five men with shaved heads, kicking two lumps on the ground.

Without a second thought, she grabbed a broken beer bottle off the ground and ran straight for the attackers.

She kicked and punched and stabbed them with the bottle, screaming, "Get the fuck off him!" What was the German word for help? "*Hilfe! Hilfe!*" she shouted. "Help!"

A group of men rushed to her side, and the attackers fled on motorcycles.

She sank to the ground and laid Cato's head in her lap. His eyes were swollen shut and he had a deep gash across his nose.

"Are they gone?" Cato said.

"Shhh. Don't talk. "Someone call a fucking ambulance!"

"Is he okay?" someone asked in English.

"Call the police!"

A siren approached. By that point, the entire club had gathered around the scene. Camera phones flashed.

She threw the bottle into the crowd. "Get the fuck out of here!"

The other victim's friends helped him to his feet then rushed him off in a car.

The paramedics arrived and lifted Cato up on a stretcher.

The next scene went by in a blur—the hospital, the doctors, the police, the reporters . . . But she didn't cry once—not until Elias walked through the emergency room door—then she crumpled to the floor.

Sobs spilled out as she tried to explain the inexplicable, that Cato had been beaten by skinheads and outed in the worst way possible.

Elias gripped his forehead, looking sad, angry, sick, and confused all at the same time. At the end of her story, he got up and left.

OSTINATO

Ostinato

"'You are sad,' the Knight said in an anxious tone: 'let me sing you a song to comfort you.'"

Soundtrack *"Coming up for Air," Philip Selway*

Machines beeped and whirred around Cato while he slept. His face was black and blue and stitches zigzagged across his forehead. A bandage covered his nose and his wrist was bound up in a splint. And those were just his visible injuries. He also had two broken ribs, a bruised lung, and a bruised kidney.

But he was alive, *thank God.* And the doctors said he would recover in no time.

The police had arrested two men after they'd been admitted to another hospital for stab wounds sustained from Effie's broken bottle.

It was bad, but it could have been much worse—he could have lost his best friend and the love of his life.

Cato's injuries seemed minor in comparison to the damage

done to his career and family. Some *puto* had taken a picture of him outside the club and sent it to the news.

It was like junior high all over again. Every day after school back then, bullies beat the shit out of Cato.

One day, Elias caught them in the act and beat the shit out of them. It was the first time Jun's karate lessons had come in handy and the last time the fuckers ever bothered him again.

After that, Cato followed him home from school every day. Elias didn't want friends though, especially friends that attracted attention. And Cato was attention whore.

But he wouldn't give up. He kept on bugging him. One day, Cato challenged him to a game of hoops.

"If I win, will you stop following me?" Elias said, figuring it was an easy bet.

"All right," Cato said. "If I win, you have to sit by me at lunch."

They shook hands. Then Cato spun the basketball on his finger like an NBA All-star. "What? Think a gay boy can't shoot hoops?"

"Mierda," Elias said.

They played ten games, and Cato beat his ass every one of them.

"You don't say much, do you, white boy?" Cato said at lunch the next day.

"And you don't shut up, do you, black boy?"

He shot him a big-ass grin. "Your mama sure liked my talking,"

"Aren't you gay?"

"Vagina-challenged, not gay."

"My mom's dead."

Cato's smile vanished. "Sorry, man."

He punched his shoulder. "I'm fucking with you."

Cato jerked back. "She's not dead?"

"She is, but I'm still fucking with you."

They became best friends after that. In high school, they started the band together.

Cato's parents were their biggest fans back in the day. His dad worked two jobs just to pay rent on a warehouse practice space.

And when they went on their first tour, Cato's dad loaned them his beat-up locksmith van.

Now, Elias had to call up his dad and tell him his son had just become the latest statistic in a hate crime.

He hung his head between his knees and rubbed the tears from his eyes. This was his fault. He should have hired security for them.

A small hand curled around his neck.

He met Effie's teary gaze and pulled her into his lap.

She buried her nose in the crook of his neck and cried. "They were monsters!" she said.

"Cato's out for the night. Let's get out of here. I'll send Annie back to check on him."

The second they got home, Effie passed out cold.

SCHERZO

Scherzo

Soundtrack *"German Love,"* STRFKR

When Cato was released a day later, Hal had to hire back-up security to fend off the paparazzi. The grounds were crawling with them.

His bassist's perma-grin wasn't quite as big it normally was, but other than that, he was back to his old attention-whore self.

He lounged on top of a pile of pillows, while Annie massaged his shoulders, Missy rubbed his feet, and Effie spooned ice cream into his fat mouth.

"You're just eatin' this up, aren't you, buddy?" Elias said.

Cato stretched his arms over the back of the couch and grinned. "Get your ass beat by a bunch of skinheads, and people start treating you like a king."

Without warning, Gail blasted through the front door with her army at her side. She marched over to Cato. "Hope you're happy. Your little stunt just cost us the RadioXM sponsorship."

Elias shot to his feet. "Get out of here, Gail."

She slapped her hands on her hips. "And go where? To the

arena that's threatening to sue us for canceling tonight's performance at the last minute?"

"I can still play," Cato said.

"No, you can't, asshole," Griffin said.

"I can stand in for Cato tonight," Effie said timidly. "I know everything by heart."

"Who's gonna play for you?" Missy asked.

"It's just one night. We can go on without a violin, but we can't without a bass player." She clasped her hands in prayer position. "Don't cancel the show, guys. I can do this. I promise."

Gail rolled her eyes and spoke over her. "Unless you want to lose more fans, don't even consider letting Pollyanna here play tonight."

Out of sheer spite, he told Gail to let the venue know they wouldn't be canceling after all.

"She's got her head so far up your ass you can't even think straight." Gail scoffed. "Think your fans paid a hundred and fifty Euros to see your girlfriend play shitty bass? Want your career to get flushed down the toilet because of some dumb blonde?"

Elias leapt to his feet. "Get out."

"Gladly," Gail said and stormed out with her lapdogs in tow.

The minute she was gone, he fled out the back.

It took almost two hours to summit the mountain behind the villa. At the top, he inhaled the crisp mountain air and took in the flower-freckled valley below. Too bad Effie wasn't with him, or he'd have proposed right there.

He just needed to be patient a little while longer. Only two more shows, then they could take off on their own. One more week was nothing, when they had a lifetime together.

PIZZICATO

Pizzicato

"But my dear, this is not Wonderland, and you are not Alice."

Soundtrack *"I Give You Power," Arcade Fire, Mavis Staples*

At the concert in Munich that night, the fever hit Effie like a tidal wave and ripped her stomach lining to shreds.

It was a travesty how awful she played. She shivered and shook and tried to keep up with the band, but never managed to catch up.

Fans booed them for the first time ever. Then someone lobbed a full beer cup at her head.

The impact wasn't half as bad as the blow to her stomach. She covered her mouth and retched.

Elias stopped playing. Missy followed suit. Then Griffin.

Hal dragged the culprit out. While he was gone, someone else threw a rock and just barely missed her head.

"Verpiss dich von der Bühne, Schwuchtel!" someone shouted.

"Hey, asshole!" Elias shouted back. "Yeah, you." He pointed at the guy. "Get up here, coward."

The guy didn't move.

Elias jumped down from the stage and punched the guy in the jaw. Griffin vaulted into the crowd to help. Hal and a roadie rushed over and pulled them off the guy.

Elias stormed out the side exit, blood dripping from his nose. Griffin followed, flipping double birds to the crowd. Missy booted the beer cup into some guy's head.

Head spinning and bile rising, Effie stood alone in front of the hostile audience. She took one step and projectile vomited on the faces of a dozen shocked fans. Then she slapped a hand over her mouth and staggered backstage, weaving down the hallway, her tunnel vision focused on the bathroom door.

Three feet from the target, she rammed into someone. "I'm sorry—" She glanced up and slammed into a pair of eyes the same color as hers—except colder and more penetrating.

"Hello, Euphemia." Only one person called her by her full name.

"Mother."

It'd been ten years since she'd last seen Greta. Except for a few new lines around her eyes, her mother looked exactly the same. Even her expression was the same—withering disgust.

Effie slapped her hand over her mouth, bent over, and vomited all over the floor. On the verge of passing out, she sank to her knees.

Her mother stepped out of the way and glared down at her. "I see you've found the perfect job for your . . . *habit*." Her accent had grown harsher since her return to Germany.

"What happened to the violin?" her mother asked. "Did you sell it for drugs?"

She glanced up at her with tears in her eyes, feeling like the same little girl, desperate for her mother's approval.

"When I saw you on the news," Greta said. "I thought maybe you'd grown up. Clearly, I was mistaken." She released a scornful sigh and adjusted the shoulder strap of her purse. "I knew you'd never amount to anything. You took after your father, after all."

Tina and her band of groupies showed up right then. They stepped over her mess and barged into the bathroom, holding their noses, and crying, "Gross," and, "Ew," and, "Disgusting."

Greta tossed her one last loathsome look, shook her head, and then disappeared down the corridor, her footsteps like bomb blasts on the concrete floor.

Effie crawled through the ladies' room door. Inside, Tina and her entourage giggled behind a bathroom stall.

All rationale vanished, and one thought pulsed through her brain: *I need to get high.*

She knocked on the stall door.

Tina peeked through a crack. "Yes?"

"Can I buy some blow off you?"

"How much?"

"Whatever you have."

Tina opened the door.

An unspeakably sad moment passed between them.

"Just take it." The groupie slapped a baggie in her hand and walked out with her entourage trailing behind.

Effie clenched the baggie in her fist until the sound of their voices vanished. Then she sprinkled coke on the back of her shaky hand and pushed it into a line.

As she lifted the drug to her nose, she glanced in the mirror and saw a woman about to make a huge mistake.

She'd just barely crawled out of the hole, and now she was diving back in.

Don't do this, she told the reflection. *You're not a little girl anymore. You have friends now—people who care. A man loves you.*

She dumped the blow down the sink and ran the faucet until it disappeared.

Once again, she stared at the reflection. Her hair was caked with beer and vomit, and her eyes were swollen shut, but she'd never looked more beautiful than right then—the moment when she fell in love with herself.

Hal burst through the bathroom door. "I've been looking everywhere for you. Are you hurt?"

She collapsed into his outstretched arms.

"Jesus, you're burning up. You've got the same crud, don't you?" He led her out to the bus.

Elias sprinted toward them. "Thank God. I thought you'd been kidnapped."

"She's sick," Hal said. "Real sick."

ELIAS CARRIED her up to her room and put her in bed. "I'm going to run you a bath," he said.

She grabbed his leg. "Don't leave me."

He swept a cool hand across her burning forehead. "*Mi amor,* we have to get your fever down. Think you can make it to the bathtub?"

In the far-off distance, a waterfall splashed. And then all of a sudden she was swimming through a sea of ice. Cocaine blocks floated like glaciers on the water. She kicked them away. "No! Get them away from me."

"*Effie,* please, let me wash your hair."

Her mother sat on the edge of the bathtub and clucked her tongue. "Pathetic. You're so intoxicated you can't even bathe yourself."

"I've changed," Effie wept. "Someone loves me."

"Of course I love you, *mi amor,*" Elias said. "You're delirious."

Someone lifted her from the ice and dried her off. "I'll be right back," Elias said.

Greta stood behind him, shaking her head.

"Don't leave," she cried. "My mother's trying to kill me."

"Jesus, I'm calling a doctor."

Everyone gathered around her deathbed while her mother sat across from her and scoffed.

"A hundred and four," someone said.

"Should we take her to the hospital?"

Her mother spoke to her in German. "Euphemia, laziness will not be tolerated. Get up and practice this instant."

Effie rolled over and moaned. "I can't play anymore. I've been playing for hours." *For days. For years.*

Elias pushed the covers around her chin.

"Who's she talking to?" someone asked.

"I don't know," Elias mumbled. "How long will it take for the fever to go down?"

"Half an hour," said another voice.

Effie's hands and neck ached. "I can't practice anymore. Please, Mother."

"Is she talking to her mother?"

"Shhh, *flaquita*." Elias wrapped his arms around her. "Your mother's not here. Close your eyes and rest."

"She is!" She pointed at the chair. "She's right there."

He hummed a lullaby and blocked out her mother's terrible voice. And then darkness swept in.

"'I AM real!' said Alice and began to cry. 'If I wasn't real,' Alice said—half laughing though her tears, it all seemed so ridiculous— 'I shouldn't be able to cry.'"

Soundtrack *"Crystalfilm," Little Dragon*

BRIGHT LIGHT FILTERED through her lids. Effie opened one eye.

Cato smiled down at her, his face still bruised. "You're alive!"

She raised her head and found Elias at her feet. "I'm so thirsty."

Elias passed her a glass of water, and she drank the whole thing.

"How long have I been out?"

"Almost thirty-six hours," Elias said.

She flopped back on her pillow. "What did I miss?"

"You had an interesting conversation with your mother," Cato said.

Elias curled around her. "You kept saying she was trying to kill you."

She stiffened. "I saw her."

"You were delirious," Elias said.

"No, at the concert. For real. She was there."

"She lives here?" Elias asked.

She nodded.

"Speaking of parents." Cato rose to his feet. "I better get back to mine."

"They're here?"

"Came in last night." He broadened his chest. "And I came out last night."

"You did! How did it go?"

"They already knew." Elias turned to his bassist. "Told you, dude."

"Said they've known since I was three." Cato raised his arms. "Free at last!"

She clapped and cheered. "I'm so happy for you."

"And they caught those motherfuckers," Cato said.

"The skinheads? Thank God. I hope they rot in prison."

"Nah, they'll love it in there. Nine out of ten homophobes are gay." He patted her leg. "Glad you're better, sis."

"Give me a hug, you big gay man."

"Vagina-challenged." He grinned and gave her a big hug. "Do me a favor?"

"Anything."

"Shower before you meet my parents."

She shoved him off. "You're such a butthole."

He fell back, laughing and kicking and slapping the bed.

"All right, get out of here, *puto*." Elias said.

After Cato left, Elias nuzzled her neck. "One more week, then I get you all to myself."

She shivered in his arms. One more week until he broke her heart.

SERIA

Seria

"It was getting dark so suddenly that Alice thought there must be a thunderstorm coming on. 'What a thick black cloud that is!' she said. 'And how fast it comes!'"

Soundtrack *"Sprawl II," Arcade Fire*

The energy onstage felt different in Prague, like there had been a cosmic explosion that night. Effie could almost hear the frenetic energy buzzing around them.

The band's chi was definitely flowing.

On their last night on tour, they played the most passionate performance of their careers. Everyone and everything was in sync, completely aligned, put back together, and made whole.

The trip had healed each of them in a way.

Griffin had sworn off women so he could properly grieve the loss of his childhood sweetheart.

Annie and LeStrange talked about moving in together.

Hal planned to meet up with the woman he'd met in Italy, after he sought counseling for his PTSD.

Missy let go of Elias and started stoking the embers of her relationship with Sam. According to her, the flames were roaring hot after his visit to Rome.

Strangely enough, Cato's tragic experience had brought him closer to his family, and for once, he seemed optimistic about finding love.

And, of course, she and Elias had fallen in love.

The whole journey seemed like a dream. And the concert that night did too.

Their fans went rabid, demanding four encores. When the spotlights finally dimmed, she wiped her tears and shuffled off the stage with the rest of the band

A mob of reporters greeted them backstage. *They must have felt it, too,* Effie thought, the band's cosmic energy that night.

Then a disembodied arm shot up and shoved a microphone in Elias's face. "Did you know your girlfriend was a drug addict before the tour?"

And then, as the reporters swarmed over them, and the air left her lungs, a ridiculous thought popped into her head: *We forgot to go sailing.*

STRETTO

Stretto

TOTAL MUSIC MAGAZINE

EXPOSED: URBAN'S SOBER LEAD SINGER IN LOVE WITH A DRUG ADDICT

By Len Neal

According to an anonymous source, Effie Murphy, Urban's new violinist, and El Love's latest heartthrob, did two stints in rehab for cocaine addiction prior to joining the band on their European tour this summer.

El Love is renowned for his drug-free lifestyle, which most likely stems from his mother's heroin overdose.

Apparently, rehab didn't take since Murphy purportedly bought coke off a fan during their Munich show.

We contacted the band's label for a statement, but they haven't commented yet.

The photos below were taken by Murphy's former roommate prior to her first visit to rehab.

Warning: Many are graphic in nature.

∾

"The Queen turned crimson with fury, and, after glaring at her for a moment like a wild beast, began screaming 'Off with her head!'"

Soundtrack *"All of Me," Big Gigantic, Logic, ROZES*

REPORTERS BANGED on the bus windows outside while she scrolled through the photos.

Back then she was nothing but skin and bones, and her hair was dirty and dreadlocked. She didn't even recognize herself.

In one shot, she was dancing at a party with one eye barely open. Another featured her half-naked and passed out by a pool.

The pictures of her passed out were aplenty—one with a burning cigarette in her hand, another in the back of Brandon's car, another on the street somewhere. She didn't even remember him taking them.

There were fifty in total on the site. How much had Brandon sold them for? What was the final price of her humiliation? Probably just enough to supply his heroin habit for a few months. It was amazing he was still alive.

Elias let out a sharp breath—his first in several seconds—and said one word: "Why?"

She kept her eyes on the photos, too afraid to see that 'look' on his face.

"That's not who I am anymore, Elias. I've changed."

"You almost did it the other night!" he shouted.

She lifted her head and braved a glance. It was worse than she'd expected. He looked broken.

"But I didn't! I stopped myself. I was sick, and my mother was there, and Tina was in the bathroom. But I didn't do it!"

He flipped through the phone. "When were these taken?"

She choked back a sob. "I don't know. I don't remember. I was twenty-one in that picture, I think."

"When was the last time you used?" His voice was tight and detached.

"Two years, five months, and four days ago." She reached for his hand.

He shook her off. "Why didn't you tell me?"

She buried her face in her hands. Nothing would fix this. It was over. "Because you wouldn't love me." She didn't just cry then —she bled.

He opened his mouth to say something then shot off of the bus.

A minute later, a red blur flew to the back. "Get your shit," Gail said.

"What? Why?"

A tiny demonic smile slid up the manager's face—an I-told-you-so smile. "You're done."

"I don't have any money."

"Not my problem," she said. "Make sure you have everything. I don't want you coming back and upsetting my lead singer."

Effie searched for her backpack under the seat, then dragged it, and her violin, off the bus.

Hal escorted her to a limo and stuffed her in without a word. As they drove away, she turned back and saw the tears rolling down the bodyguard's face. "Oh, Hal," she whispered.

"Where to?" the driver asked.

"Just pull over," she said.

Callie answered her call on the first ring. "I saw the news. Where are you?"

She answered the question with a wail.

"We're on our way to the airport," Callie said. "Where do you want me to meet you?"

"I don't know. I'm in Prague. In a car…somewhere. Fuck!"

The line went silent for a moment. "I've always wanted to go to Greece," her sister said. "Want to meet me there?"

"I guess."

"You need money?"

She looked down at her violin. "No. I've got to go. I'll call you back."

She pulled out the museum director's card from her wallet. "Can you drive me to Salzburg?" she asked the driver.

He glanced up in the rearview mirror, his gaze full of pity, and nodded.

SALZBURG, AUSTRIA

"Who in the world am I? Ah, that's the great puzzle."

AT FIVE O'CLOCK THAT MORNING, Effie knocked on the Mozart Museum director's door.

He gave her a sad smile and handed her the receipt for the money he'd wired to her account.

Without a word, she gave him the violin, but kept the bow Elias had given her.

The last connection to Greta had finally been cut. In a way, it was like throwing a handful of dirt on her grave. All of this was her mother's fault, and as far as she was concerned, the woman was dead.

REQUIEM

Requiem

"You're not the same as you were before. You were much more, more . . . muchier. You've lost your muchness."

Soundtrack *"Creep," Daniela Andrade*

Thirty-six hours later, Effie sat on the edge of a Santorini cliff and watched a dark, shapeless mist roll over the indigo sea below.

She'd had thirty-six sleepless hours on the way to there to think about her life. And so far, none of it made any sense.

She closed her eyes and let the nothingness fill her ears. The sound of love lost. The requiem.

Someone sat next to her. "How long have you been out here?" Callie asked.

She didn't answer.

"You're sunburned."

She felt nothing.

"Come inside," said her sister.

Effie raised her hand and blocked the violent sun. "Did you just get here?"

"Yeah," Callie said. "Come inside. It's fucking hot here."

Back in their room, they climbed into bed together and clung to each other for the first time since leaving their mother's womb.

"It hurts," Effie cried.

Callie squeezed her tighter. "I know."

"I feel like I'm going through withdrawal."

"I know."

"I saw our mother. I saw Greta."

Her sister loosened her grip. "You did?"

"At the concert in Munich."

"Fuck."

Effie relayed the events over the last week.

Her sister was quiet for a long time. "I should have done something. Stopped her."

"I hated you," Effie said.

Callie lowered her damp lashes. "I thought she loved you more. Because you were so talented."

"I went through hell."

Her sister burst out sobbing. "I didn't know. I'm so sorry. I didn't know. And then the drugs. And you ran away. I didn't know what to do." She let out a sickly moan. "And those pictures of you. Thank God Skip found you. I hate that he was there for you, and I was with that asshole, Daniel."

"I punched Daniel. Well, Elias punched him, and I punched Hillary."

Callie wiped her nose. "What? When?"

"Skip made me dress up like you, so I could accept the award for the dildo campaign. Daniel was there with Hillary."

Callie covered her face and bawled. "You've done everything for me, and I've done nothing for you."

Effie rolled her eyes. "You loaned me fifty grand."

"No, you *stole* fifty grand."

"I can pay you back now. I sold the violin."

"You what! What are you going to do now?"

"Be sad for a while. Then I'm gonna get up, dress up, show up, and get on with my life." Because that's all she could do, just go on living.

"Wow," Callie said. "You sound so well-adjusted."

A gust of wind blew through the door and whipped the curtains against the wall.

Callie regarded her for a moment. "What about Elias?"

All at once, blinding pain swept in. She'd probably never see him, or the band, again.

"Has he called you?"

She shook her head.

Callie pushed the hair off her face. "If he loves you, he'll come for you. Real love heals and forgives. It's not conditional. Love doesn't bolt out the door after finding out you used to be a fuck-up."

Effie pulled the covers up to her chin. "I just want to sleep."

Her sister closed the curtains. "I've got to call Hot Cock. He's worried to death about you."

She tried to laugh but nothing came out. Instead, she closed her eyes and tumbled down a dark, dark hole.

TUTTI

Tutti

"'Once,' said the Mock Turtle at last, with a deep sigh, 'I was a real Turtle.'"

Soundtrack *"Big Decision," Elliot Smith*

After searching the entire city, Elias finally found Len Neal, seated at the bar of a sleazy airport hotel.

Four empty bottles of cheap Czech beer and a basket of pretzels surrounded the reporter. He popped a pretzel into his mouth and chuckled to himself as he scrolled through his phone.

Elias grabbed the back of Len's shirt and hauled him off the stool.

His rubbery form lay in a heap on the floor.

"Get up, asshole. I want to talk to you."

Len shielded his face with a forearm and rose to his feet. "Hey, dude, how's it going?"

Elias pointed toward the patio and shoved the reporter out the door.

Outside, screaming jets took off and multiplied his rage by tenfold. "How much did you pay that prick for those photos?" His voice was shockingly calm.

"I can't tell you," Len said.

He punched his nose.

"Okay. Okay." Len's hands covered his bloody nose. "I didn't pay him. Your manager did. She hired a detective, who found the guy in LA and paid him off."

"No, *you* paid him off. It's your website that published them." He cocked back a fist and threw another punch.

Len ducked. "I didn't! Gail did."

A red mist of rage blurred his vision. *His manager paid him?* Gail fucking paid that *cara rota de mierda* off? He was going to murder her. He hurled a chair to the other end of the patio. "*Hijo de remil puta,* motherfucker, I want those pictures off your site."

"It's not my call," Len said.

He heaved a chair over his head, ready to smash it into the reporter's face. "I'll sue you for every penny you own. Defamation of character, invasion of privacy, harassment—"

"Okay, okay!" Len crouched and covered his head. "I'll talk to my boss."

Elias kept his glare locked on him for a long drawn-out minute, just to make the asshole squirm. Another plane lifted off and drowned out the silent tension rippling between them.

Once it was out of earshot, Len spoke to the ground. "For the record, I didn't want to do it. Gail went over my head."

He examined Len's bloodied expression and found the truth there.

Len cast his gaze to the ground. "I hate this job. It fucking sucks. If I didn't have a greedy ex-wife and two kids in college . . ."

"Think I give a shit about your family, motherfucker?" he said.

"You're nothing but a maggot, living off the shit in everybody's life. You ruin careers and destroy relationships. How do you live with yourself?"

Len let out a long-suffering sigh. "The music's the reason I stick with it. It's the only thing that keeps me sane. And yours . . ." He rocked back on his heels and stared at the sky. "Fuck, man. I wasn't kidding about being your number one fan."

"Is that supposed to make me like you?"

Len wiped the blood from under his nose. "I'm sorry, man. Really. Truly." Slow as fucking a turtle, Len limped back inside the bar with his back hunched and his head hanging so low his neck disappeared.

Elias didn't move from his spot, still stricken by the crushing blow of the evening's events.

The images of his sweet, sunny love, splayed out on the ground like human waste, looped endlessly through his mind. And when those images grew old and tattered, his mother's images played on repeat.

He'd spent the better part of his childhood a secondhand victim of drug abuse. Even the thought of Effie in that condition sickened him.

But she'd said she wasn't that person anymore. Who was she, then? And why did she try to buy drugs the other night?

Another plane ripped through silence. He gripped the railing and shouted, "Fuck you!" to the sky so loud his vocal cords almost snapped in half.

Then he broke down and cried. He didn't even cry when his mother overdosed. But this was different. Effie was everything. If felt like half his heart had been sliced off.

The sunrise tinted the sky pink, and the birds began to chirp. And as the night disappeared, some of the heaviness lifted. His throat ached, and his limbs felt like rubber bands, but he managed to make his way out front and flag down a cab.

∾

"'We must fight for her, then,' said the Red Knight."

Soundtrack *"250 Miles," Radio Moscow*

THE CAB PASSED over the Vitavia River, and as the city's sharp cathedral spires came into focus, the fog in his mind began to clear.

He didn't know anything about Effie or her mother or her addiction or her childhood. She hadn't had a chance to tell her story.

What an unfair thing he'd done—run away when she'd been so cruelly exposed. She would never have done that if the situation were reversed.

"Can you go a little faster?" he told the driver.

The driver shot him an evil smile and slowed down instead.

At the hotel, he sprinted up five flights of stairs, then pounded on the band's door.

Hal swept it open so fast he almost fell on top of him. "Aw, shit, it's you. I thought you were Effie."

Elias rushed to the living room. Everyone sat frozen, stiff as corpses. It looked like he'd just stepped into a wax museum. "Where is she?" he shouted.

No one answered.

"Where the fuck is Effie?"

Annie wept into a wadded-up tissue.

"She's gone, man," Cato said.

"What do you mean, she's gone? Where'd she go?"

Hal started bawling. "I put her in a limo. I thought she'd come here, but she never showed up."

"You what!" He grabbed a vase off the table and hurled it against the wall.

Then he really lost it.

Anything he could pick up—dishes, paintings, lamps—he smashed them all. When he ran out of small objects, Cato and

Griffin helped him rip the big-screen TV off the wall and toss it over the balcony.

Then everyone joined in.

Missy stabbed a knife into the couch cushions and threw the stuffing everywhere.

Hal tipped over the fridge in the kitchen, shouting, "Fuck everything!"

Annie grabbed a broom from the closet and beat the shit out of the chandelier, raining glass shards down on everyone's heads.

They didn't stop until LeStrange ripped out the bathroom sink and tossed it into the living room.

All eyes landed on the petite French bus driver. He pounded fists on his chest. "*Sheet,* that felt good."

Elias bent over and roared. *Why the fuck was he laughing?* He snapped back up and dragged his hands down his face. "*Hijo de puta!* What am I going to do?"

A hush fell over everyone.

Griffin interrupted the silence. "Did we just destroy our first hotel room?"

Cato fist-bumped the drummer. "We're rock stars now."

Annie shook her head. "This will cost a fortune."

"Make that bitch Gail pay for it," Griffin said.

And the tension sprang back into the room.

"She hired a detective to dig up that scum Effie was with," Elias said. "She's the one who sold those photos to *TMM.*"

"That's a big shocker," Missy said dryly.

He sat on what was left of the sofa and closed his eyes. "I need help. I need to find Effie. I need to fire Gail—"

"You need sleep," Annie said and led him to the back bedroom.

"Close your eyes." She tapped needles into his scalp until he felt overcome with exhaustion.

"What am I going to do?"

"Find Effie and ask her to marry you."

"What if she relapses?"

A Zen-like wisdom filled the woman's gaze. "She won't."

"How do you know?"

"You healed her."

He swallowed the razor blades in his throat. "*She* healed *me*."

Annie rose from the bed. "We'll find her. You rest." A short while later, she removed the needles and kissed him on the forehead.

He sat up. "I love you, Mom."

She smiled and patted his leg. "I love you, too, *Érzi*. Don't worry. We'll get her back."

SERENADE

Serenade

"'Wake up, Alice dear!' said her sister. 'Why, what a long sleep you've had!'

'Oh, I've had such a curious dream!'"

Soundtrack *"Stillness," Hilary Hahn and Hauschka*

For over a week, Effie lay suspended in a fantasy world. In her dream, she was a little girl again, living in a strange animated land, filled with flowers and animals that talked.

The red queen appeared in her reverie and barked orders for her execution. After that, a white knight, riding a black horse, saved her and then galloped away, leaving her with a giant hole in her heart.

Voices faded in and out. "We've got to get her up," Walker said.

"Soon," Callie said. "She'll get up when she's ready."

Effie tried to climb out of the dream, but she was far too small.

One day, the scent of orange blossoms floated through the breeze, and her sister called to her.

"Effie, sweetie," Callie said. "Wake up."

She rolled over and opened her eyes. "I'm too tired."

Callie yanked off the covers and dragged her by her ankles to the edge of the bed. "Enough of this depressive bullshit. Get up and take a shower. You stink."

"I don't wanna," she whined.

"That's it." Callie stomped over to the table, grabbed a pitcher of ice water, and dumped it over her head.

Effie jolted to her feet.

"Now get in that shower!" she shouted. "Before I kick your ass."

She loped to the bathroom and took off her nightgown.

Callie turned on the faucet and shoved her under it.

The cold water sliced though her skin like razor blades. "It's freezing!" she cried.

Callie dumped a bottle of shampoo on top of her head. "Wash that mop!"

For the next ten minutes, Effie followed Commander Callie's grooming orders.

Once the torture session was over, her sister dried her off with all the tenderness of a pro wrestler, and then slapped a dress over her head.

While her sun-freckled sister braided her hair, Effie studied herself in the mirror. Her cheeks were hollow, and her eyes looked bruised, but she was alive, and that was something. "Remember that time you cut my hair?"

An evil half-grin crept up her sister's cheek. "Not all of it. Just the back."

"And I'm the bad twin?"

Callie gripped her shoulders and whipped her around. "You are not bad. Do you hear me? You are beautiful and talented and kind. You paid dearly for your mistakes. Now it's time to move on." A tear rolled down her fragile smile. *"Literally.* And you know how much I hate when people misuse that word. It's *literally* time to move on. Now get your fucking shoes on. It's time to go."

Effie gave her a blank stare.

Callie grabbed a dirty rag from her luggage and waved it front of her face. "I have a surprise for you."

"A dishtowel?"

"Turn around."

"You're not putting that on my face."

Callie yanked her braid then tied the rag around her head so tight her eyeballs almost imploded.

"Let's go, assface."

"'So I wasn't dreaming, after all,' she said to herself, 'Unless we're all part of the same dream.'"

Soundtrack *"Daphnis et Chloe Suite No. 2," Maurice Ravel*

THE SUN WARMED her chilled skin as her sister led her blindly down a path. The bells on her sandals tinkled, and the birds in the sky tweeted, and the soft buzz of conversation floated through the breeze.

Why do I smell oranges?

Then she heard something—music—and froze in her tracks. "Is he here?"

Callie kissed her cheek and removed the dishrag. A group of musicians were playing out by the pool—Missy and Griffin and Cato. Next to them, stood a bodyguard, an acupuncturist, a Disco Bus driver, and Walker, wearing a big dimpled grin.

And in the center of them all, under an arc of flowers, a handsome man with long dark hair played guitar.

He sang about secret gardens and candy slides, lollipops and horsey rides, tree houses and pale skin, chaos and identical twins, puffy clouds and bright blue skies, violins and disguises, half oranges and pretty little trees, and making music with his wild Effie bomb—his heaven, and the love of his life.

On the last note, an explosion followed, and the door to her soul burst open, and love beamed out of her, brighter than the sun.

Elias set down his guitar and knelt in front of her. "F-bomb Murphy, *te amo*. I love you. Will you marry me?"

"Are you sure?" she whispered.

"Oh, for fuck's sake," Callie said.

Walker covered her sister's mouth.

Elias answered her with a warm soulful smile. "Yes, *flaquita*, I'm sure."

She kneeled down with him. "Then, yes, I'll marry you."

He slipped a beautiful blue ring on her finger, and everyone cheered and banged on instruments.

It was the sound of love, true love, and also the finale of her opera.

FINALE

Finale

MANHATTAN, NEW YORK

ONE YEAR LATER

"As the Knight sang the last words of the ballad, he gathered up the reins, and turned his horse's head along the road by which they had come. 'You've only a few yards to go,' he said, 'down the hill and over that little brook, and then you'll be a Queen.'"

Soundtrack *"Ate the Sun,"* Mr. Gnome

In the Lincoln Center audience, Elias and Effie held hands and watched the New York Philharmonic perform her first symphony titled: *Lovely Chaos.*

Effie glanced over at him with her twinkly blue eyes wide with excitement. "I did it," she whispered. "I'm successful."

He kissed her hand. "It's a masterpiece, *mi vida.*"

She leaned her head on his shoulder. "I wrote it for you."

AFTER THE TOUR, Effie entered Juilliard's composition program in the fall and finished her first symphony. The Philharmonic had chosen her work to headline their modern composer series.

Shortly after they returned from Greece, Effie enlisted the help of her friend Skip's PR person to repair her reputation after Heart Records ruined it.

When they spread the news about Effie's free lessons to the Brooklyn schools, people stopped talking about her addiction and started talking about her recovery.

It took almost a year, but Elias sued Heart Records and won. Urban's song royalties finally belonged to the band.

Once the court case was over, he went on camera and told the world what Gail had done. No one wanted to work with Heart Records after that, so Mr. Heart sold the company and retired.

Gail hadn't been seen since.

Effie bought a new violin and played it left-handed with the band a few times before they decided to take an indefinite hiatus. Since then, she rarely played, but once in a while, she put on a naked recital for him.

Speaking of home, Eli St. James moved out, and Effie moved in.

Though he and Effie shared an apartment, they chose to hold off getting married until after a year of counseling together.

As for the rest of Urban's members, Missy and Sam were trying to get pregnant. They visited often, along with and Cato and his new boyfriend, Tito.

Griffin decided to do some soul-searching in South America. He was somewhere in the Andes now.

Annie and LeStrange expanded the Disco Bus operation to the States. And Hal moved his Italian sweetheart to New York. They were all in the audience that night, along with Callie and Walker.

Effie's sister recently found out she was pregnant with twins. After the performance, they were riding down to Georgia in the Silver Dildo camper with Walker and Callie, to plan a double wedding.

As for Elias, he hooked up with a buddy in LA and started scoring films. Now he got to make music all day long, without having to step foot into the spotlight.

AFTER THE SYMPHONY FINALE, Effie received a standing ovation. She insisted he take a bow with her. "Get up here," she said. "You're my half orange."

He laughed. "I'm crazy about you, F-bomb."

"I'm crazy about you too, Elvis."

Making music, making love, and making each other laugh—life with his half orange was pretty damn sweet.

"Of all the strange things that Alice saw in her journey Through The Looking Glass, this was the one that she always remembered most clearly. Years afterwards she could bring the whole scene back again, as if it had been only yesterday—the kindly smile of the Knight—the setting sun gleaming through his hair, and shining on his armor in a blaze of light that quite dazzled her—the horse quietly moving about, with the reins hanging loose on his neck, cropping the grass at her feet—and the black shadows of the forest behind—all this she took in like a picture, as, with one hand shading her eyes, she leant against a tree, watching the strange pair, and listening, in a half dream, to the melancholy music of the song."

GLOSSARY

CHAPTER 2

Gil—Spanish insult similar to dumbass.
Puto—Bitch.
La puta madre—Similar curse to motherfucker.

CHAPTER 3

Hijo de puta—Son of a bitch.
Estás más loca que la mierda—You're fucking crazy.
Mujer salvaje—Wild woman.

CHAPTER 4

Ella tenía una buena onda—She had a good vibe.
Cero—Zero
Mina—Chick.

Flaquita—Term of endearment similar to babe. Literally means skinny.
Porfa—Familiar version of please.
Mierda—Shit

CHAPTER 6

Tranquilo—Tranquil.
Dios—God.
Riquísimo —Delicious.
Tesoro—Treasure.
Princesa—Princess.
Me estás jodiendo!—No fucking way

CHAPTER 7

Podría metértela en la boca—I could put it in your mouth.
Mi pija—My dick.
Vamos—Let's go.

CHAPTER 8

Ghetto de mierda—Similar to fucking ghetto.

CHAPTER 9

Lǎobǎn—Derogative term for boss.
Jianren—Slut or bitch.

CHAPTER 10

Tenés una boca tan hermosa.—You have such a beautiful mouth.

CHAPTER 11

Quiero comerte la boca—I want to eat your mouth.
Mierda—Shit
Cásate conmigo—Marry me.
Por favor—Please.
Ton amour est ma musique—Your love is my music.

CHAPTER 13

Chau—Bye.
Hasta la vista—See you later.

CHAPTER 15

Ta gueule!—Shut the fuck up.
Je ne peux pas conduire ce putain d'autobus avec toi hurlant, comme ça—I can't drive this fucking bus with you screaming like that.

CHAPTER 16

Que lío de mierda—What a fucking mess.

CHAPTER 19

Mi amor—My love
Andá a cagar, puto!—Go take a shit, bitch. Similar to "kiss my ass."
Puto de mierda—fucking bitch.

CHAPTER 20

Non, ce n'est pas étrange, connard—No, it's not strange, asshole.
Idiota de mierda—Fucking idiot.
Mes testicules ont rampé à l'intérieur de moi pour garder au chaud—My testes crawled inside me to keep warm.
Qu'est-ce que c'est bordel—What the fuck is this shit?

CHAPTER 21

Buenos días.—Good morning.
Hola.—Hi.

CHAPTER 23

Perdoname—I'm sorry.
Te prometo—I promise.
Cojónes—Balls.
Jefe—Boss.

CHAPTER 26

Soñá con los angelitos, mi vida—Dream with the little angels, my life
Quiero cogerte esa boca linda—I want to fuck your beautiful mouth.
Pendejo—Asshole.
Sí, mami —Yes, ma'am.
Tan vivaz—So vivacious.
Me gustás mucho—I like you a lot.

CHAPTER 27

Quiero coger con vos toda la noche —I want to fuck you all night.

CHAPTER 29

Là-bas—Over there.
C'est bon pour l'énergie sexuelle—It's good for sexual energy.
Il y a du fromage et des fruits au frigo—There's fruit and cheese in the fridge.
Ce sont pour le système de son—This is for the sound system.

CHAPTER 30

Vous ne pouvez pas faire ça ici—You can't do that here.
Mon Dieu!—My God.
Mais, bien sûr—Well, of course.

CHAPTER 31

Los Submarinos—Argentinian hot chocolate.
Esperá un momento—Hold on a second.

CHAPTER 32

Estoy loco por vos, mi amor—I'm crazy about you, my love.

CHAPTER 36

Putain!—Fuck.
Ça va, chérie—You okay, honey?
Crevé—Flat, crushed.
Croque-monsieur—Grilled ham and cheese.
S'enfuir—Fly away.
Si. Tu vois, I am older, donc beaucoup plus intelligent—Of
course it will. You see, I am older, and therefore, much smarter
than you.
De Le merde—Shitty.

CHAPTER 37

Qué carajo—What the fuck?

CHAPTER 39

Voy a devorarte—I'm going to devour you.

CHAPTER 40

Pelotudo—Asshole
Qué pasa, che?—What's up, dude?
Habrá música y baile y tapas—There will be music and dancing and tapas.
Ce n'est pas ici—It's not here.
Moi, non plus—Me neither.
¡Qué lo parió! ¡Qué chanta! — What the fuck! What a con artist!
Chupámela, pelotudo —Suck my dick, asshole.
Sos divina—You are divine.
Tenés los ojos más lindos del mundo—You have the most beautiful eyes in the world.
Tu concha está mojada—Your pussy is wet.

CHAPTER 42

Putain de merde—Motherfucker. Literal translation: whore shit.
Qu'est-ce que c'est bordel—What the fuck is this shit?
The bus is baisée—The bus is fucked.
Exactamente—Exactly.
Chante une autre—Sing another.
Ay! La puta madre!—Motherfucker
Mauvaise idée, les gars—Bad idea, guys
Mes couilles—My balls.
El Semental—Stallion.

CHAPTER 45

Qué carajo—What the fuck?
Érzi—Son.

CHAPTER 46

Sos mi media naranja, mi cielo — You are my half orange, my sky.

CHAPTER 47

Guten abend—Good evening.

CHAPTER 51

Verpiss dich von der Bühne, Schwuchtel!—Piss off the stage, dike!

CHAPTER 55

Cara rota de mierda —Shameless fuck. Literal translation: broken face of shit.
Hijo de remil puta—Fucking asshole!
Hijo de puta—Son-of-a-bitch.

ACKNOWLEDGMENTS

Everyone deserves love, even fuck-ups. That's why I wrote this book. Sadly though, we all have to grow up at some point. But that doesn't mean you have to stop having fun. List the things you loved as a kid, and do them often. And above all, laugh. Even when things suck. That's the moral of the story, in case you didn't figure it out.

I couldn't have written this book without help. And lots of it.

Mark Landon, a composer and violinist at the Dallas Symphony, spent hours talking to me about music and issues with violinists. He was amazing.

My friend H, a PhD student from China, provided all the Chinese language information. Penny Sparkles checked my Argentinian Spanish.

I also want to express my gratitude for a few authors who've helped me on the bumpy road to becoming an Indie author.

Penny Reid, whose fabulous books inspired me to write rom-com, advertised my book Road-Tripped on her page when I didn't know a soul in the book world.

I'd also like to thank Melanie Harlow for helping me and other aspiring authors navigate through the rough waters. And lastly, I'd like to thank author, J.D. Hawkins, for helping me with my introverted male character. He supplied Elias's line, "My dick's not shy." His sense of humor is always a bright spot in my day.

All the quotes in the book were from Lewis Carroll's *Alice in Wonderland* and *Through the Looking Glass*.

Effie and the others in the story were loosely based on the characters in these books.

Also, the band Arcade Fire was the inspiration for Urban. They have a kick-ass violinist too.

Child prodigies often struggle when they grow up. Many turn to substance abuse. Check out these articles: The Mind of the prodigy | How to Raise a Child Prodigy | Child Prodigies All Grown Up | The Downside of Being a Child Prodigy.

Effie probably has a mild case of undiagnosed Asperger's, which often manifests differently in women.

Research has found that people with ADHD often turn to cocaine addiction to self medicate.

And sadly, Neo Nazism is on the rise all over the world, including in the United States.

Readers of romance, please stand up against hatred and give everyone the love and respect they deserve.

REVIEW ME

Hey, Fabulous Reader! Raise your hand if you liked this book? Or better yet, leave a stellar review everywhere. Positive reviews are critical to the survival of new Indie authors, and I'd be ever so grateful if you took the time to write one.

Also, did you know that when you flick off a star rating at the end, it doesn't actually show up unless you write a few words?

Please review me wherever you purchased your book.

Love, Nicole

ABOUT THE AUTHOR

Nicole Archer's lengthy career as an advertising copywriter not only polished her writing skills—it provided a lifetime of book material. As a single, full-time working mom of a beautiful, brilliant, and horrifically energetic son, she has little time to do much else besides work, write, read, drink wine, and breathe. She's originally from Colorado, but lives in Dallas now. Head-Tripped is her second book.

Newsletter: http://eepurl.com/b6JPsn
Website: Nicolearcher.com
Facebook group: http://bit.ly/2mF6ZT4
Facebook author page: http://bit.ly/2eWjxgY
Twitter: @nicolearcheraut
Instagram: authornicolearcher
Goodreads: http://bit.ly/2eFT5XW
BookBub: http://bit.ly/2fARKnF
Pinterest: Pinterest.com/nicolearcheraut

ROAD-TRIPPED– AD AGENCY SERIES, BOOK 1

What's worse than driving across country in a phallic-shaped RV with a coworker you hate? Falling in love with them

Copywriter, Callie Murphy, has a bad attitude, a vicious tongue, and a serious aversion to Shimura Advertising's resident manwhore, Walker Rhodes. Know where he can stick his good looks and Southern charm? She can think of a few creative places. Avoiding him wouldn't be a problem, except her boss threatens to fire her if she doesn't go along with him on their RV client's cross-country tour.

Walker is sick of his job, tired of women, and in a big old creative rut. The upcoming client road trip is just what he needs to shake things up and rediscover his lost passion. But his plans go south when his partner drops out at the last minute, and Callie, the foul-mouthed tiny terror, takes her place. Unless he can find a way to thaw his icy coworker, he's looking at two months of pure hell.

FIELD-TRIPPED-AD AGENCY SERIES, BOOK 3

I WAS DONE WITH GAMES. BUT PLAYING WITH HER IS SO MUCH FUN.

Ten years ago, I was all set to compete in the winter

Olympics. Then I lost everything—my career, my best friend, and my girlfriend.

After that, I stopped playing games for good. I swore never to go back to Colorado. Too many bad memories. Plus, she's still there.

Now I live a simple life as a creative director at Shimura Advertising in New York. All is good, until my boss cons me and my coworkers into spending two weeks in Colorado at Proton Sports' sleep-away camp for adults, pitching their business. Turns out Proton's idea of a pitch is making the agencies battle each other in a bunch of ridiculous winter games.

Guess who owns the rival company? Her. And she's out to get me.

I might just let her win.

Field-Tripped is Book 3 in the in the Ad Agency Series and can be read as a standalone.

GUILT-TRIPPED—AD AGENCY SERIES, BOOK 4

Coming summer 2018. Sign up for updates on nicolearcher.com.

www.ingramcontent.com/pod-product-compliance
Lightning Source LLC
Chambersburg PA
CBHW050522110726
47899CB00005B/1552